the Mistress

Martine McCutcheon is a much-loved household name. A TV and film actress, probably best known for her starring role in *Love Actually*, she is also an award-winning musical star, chart-topping pop star, presenter and bestselling writer. Martine lives between Richmond and France with her partner Jack, and continues to write, sing, act and design.

MARTINE McCUTCHEON

the Mistress

PAN BOOKS

First published 2009 by Pan Books
an imprint of Pan Macmillan, a division of Macmillan Publishers Limited
Pan Macmillan, 20 New Wharf Road, London N1 9RR
Basingstoke and Oxford
Associated companies throughout the world
www.panmacmillan.com

ISBN 978-0-330-50448-5

'Part Time Love' words and music by David Gates © 1975, reproduced
by kind permission of EMI Music Publishing Ltd, London W8 5SW

9 8 7 6 5 4

A CIP catalogue record for this book is available from
the British Library.

Typeset by Ellipsis Books Limited, Glasgow
Printed and bound in the UK by CPI Mackays, Chatham ME5 8TD

Visit **www.panmacmillan.com** to read more about all our books
and to buy them. You will also find features, author interviews and
news of any author events, and you can sign up for e-newsletters
so that you're always first to hear about our new releases.

To Jack

You were always on my mind . . .

x

I was never the type of woman to settle for second best.

I was never going to be someone's silver when I should be their gold.

I never dreamed I'd be the mistress.

ONE

The Birthday Girl

As Mandy heard the taxi pull up she spun round in the hallway, making sure she had everything. She was always running late, but tonight was special: tonight was her night, and she just had to be on time.

She'd better tell the taxi driver to wait. She grabbed her copy of *Grazia* from the antique table to cover her head from the heavy rain.

'Hi,' she smiled to the taxi driver. 'Can you wait five minutes? I need to lock up.'

'No problem, love,' he said.

She skipped down the stairs in her satin high heels, trying to avoid slipping in the puddles, and back through the door.

Mandy loved her home in the basement of a grand stucco property in Queensgate, South Kensington. As she walked into the entrance she checked herself out in the mirror. She felt good, more confident than she had expected to at this turning point in her life. She reached for her lip brush and added one final coat of luscious gloss. She cleaned any remaining stains off her teeth with her tongue and smiled at herself in the mirror. Her hair was dark as ebony and it fell in shiny waves over her shoulders; her skin was flawless, even and gleaming, her long dark lashes framing her beautiful big brown eyes perfectly. Her lower lip was fuller than the top and when she smiled she lit up the room. She grabbed her keys and her clutch bag and quickly squirted some perfume.

'One last check,' she said to herself, looking at her reflection. Tonight was a big night. She had to look great. 'Have I got everything? Right, bag – check, lippy – check, keys – check.'

She grabbed her slightly sodden copy of *Grazia* again and headed out of her heavy black door, pulling it shut by its knocker. She fumbled with the umbrella: 'Oh bloody hell, it never works, why do I bother?' She ran and jumped into the taxi.

'Ready, darlin'?' said the cabby with a twinkle in his eye – he clearly found Mandy attractive.

'Ready!' she replied with a big smile, relaxing into the back seat. Mandy looked out at the rain falling hard.

'You look nice,' said the cabby. 'Are you going somewhere special?'

'Yes,' Mandy replied, 'I'm off to the Wolseley.'

'Ooh,' the cab driver said, laughing, 'very posh. Special occasion?'

'Yes, actually. I'm turning thirty!'

The cabby looked at her in the mirror for about the tenth time in as many seconds, openly enjoying the view.

'You don't look it,' he said with a grin. 'I'd have you down as twenty, easy.'

Mandy laughed and rolled her eyes, knowing that, yes, she looked pretty good – but not twenty!

God, she loved London. Even in the rain, she found it romantic. As they drove past the Natural History Museum, Harrods and one of her favourite hotels, the Lanesborough at Hyde Park Corner, the old streetlights glowed a deep orange and fairy lights twinkled in the trees, building up the momentum for Christmas. She felt the driver's eyes on her again. Now he was swerving over the wrong side of the road.

A car honked its horn with a loud *beep*, and the driver yelled, 'Keep in your own bloody lane!' as he sped past.

Mandy's cabby just laughed and carried on with his friendly banter. 'So who you meeting then, anyone nice?'

'I'm meeting about ten lovely people actually,' Mandy said, thinking how thrilled she was that so many of her friends could make it. They were colourful characters all of them, with fast-paced lives, and pinning them down wasn't always easy.

'Bet a gorgeous girl like you has to beat them off with a stick,' the driver said with such a grin that Mandy had to humour him.

'Only the ugly ones,' she joked, raising her eyebrows. She looked out on to the rainy streets and people-watched for a moment. It was nearly eight o'clock in the evening and people were rushing around, trying to fit everything into their undoubtedly jam-packed diaries. London was such a fast place, full of different nationalities, different religions. On a bad day it could feel suffocating, but generally it felt to Mandy like the most exhilarating city in the world, with the speed of New York but the history of a Paris or Rome. If you went for it, truly went for it, you could get the life you wanted here, and that was Mandy's aim – to have it all. And why not? She'd read a greeting on a card once in Paperchase on the King's Road that had truly stuck with her: *Reach for the moon, and even if you miss, you'll land among the stars.* She loved it and used it as a mental pick-me-up whenever she felt low.

And God, had she been low recently! She had spent the last couple of years settling for less than she should in almost every way, from her old flat and job to the men in her life. None of it had been good enough, and some of her old sparkle had gone. Mandy checked herself in her mirror one last time before they entered Piccadilly.

'Oh no,' moaned the cabby. 'Sorry, love, Piccadilly's rammed.' He squashed his face up to the windscreen. 'But at least it's moving.' He was a sweet, cheeky chappie in his thirties with cute dimples – a typical black-cab driver in his Ralph Lauren jumper with polo-shirt collar poking up from underneath. 'Bet your boyfriend won't be happy,' he smiled.

'God you're nosy,' Mandy laughed.

'I'm a black-cab driver, it's part of the job description,' he countered throatily.

Mandy felt relaxed with her new friend of five minutes. 'Actually my main man waiting for me is gorgeous, but gay – very, very handsome and my best friend. But I'm single now and couldn't be happier,' she lied. 'I can't be bothered with you men any more.'

Mandy had always loved dating and having fun with the opposite sex. All through her twenties the attention made her feel fantastic, and dating different men was exciting but, turning twenty-nine, she had realized she dreaded hitting thirty. There was so much she wanted to do, and life wasn't working out as she'd planned. She had been with many different men because no one man seemed able to tick all the boxes. If they were funny, they were ugly; if they were clever, they were dull; and if they were great lovers, they were normally stupid. Their best way of communicating with you was obvious.

Of course, Mandy had had lots of fun coming to that conclusion, but that was the unkind thing about growing up. She'd got to the stage of finding out what did *not* suit her. At twenty-nine it no longer felt right to share her body with someone she knew right from the off was wrong for her. How dull, but oh so true. So she had decided to get a grip. She took control of her finances, making sure she was on top of tax payments and savings, and realized that if she worked her butt off, she could not only buy a bigger flat but a Gucci bag too. Hurrah!

Mandy heard a song that reminded her of her father: Nat King Cole, 'Let There Be Love'. She realized she was humming along.

'Do you want me to turn it up? I love all the old stuff on Magic,' said the driver. He whistled along as if he hadn't got a care in the world.

'Please,' Mandy replied, looking out at the bright lights of the Ritz as they drove beyond it and pulled over.

She felt excited: tonight was going to be perfect, apart from one thing. God, she wished her dad could be there.

The driver snapped her back to reality. 'Here you go, love. Watch you don't slip, it's chucking it down out there.'

Mandy tipped him and tried her umbrella, arms stretched out of the taxi. 'Eureka, it works!' she trilled, as if discovering a new invention.

The lovely Irish doorman, Callum, helped her to the main doors of the restaurant.

Mandy swept through the doors of the Wolseley, shook the raindrops off her umbrella, and gasped at the beauty and opulence that filled the room. Everyone looked so beautiful, polished and stylish. This wasn't just a restaurant, this was like the perfect scene in a film.

'May I take your name, madam?' asked a friendly-faced member of staff.

'Yes, it's Mandy Sanderson. I'm here with quite a large party of people.'

No more introductions were necessary.

'SURPRIIISE,' yelled a group of people sitting at a large table just to the right of Mandy's view. Oh my God, thought Mandy. There, standing up and clapping, whooping and singing 'Happy Birthday', were about ten of her friends. Mandy was rooted to the spot.

'Come on, darling,' beckoned George, 'we're making complete arses of ourselves for you!'

Mandy could contain herself no longer. Suddenly, all the happiness and exhilaration hit her at once. She bounced over and kissed all her guests as a massive round of applause broke out, not only from them, but from the whole restaurant.

'It's her birthday, it's her thirtieth!' George announced to the room. He was showing Mandy off as if she was a prize on a game show.

'Happy birthday, dharrling,' purred her Russian friend Assia. 'The fur jacket and dress are both divine.'

'Happy birthday, Mandy.' Mandy looked up and saw Andrew. She worked with him and he'd always had a little crush on her. He was a bit preppy, but Mandy liked him – as a friend. 'I've got you a little something,' he said. 'It's not much but it's not every day you turn thirty.' He blushed and shuffled from foot to foot.

'Oh thanks, Andy! You didn't have to do that.' Mandy looked at him sweetly. 'Shall I open it now?'

'NO NO,' stumbled Andrew, going red. 'Just open it later – you have all of these friends to meet and greet.'

One friend after the other kissed and hugged Mandy in greeting. Deena, a tall red-haired couture hippie, presented her with a bunch of sparkly red balloons and placed what seemed to be a pebble in her palm. Deena winked and held Mandy's hand tight in hers, and with a misty air of spirituality she looked Mandy straight in the face and whispered loudly, 'This is a rose quartz. I got it from the tree festival. It will bring you love.'

As Mandy looked down at the light-pink stone, she felt she was being watched intently, to the point that it caused a burning sensation to the side of her head. She looked to her left, and straight away she found him.

There, at the other side of the room, was a gentleman at the bar. His suit jacket had been removed and the sleeves of his crisp white shirt rolled up. He was sitting on a tall stool and had swung round in her direction. He had one hand placed on a drink and the other on the thigh of his beautifully tailored black trousers. His skin was tanned and his hair mousy. Mandy looked down and up again, as if she needed a reality check. Yes, he was still there, almost glaring back at her.

Mandy's heart flipped, her face felt hot and the voices of all the well-wishers faded until she couldn't hear a thing other than the buzzing in her head. Other customers and staff at the restaurant slipped away and the man's face seemed closer and closer, until—

'Mandy, Mandy.' George slipped his arm around her waist, bringing her back to reality. 'I want you to sit next to me. You look so beautiful that it will only make me look better,' he giggled.

Mandy just about managed to pull her gaze away from the man at the bar to focus on what George was saying.

George was amazingly stylish, and extremely witty. He was slim, with short buzzed hair, piercing blue eyes and full lips. Women loved him, but George maintained the rule, after a 'bad experience' with a woman, that 'Girls are for gossip and shopping, and men are for sex.'

He worked for a fashion magazine. A passion for fash ion was something the two had in common, and many a Saturday lunchtime would be spent in the Bluebird café in Chelsea, flicking through the latest must-haves in *Elle*, *Vogue*, *Bazaar* and *Grazia*. More often than not, after an espresso and a Diet Coke, hours of fun would be had, and Mandy would find herself laden with bags of shop-ping and a great big credit-card bill. George understood Mandy completely. In many ways they were so similar: they both liked to party, but never to the point that it damaged their careers; they were both ambitious; they both loved sex and lots of freedom, but secretly yearned for 'The One'; both loved food but could never have much of it as their waistlines would suffer. Ninety-nine per cent of the time they would know exactly why they shouldn't do something, but then occasionally at the eleventh hour they would go and do it anyway.

George had once explained, 'I constantly feel like I have this red glowing button on my forehead and the finger on one hand is pointing towards it and dying to push it. The other hand is constantly trying to hold it back. It's the self-destruct button. When it's pushed the initial buzz is fucking amazing, but the consequences are catastrophic.'

Confiding in each other about their weaknesses and strengths was a great comfort to them both, and in the fabulous but equally fake world they lived in it was great that they could relax and be anything they wanted to be with each other. Although George drew the line at *ever* being badly dressed.

'No matter how bad things are, darling,' he once whispered as Mandy hugged him, crying after a break-up, 'wearing a beautiful coat and diamonds will always make you feel better, even if it's just slung over jeans and a sweatshirt. No one will ever know what's lurking beneath.' He had stroked her hair back and smiled. 'So wipe your eyes and get that fucking awful tracksuit off! You look like Vicky Pollard! I wouldn't be seen dead in it!' Tough words, but said with heart.

Yes, they were camp together and sometimes enjoyed the shallow things in life, but deep down there was a true loving friendship.

As everyone sat down and looked at their menus, Mandy could feel the man's eyes on her the whole time.

The beautiful candlelit tables twinkled, and the waiters rushed around busily, catering to everyone's needs. Starters came, pink champagne was served, and the evening was already shaping into one of the most memorable ever. As Mandy looked around the table at Deena, Assia, George, Andy and her other wonderful friends, she realized just how lucky she was. Her friends were all so different – some wealthy, some not so, some quirky, some talented, some beautiful – but all fascinating, with a story to tell. Yet the person who intrigued her most right now was not at this table, it was the man sitting at the bar. He was saying good-bye to a male friend who was putting on his raincoat and picking up a black leather briefcase. They looked like good friends; probably long-term work colleagues, thought Mandy.

'Gorgeous, isn't he?' said George, following the direction of her eyes. 'I'd like to think he was gay, but the farewell to the raincoat guy was definitely a heterosexual one.'

Mandy found herself momentarily unable to speak.

'Keeps staring at you, too. Get in there, darling!' Smiling, George looked down at his food, 'Tuck in, sweetness, or have you lost your appetite?' George took a mouthful of risotto and tried not to chuckle. He could be a devil and Mandy loved it.

'I'm going to the ladies'. Coming?' she joked to George.

'Hmmm, toilets aren't my thing.'

Mandy raised an eyebrow and giggled.

She found herself in front of the mirror in the ladies' room with all her make-up sprawled on the shelf in front of her, making sure she looked great for her return to the restaurant.

'You're being ridiculous,' she whispered under her breath. 'You don't even know him and you're making yourself up like he's your bloody date.'

She stuffed her alligator clutch bag with all her lotions and potions, quickly squirted some Chanel Cuir de Russie, and made her way upstairs. One last check before she opened the door, and *voilà*!

She was walking back to her table, gracefully, elegantly and as naturally as possible, when Shit, she felt him look up at her. He was about ten feet away. He'd already seen her, of course. She moved to walk away, her body turned round – but her feet stayed firmly planted on the floor. Mandy found herself hopping from one foot to the other and feeling like a complete prat.

She chided herself: For God's sake, Mandy, how hard can it be? Just walk in a bloody straight line and don't look at him, look straight ahead whatever you do. Look important and look busy but don't look at him, *not at* him. At last she glided by the bar, feeling absolutely fine, keeping her head up. She was just about past him when she heard a voice say, 'Happy birthday' over her shoulder, and the man at the bar was smiling.

'Thank you.' Mandy smiled back.

He looked tired, but devastatingly handsome and extremely sexy.

'Can I get you a drink?' he said, and then looked down shyly at his empty Scotch glass and swirled the remaining ice cubes round and round as they melted.

Mandy desperately wanted to say yes, but 'No, thank you' were the words that, remarkably calmly, came out instead. 'It's my birthday, all my friends are here to see me and I should get back to my table really, but thanks.'

The man looked up at Mandy. His eyes were beautiful, and despite being tired they sizzled, full of knowledge, some sadness but most of all kindness.

'I know it's your birthday,' he replied, looking upbeat. 'I've had a great day myself, actually. I'm celebrating a big new deal, and so the least we deserve is a celebratory drink. I'm sure your friends will be all right just for five minutes.' Before Mandy had a chance to reply he had a cocktail list in his hand. 'So what's your tipple, birthday girl? Vodka champagne?'

'I love mojitos actually.'

'Mojito it is, and a Scotch on the rocks for me, please.'

The barman bustled off and there Mandy was, left with the stranger.

As he swung back around towards her, she caught the scent of his aftershave; it was musky and she found herself looking at his lips for that second too long.

'So, birthday girl, are you enjoying your night so far?'

'I'm loving it, absolutely loving it. My friend George planned the whole thing. He has great taste and . . .' Mandy felt clumsy with her words, 'oh and my name is Mandy, Mandy Sanderson.'

The man extended his hand to grasp hers and said politely, 'Jake, Jake Chaplin. Absolute pleasure to meet you.'

Jake didn't let go of Mandy's hand. They both smiled at each other, almost as children do when they've decided to be best friends.

The bartender returned with the drinks.

'Cheers, Mandy, and happy birthday. May this year bring you lots of health, wealth and happiness.'

'And sex,' Mandy blurted out.

Jake looked slightly taken aback. 'Erm yes, and lots of that!'

Mandy laughed, shocked at her own outburst. 'Sorry, must be habit,' she giggled. 'Always say that to my friend George when we toast, and we have to look each other in the eye or it means lack of sincerity and *seven years of bad sex*! He's a red-hot-blooded gay man so we make sure we say it every time!'

Mandy giggled and toasted Jake, looking him right in the eye. 'So, to seven years *great* sex, going for our dreams and being happy.'

Mandy sipped her mojito through her straw and saw Jake's gaze taking her in.

'What do you do, Mandy?'

'I work for an events company,' she smiled. 'We do everything from weddings to premières and corporate functions. I love it, actually, and the good news is I've just been promoted.' She smiled and raised an eyebrow. 'I don't have to fulfil someone else's vision any more. I can come up with my own ideas, from the fabric on chairs to lighting to colour schemes – you name it!'

Jake looked important, a powerful man, and he seemed impressed by her. She felt extremely flattered. She had met many different characters in her job and could normally 'place' people pretty quickly, but Jake was a mystery.

'Well, you know about me,' she quipped: 'how about you? What do you do, and what are you celebrating?'

Jake smiled, as if he was drained by but also proud of the answer. 'I run my own advertising company. We won a huge pitch with a sportswear brand today. Our company has wanted this client for a long time, so we're very happy. We have also been expanding and going down new avenues.

It's all good, but it can take up your life.' He looked at his empty glass.

'That's why it's so important to love what you do for a living,' Mandy sighed. 'I see more of my work colleagues than I do of my own family.'

Mandy glanced over at a family sitting together at one of the tables and thought of her own mother and sister. They lived just out of London, in Surrey, and she felt bad she didn't see them more often, especially since her dad had died. It had been two years now and when Mandy visited, it made her miss her father even more. That was partly why she kept so busy: she wouldn't have to see them so much and as a result she didn't have to be reminded that Dad was gone for ever. She wanted to change the subject and Jake sensed it. She gave him a big smile.

'Listen, you must need to have the odd party, put on events et cetera. Why don't I give you my card?' She placed her drink on the bar, rummaged through her bag for her business card and offered it to Jake. 'Then when something comes up and you need an events organizer you can give me a call.'

Jake took the card and stared at it for what seemed like an eternity.

Mandy continued, 'My bosses would absolutely love me getting a big player like you on our books.' She smiled confidently. 'I just know you'd love what we can do. You wouldn't regret it.'

Mandy's attention turned to her friends at the table. They were all looking over now, wondering what she was up to. They were trying to be subtle, apart from Deena, who was waving her arms around indicating that Mandy needed to come back.

Jake continued to look at her card and Mandy sensed something was wrong. Lots of thoughts flooded her head, bizarre notions of seeing him again, where it would be, how she would act, what she would wear. She was captivated by his face. He was by no means perfect, but something about this man made her feel intensely emotional.

Jake finally looked up. 'Thanks for the card, Mandy,' he said quietly.

'You're welcome.' She closed her clutch bag and slid it under her arm.

'But I can't take it.'

Mandy's face dropped. She bit her lip and looked right into his eyes. What the hell was this man playing at? Staring at her for half the evening, smiling all starry-eyed and buying her a birthday drink, and all she does is give him her business card and he rejects it? Mandy normally knew a player when she saw one and she didn't have Jake down as one of them.

Continuing to hold her gaze, he said deliberately, 'Mandy, if I was to take your card it wouldn't be for business.'

The silence seemed to go on for ever and Mandy was anticipating bad news from a man she hardly knew. She was confused, but tried to remain calm. 'And what's so wrong with that?' She gave him a half-hearted smile.

Jake twiddled the card and repeated, 'What's wrong is that I wouldn't call for business.' He looked at her beautiful face. 'I'd call because I think you're . . . absolutely gorgeous.'

Mandy looked at him with a mixture of relief and anticipation. 'And? I don't get your point.'

Jake was obviously choosing his words as carefully as he could. 'And I'm not in a position to act on the fact that I think you're gorgeous, because I'm married, and not only am I married but I have two kids – two beautiful boys.'

Mandy had only known this man for the shortest amount of time, yet, ridiculously, she felt he'd betrayed her. He had been sweet, bought her a birthday drink – and owed her nothing. He was actually one of the good guys: he came clean! He didn't have to tell her he was married, he could have kept quiet, told her what she wanted to hear and attempted to woo her straight into bed. She must have got it all wrong, misread the signals, and yet why did he look so sad? Why had he stared at her all night? Mandy remembered her mother's words: 'If in doubt, be a lady and keep a dignified silence.' Mandy hadn't always managed to follow that rule, but right now she did her mother proud.

'I couldn't take my eyes off you, though.' Jake looked at the floor. 'I tried not to look but I found myself gazing at you again before I knew it.' He looked up to Mandy and gave her a lovely warm smile. 'I'm not a bastard, Mandy. I don't chat up girls in bars, birthday or no birthday.'

Something about his sincerity made Mandy want to laugh. Maybe it was nervousness at such emotional honesty. There was a tickle in the air and the two of them burst out giggling like schoolkids as if it was some kind of forbidden release. Mandy saw an even more gorgeous side of Jake when he was laughing so much. He seemed lighter, more alive.

'What *are* we laughing at?' he said between guffaws.

'I don't know, but at least it broke the ice!' Mandy giggled.

Mandy looked over at her friends. George was mouthing, 'Birthday cake,' with wide eyes and such a dramatic gesture he looked as if he was presenting a children's show. Mandy sighed. 'Listen, my so-called "surprise" birthday cake is coming out any second and I'd better get back to everyone.'

Jake nodded, looking like he didn't want to let her go at all. He smiled again, his eyes sparkling. 'You are absolutely lovely, such a special girl. Whoever ends up having you in their life is a very lucky person, and if things were different—'

Mandy cut him off. 'But they're not, are they?' She put her hand on his and felt brave suddenly. 'Some people say that people know each other from previous lives, that's why they have a connection and get married. Soulmates, if you like. Maybe we're setting up things for next time?'

Jake glanced at her. A thousand words were said in that one look. Taken aback, Mandy felt her eyes well up ever so slightly.

'Good-night, Mandy . . .' He lost his words. 'So – so lovely to have met you.' He squeezed her hand tight. As Mandy left to go she took the card back from his grasp, but he grabbed it back urgently.

'I would like to keep this after all,' he said.

Mandy looked at him, not sure what to say, and went back to her friends, who started to sing, 'Happy birthday to you, Happy birthday to you, Happy birthday, dear Mandy' – a big cake with lots of candles was placed in front of her on the table – 'Happy birthday to you!' Mandy looked up and Jake was cheering along with the whole restaurant, smiling like he'd known her for ever and was proud to be there.

'Who's the cute man up at the bar, Mandy?' Assia asked the question every other friend at the table was dying to.

'Ssssh, everyone,' said George. 'Mandy's got to blow out her candles and make her wish.'

Mandy did just that. Closing her eyes tight, she wished as hard as she could. All the candles went out in one go and everyone cheered.

'That wish will certainly come true!' said Deena as she kissed her on the cheek.

Mandy looked up. Where Jake had once sat was an empty chair. He had gone

TWO

It's a Family Affair

The traffic was murder. Mandy was driving her much-beloved Nissan Figaro, fondly referred to as Figgy. She was a cute and chic shade of 'topaz mist' and seemed to have a very temperamental, almost human personality. If Mandy was nice and had her valeted once a week, she drove like a dream; if not, Figgy didn't want to play the game and Mandy would be lucky even to get her engine running. Figgy also chose all of Mandy's music. Any tunes Figgy didn't like, she simply didn't play: they were spat out of the CD loader and nothing could change her mind. Today Figgy was in the mood for a bit of Prince and Mandy sang along to 'Raspberry Beret'. Mandy pictured herself in the beret, naked with matching raspberry-red heels. Suddenly a man's hands cupped her tits from behind her, turned her face to his and French-kissed her hard. 'Fuck!' exclaimed Mandy; it was the gorgeous married man. 'Think of something else, you dirty cow,' she mumbled, shocked that he had flashed back into her head in such an intimate way.

She turned up the music and focused on the tune as hard as she could, anything to stop that happening again. She pulled up to the Berkeley Hotel and whacked some change into the pay-and-display meter, then ran in to meet Assia and Deena. Both were already a tad tipsy, and it was only one in the afternoon.

'Is this the AA meeting?' Mandy giggled.

'Dharrling, come and have some fun with us, don't be a bore,' ordered Assia. She was a very tough-talking, to-the-point Russian who had landed on her feet completely when she met an older businessman. He'd fallen in love and married her – and he just happened to be worth a cool one hundred million. As usual, Assia was dripping in diamonds, her blonde hair tightly slicked back in a classic bun but with her dark roots just peeping through.

'I am *not* broke or tacky, dharrling, it's the fashion,' she pointed out, noticing Mandy's eyes on her get-up. 'Sit, sit,' she ordered. 'A glass of champagne for my dharrling friend,' she added, clicking her fingers to the bemused barman. 'So, how are you? Is hair of the dog needed after last night?'

'I feel OK, actually, didn't mix, just stayed on mojitos all night.'

'I feel hideous!' said Assia. 'Just hideous.' Rolling her eyes, she slicked a stray hair tightly behind her ear. 'Marius was not happy when I rolled in at three in the morning and threw up everywhere, dharrling. I was just like the exorcism!'

'*The Exorcist,*' Mandy corrected, laughing.

'Whatever, it was hideous, dharrling, simply *hideous*. Anyway, enough from me, dharrling, we'll get to that later. What's happening with the hot guy from last night?'

'What guy?'

'"What guy?" she asks, what guy?! Come on, Mandy, don't pull the jumper over my eyes.'

'The wool.'

'Whatever! He was just *sooo* hot, huh?'

'So hot and sooo married,' said Mandy firmly.

Deena choked on her watermelon-fizz cocktail. 'Married?' she gasped.

'Thank fuck! She's alive!' drawled Assia, looking at Deena. 'I thought she was drowning in that bloody fizz drink. That's the first thing you've said since Mandy got here, Deena.' Assia slapped her thigh and laughed too long at her own joke.

Mandy looked at both the girls. They were clearly a little giddy.

'Been here a while?' she smirked.

'My life is one long party lately,' smiled Assia. 'Marius is away so much, and he can't get it up any more, so I'm bored, you know? And when he does, I have to feign interest.' She pondered a moment. 'It's small, so I'm seeking adventure, you know?'

Deena choked again, but this time on laughter.

'You are so wicked, Assia,' she said, making a racket

sucking the last of her watermelon fizz through the straw. 'Marius loves you, and you knew how old he was when you agreed to marry him. Maybe if you opened up a bit spiritually and emotionally, let him in, the rest would follow.' She smiled at Assia sweetly.

Assia yawned. 'You're so full of poop, you know that?'

Deena shrugged, placed her hand on Assia's knee and said with all the sweetness of a saint, 'One day you will believe.' She gazed with a mystical stare at Assia that she must have copied from some guru and had clearly practised too much.

Assia turned her attention to Mandy. 'Anyway, the married man: are you going to see him again?' Her eyes twinkled as her red lips opened up into a Cheshire cat grin.

'God, no,' Mandy retorted. 'I'm not some home wrecker. I can't stand those ruthless women who callously take what they want and don't care about the consequences.'

'But Assia is a friend!' Deena smiled sweetly.

Assia just shot her a deadpan look.

'And the impact it has on any children is tragic,' continued Mandy in earnest. 'I've seen it with friends of mine from schooldays: it truly affected them so much. Anyway, I think it's tacky, and these women get their comeuppance.' She paused thoughtfully. 'And they never truly feel comfortable: the first woman is always there ready to pounce and to make your life hell for taking her man.'

'Not thought about it that much then?' Assia grinned.

Mandy fidgeted with the buckle of her Burberry mac and felt embarrassed. Where the hell had all that come from?

'I just think it's out of order,' she concluded firmly.

Mandy's champagne arrived to silence and a bit of an atmosphere. Mandy sipped her drink and said, raising her glass, 'Anyway, happy birthday to me! Again! I love dragging my birthday out for a week – well anyway, that's the plan.' She chuckled.

'I think being a mistress is sexy,' Assia interjected regardless.

Mandy felt uncomfortable; why couldn't Assia just drop it?

'It's not tacky, dharrling, it's a modern woman's dream.'

Deena looked at Assia disapprovingly. 'And how the hell did you come up with that notion?'

'It's true,' Assia purred, popping a fancy floral crisp into her mouth. 'I know so many women who have been or are having an affair.'

Deena sighed sadly. 'But these women are victims in my mind. Why would you put yourself through that heartache, knowing that you will never be number one on his list? They must have such low self-esteem.'

Assia snorted. 'You were with Mark for years and have never met anyone since. Pot calling kettle black springs to mind.'

Exasperated, Deena said witheringly, 'It's hardly the

same, Assia. Mark was separated for a long time and going through a divorce. He wasn't happily married.'

'And did he get it?' Assia raised an eyebrow.

Deena just stared at her. 'The divorce? No, he didn't, and now he is back with his wife. But there was no trickery or cheating. Everyone knew where they stood. Mark lived with me, for Christ's sake, visited his children at weekends!'

'Maybe the trick was on you,' replied Assia. 'You can't label things, just like that. Everyone's different, you know, we all say and do things that make us feel a bit better about a situation, but the truth is that we all like to think that we know what our partner wants and that everything is out in the open, but in truth we never *really* know, do we? When Marius is fucking me, thinking he's the king of the castle, I think of Roger Federer. Is that cheating? Where do you draw the line? If it was not for Federer in my head, Marius and I would never even kiss goodnight.'

Mandy took this all in. 'OK, but you must admit that it's not ideal, Assia?'

Assia looked upwards. 'For some mistresses, no.' She shrugged. 'They are the sensitive kind, looking for old-fashioned love, but I have a few friends who would genuinely not have it any other way.'

'Oh yeah, like who?' Deena said scathingly.

'Women with careers that are their babies, if you like. Their passion is life itself, they are busy jetsetters who don't have time for a demanding or controlling man. Their personalities wouldn't suit being with a man who wants to become the whole of their life; they have their own success, big houses and flashy cars. Their love affair is with their friends and they are fulfilling different kinds of dreams.'

'Sounds a bit shallow and lonely to me,' mumbled Deena.

Assia shook her head. 'No, they are just strong and different. They don't have a problem about Christmas without their men; they spend it with their own families and then have a naughty weekend away, dressed as one of Santa's little helpers. These women don't yearn for babies, they yearn to travel and experience. So why is that wrong? It's what they want and they've earned it.'

A waiter arrived with three fancily presented club sandwiches, complete with trimmings. Assia took a bite of one and looked at both of her friends. 'I'm not saying that it's always right,' she spluttered with her mouth full, 'but it's not always wrong either, and sometimes the mistress is the trigger for things to change. The unfulfilled wife always senses that something is wrong. If she's lucky, she gets a huge payout, and fucks her own bit on the side more often. Maybe *she* falls in love, marries again, but she keeps her kids and has a link with the father for ever. Sometimes he does things far better second time round. He'll pick a woman better suited to the man he wants to be in the future, and the mistress finally gets the man she has yearned for all along. At last she has him all to herself – well, as much as possible when he has a history of a wife and kids from before.' Assia took a breath and another bite of her delicious sandwich. 'But sometimes things can get sticky, if he keeps going back to his wife and sleeps with her too.'

'How on earth do you know all this?' Mandy blurted out, amazed.

Assia shrugged. 'Oh, you know, for years I lived in Paris. It's the norm there.'

Leaving the girls earlier than she'd planned, Mandy felt unsettled. She had booked a day off but didn't want to be alone with her thoughts, so she popped in to work at the offices in Fulham to catch up on some admin. After a few phone calls and replying to some emails, she left and drove home. Parking her car in Queensgate, she sat motionless for longer than she realized, the engine stilled. It was strange and uncomfortable, for she couldn't get *him* out of her head. She batted the thought of him away, sure that he at least would have forgotten her by now. She gathered her things from the car. Just as she was about to pick up her mobile from the passenger seat, the phone signalled a text message.

Bleep, bleep, bleep, bleep!

Mandy checked the screen. 1 NEW MESSAGE. It was a number she didn't recognize.

I CAN'T STOP THINKING ABOUT YOU. CAN WE MEET?

Mandy knew straight away who it was, there was no doubt, but at the same time couldn't quite believe it. She shut the car door, put her bag over her shoulder and as she walked to the top of the stairs she flipped up her phone and looked at the text again.

I CAN'T STOP THINKING ABOUT YOU. CAN WE MEET?

She hated to admit it, but the man had read her mind. She was excited but scared, all at the same time. As she raised her eyes, she couldn't believe the vision before her. Diva Watson, an elderly neighbour from the flat above, was outside the main entrance of the building. Mandy adored her: she was easily in her late seventies, and incredibly grand. Today she was dressed in smart black trousers and a se-quinned cape, and wore a beautiful shade of coral lipstick. Diva nodded her head in Mandy's direction: 'Mandy darling, hope you don't mind, but I used your spare key today. A huge vanload of flowers came for you and I was worried that if they were all left outside they may be stolen, so I took the liberty of letting the delivery man in. Don't worry, I watched him the whole time so that nothing was stolen.'

Mandy was stunned. 'There are flowers inside?'

'Yes, dear,' laughed Diva. 'Must dash, got the girls coming over for tea and biscuits.' Mandy smiled, knowing that 'the girls' would each be at least seventy.

'Enjoy,' trilled Diva, disappearing through the door.

Mandy opened her front door and stepped inside her flat carefully. The most amazing array of flowers and balloons filled her sitting room and the scent of powder-pink and red roses filled the air. Mandy dropped her bag at her feet and placed her hand over her mouth in astonishment. She'd never received anything like this before. She spun around on her heels and laughed out loud, shrieking, unable to believe it. On one huge bouquet she noticed a beautiful simple cream envelope with brown italic writing on the front. It read simply:

For Mandy x

She opened the envelope and read the card inside.

A belated Happy Birthday, thinking of you. J x

Mandy sighed and held the card to her chest. How could something feel so good so soon?

Over the next couple of weeks, Mandy tried to carefully select the emotions she could live with and shut out the rest. The flowers were breathtaking and were still blooming beautifully. She loved looking at them, displayed artfully in each room. In truth she also felt good about herself whenever she thought of who they were from. However, in her mind she had done the right thing, justified things as far as she was concerned. She had not contacted Jake at all, other than one text to say:

THANK YOU FOR THE BEAUTIFUL FLOWERS. X

She pondered over the kiss in the text, but decided that she would send that one kiss to anyone else who had been so generous and, to be fair, this man had taken generosity to a whole new level. She hadn't encouraged him any further and felt good about that.

Now she grabbed her Moncler padded ski jacket and as she snuggled into it she felt warm and cosy, the black fur around the hood making her look like an exotic Eskimo. George would be happy! She picked up her Yves Saint Laurent tote bag and as always checked she had what she needed.

Keys – check.
Mobile – check.
Cash – check.
Lippy – check.

And with that she whizzed up the stairs and into Figgy.

It was a Saturday and the traffic on the A3 was pretty good. It was a cold and frosty afternoon but the sun was shining and Mandy enjoyed the drive to Esher to visit her mum and sister. It had been nearly two months since she'd seen them and Mandy missed them and her two nieces desperately. Robyn was the eldest, eight years old going on thirty, and spoiled rotten. She had light-brown hair and a face full of freckles with cheeky dimples. Mandy knew she would be trouble with a capital T, but she was also so loving, simply craving reassurance and attention. Milly was four and adorable, with big brown eyes and a cute bobbed haircut. She was fabulous. Nothing really rocked Milly's world; she was the most chilled-out four-year-old Mandy had ever seen.

As Mandy pulled up outside her sister's grand Victorian house, she noticed the new driveway with the new Range Rover parked on it. She couldn't help but realize how different she and Olivia had become since Dad had died. Olivia, more than ever, was on a mission to keep up with and surpass the Joneses. Everything had to be as if it was a feature in *Elle Décor* magazine. The house was minimalistic inside and everything had its exact place. During the week Olivia had a cook and a cleaner – and of course there was always Valerie, their mum. Valerie and Olivia had always been especially close, but since Dad had died their mum seemed to want to be around her grandchildren more often. She had mellowed, only slightly, but enough all the same.

Through her open car window, Mandy heard the giggles of her nieces just as she saw Robyn frantically pointing to the bush and then placing her finger to her mouth as if to shush Mandy. Mandy twigged straight away: Milly wanted to play hide-and-seek. Mandy got out of her car and went along with the game.

'Hello, gorgeous, I've missed you so much.' Robyn ran over to her and hugged her tight.

'Hello! Have you heard the new Girls Aloud song? It's

brilliant!' Her green eyes looked up adoringly at Mandy. 'Mum says you've actually met them!'

'Yes, darling. We threw one of their parties and they were all lovely – very beautiful, as you'd expect.'

'Kimberley is my favourite,' said Robyn confidently as they both walked up the driveway.

'Cheryl's the best, not Kimberley!' said a little voice from behind the bush. Mandy tried not to laugh. Milly was useless at hiding, you could always see her, yet she of course thought she was invisible.

'I think I know that voice,' mused Mandy. 'Is that my little minx?'

Milly jumped out of the bush with a huge growl.

'Oh, you frightened me,' gasped Mandy, tickling the girls and loving their company already. She adored their openness and genuine love for her. 'Mummy and Granny are cooking lunch,' Robyn said, skipping her way to the back door.

The minute Mandy walked in, she sensed something was wrong. A strained heaviness filled the air. Yet Mum was in her usual winter uniform of brown roll-neck sweater and jeans, standing at the kitchen stove cooking, and Olivia was dashing around picking up toys, her blonde highlights swept back in a ponytail. She was wearing a white cashmere V-neck and slim-fitting faded blue jeans and was barefoot, exposing her tanned feet. Her figure was great, especially after two children; she was tight and toned, no skinny minny but perfectly in proportion. Whilst she pretended that she owed her fit body to rushing around, she actually worked out with a personal trainer three times a week and ate whatever she liked to eat, apart from a 'forbidden' list of:

Bread
Wheat
Starch
Sugar
And dairy.

That was Olivia all over: something about her was ashamed to admit to being anything less than perfect. She threw amazing dinner parties but only invited celebrity friends, friends who would not bring up her past or embarrass her – and she was easily embarrassed. She was a natural with interior design, flower-arranging and anything creative. She would never admit to having to work hard at anything, though she frequently put herself under unbelievable pressure. The pretence of achieving her perfect life with ease was part of the image.

Mandy had often wondered what drove her sister. Was she bored or unfulfilled, focusing so much on the home and children because she was never really brave enough to go for her dreams big time? Olivia was always so busy compared to everyone else, you had to book to see her weeks in advance and she simply didn't have the time for Mandy any more. They were definitely not as close as they had been and Mandy missed her sister desperately. But she had learned that being open or seeming vulnerable with Olivia just didn't get you anywhere; she was too like her mother.

Despite the slight atmosphere, Olivia kept her tone light and was polite in her conversation, almost to a fault. Sometimes Mandy felt like she was a mere acquaintance, one of the mums from her nieces' school rather than her sister.

'Hi, Mand, are you OK? Mum's making some pasta and salad, if that's all right with you?'

Mandy walked over to Olivia and kissed her on the cheek, and then did the same to her mum.

'Yeah, that sounds great, thanks. I've brought some wine for you – not the best in the world, but I thought it might be nice for later.'

'Oh, lovely,' acknowledged Olivia, opening the fridge and pushing the wine bottle to the back. 'Robbie has had some truly gorgeous wine given to him for some work he did for a client and I thought we could have that today?' Olivia closed the fridge door and smiled. 'No doubt we'll have yours too, thanks, darling.' Mandy knew they wouldn't get to it, and wondered why she had bothered. However, she persisted:

'I also got some bits for the kids, just from GAP, but really lovely white linen pyjamas.' Mandy handed them over.

'Oh, you didn't need to do that,' Olivia said. 'Mum bought us some Ralph Lauren ones for our holiday in the new year.

They'll need a second pair though, so these will come in handy. Thanks, darling.'

With that, Olivia efficiently folded them and whisked them upstairs.

Mandy rolled her eyes, sighed and sat down on the big plush velvet sofa.

'She doesn't mean it, you know.' Valerie was slicing tomatoes for the salad.

'Well, Mum, you wouldn't say anything if she did, so let's not go there, shall we?' Mandy snapped, exasperated by her sister's behaviour.

'What's that supposed to mean?' Valerie asked without even lifting her eyes.

'You know what it means, Mum,' Mandy said quietly. 'But look, I want a nice day and to see the kids. It's fine, so let's just leave it.'

At that moment, Robbie bounced down the stairs and into the kitchen.

'Hi, darling, how are you?' He greeted Mandy with a kiss on the cheek. 'Olivia just showed me the bits you bought for the kids. Thanks, babe, very generous of you.'

'No worries,' Mandy smiled, pleased that at least someone was grateful.

Robbie was clearly happy to see her, but he looked drained. Something was off, out of synch. He was a good man, handsome but not pretty, slender and tall, and he reminded Mandy of Paul Weller. He was always dressed casually and seemed rather cool. He was an architect and quite well known, with a growing reputation. Olivia had met him when his firm was looking for a PA/accountant. She was useless with maths, but fancied Robbie like crazy and lied and said she was qualified in both. She gave him some cock-and-bull story about the people she had worked for and he swallowed it and took her on. (He later confessed he knew she was lying, but really fancied her too.)

At that time Robbie had been seeing a girl for a couple of months, but he and Olivia were crazy about each other very early on. Olivia was far from the control freak she was today: she was fun, vivacious and at times reckless. She still had a hard edge, like her mum, but she had a youthful freeness to her soul, and as a result was sparkly and attractive, and many men wanted her. Olivia had a boyfriend at the time called Patrick, with whom she had the most amazing sex. But Patrick was abusive too, and when she became pregnant by him she realized that Robbie meant more to her than she'd thought. Robbie was wonderful to her, and they became close. More importantly to Olivia, he ignored her bruised arms and eyes covered in make-up, and even drove her to the hospital after she miscarried following another beating from Patrick. Life had not been easy for her, and she always felt safe and comfortable when Robbie was around. Robbie was still seeing his girlfriend, and Olivia's duties as a PA included arranging their dinner dates and weekends away, but one day something snapped inside her. She could not lie to herself. Robbie was gentle and kind and she realized she loved him.

She wasn't used to a healthy love, only the rollercoaster of a bad relationship with all its dramas. She worried that Robbie and this whole new experience of him loving her would bore her, that she herself would one day sabotage a good relationship. Mandy believed her sister had met The One, and told her she deserved him and not to fuck it up.

That day, with her things packed, Olivia told Robbie that she was leaving, that working for him as his PA, booking romantic dates for him and his girlfriend, was proving too difficult. This was a big thing for Olivia to actually say, and Robbie knew it. He took her in his arms and kissed her deeply, then kissed her some more. He knew he had to wait for her to be ready.

Now, in their state-of-the-art kitchen he stretched his arms up and said, 'Right, I'm off to meet the boys down the pub to watch the footie.' He dawdled for a moment. 'Bye,' he said to Valerie, but she chose to ignore him, looking down at the cutting board and expertly slicing the cucumber.

'Bye, Mand, have a lovely day with the girls.' Mandy hugged Robbie goodbye and after she'd closed the door behind him turned to her mum.

'What the hell is the matter? *What's* going on here?'

Valerie's manic slicing stopped. Looking directly at Mandy

and with no emotion in her voice she said bluntly, 'I think he's having an affair.'

Mandy froze.

Valerie wiped her hands on a tea towel, and spoke in a lowered tone. 'I heard him on the phone earlier – a woman had left him a message and I could hear it from here. Whoever she was, she was in a noisy place and so obviously she had to talk loudly.'

Mandy shook her head in disbelief. 'But it – it could be anyone, someone from work.'

Valerie scoffed coldly. '*This* was not from work!'

'Does Olivia know?' was all Mandy could ask.

'Who knows with that one?' countered Valerie, looking sadly up the stairs towards her daughter's bedroom. 'She sees what she wants to see.'

'What did Robbie do when he knew you'd heard the message?' Mandy spluttered. 'I mean, did he say anything, anything at all? Does he know?'

'I don't think he *really* knows exactly what I heard, but he knows I know, put it that way. I've no idea what is going on with those two and I'm not going to cause mayhem over one muffled message, but Olivia suspects something, I'm sure, and when she's ready to speak to me I will be there for her, no matter what. Fucking men: they fuck you about when they are around and then they fuck off!'

The tension was unbelievable and Mandy was astonished. She didn't know whether to comfort her mum or slap her. She wasn't sure whether she was insinuating something about her dad. Mandy was furious. It wasn't as if her dad had left out of choice; he died. Silence reigned for a moment.

Finally Valerie looked at Mandy with what seemed like slight tears in her eyes and, biting the inside of her lips, said, 'But that's enough of all that now. Lunch is served.' She placed the pasta dish proudly on the beautifully arranged table. 'Call the girls for me?'

After lunch, Mandy could hardly see her way home – Figgy's heating was playing up and the mist on the windscreen had thickened. On top of that, it was now chucking it down, and the rain seemed relentless.

Mandy finally made it back home, stop-starting through the usual London traffic, and felt unsettled for the rest of the evening. She kept taking deep breaths every sixty seconds or so, thinking back to her lovely girls and how they had played around, simply oblivious to the mess of their parents' marriage. Mandy wondered how she would feel to be the other woman, a home wrecker who could change a happy family for ever. It was something that would never sit happily with her, she was sure of it.

Jake sat alone in his huge office late on a Saturday evening, looking at the twinkling London skyline through floor-to-ceiling windows, and acknowledged to himself that he had it all. A beautiful wife, two lovely children, money, an amazing career and a stunning home. He had travelled extensively, achieved many dreams and on paper everything seemed perfect, every box ticked. So why did he feel so lonely? He felt guilty for even thinking it, but he knew, deep down, he did not feel complete.

He was a man who thrived on living life, yet he was merely existing. He had forgotten the buzz that came with being his true self. Somewhere along the line he had lost his way. Money, power and fast cars were undoubtedly a huge part of what made him tick, and he yearned to be a great father and husband. Most of the time he succeeded, but something was missing and he had not realized what that something was until one night he had seen her, standing right in front of him. That feeling had not burned in him for a long time – God, he had missed it! His fire was back. An unopened door beckoned him. It had always been there, but buried for so long. He knew Mandy was the key, he had found her at last. Jake had been denying himself some thing that was part of him, like a second skin. He didn't know exactly why or when, but he knew a big change was on its way.

He felt relieved, happy, guilty and petrified. He looked at his happy family photo and for once in his life he truly felt powerless. He sensed that, for a long time to come, that was not going to change.

THREE

The First Kiss

The following Sunday morning Mandy awoke to her mobile vibrating on her bedside table. Half asleep, she fumbled for the phone and without checking the number she answered groggily:

'Hello.'

Silence.

'Hello.'

Silence. Now she felt grumpy. 'Oh, whoever you are, you've bloody woken me up and now you're not talking. Call me back when you have something to say, weirdo.' And she hung up.

The phone vibrated again.

'Hello . . . Speak to me. Is that you fucking about, George?'

'Hi, sorry, it's Jake,' a voice said gently.

Mandy sat up so quickly she felt dizzy.

'Oh God, sorry, I'm . . .' She hadn't a clue what to say. 'Sorry, I didn't sleep very well last night, and I took a

42

few Nytol, so I don't know what the hell I'm saying or doing.'

Jake's voice continued calmly. 'Listen, I've left various messages and a text and not heard back from you. I just need to see you, just once, to see if all I'm feeling is real or not. I could be driving you nuts, and myself too for that matter, and all for an idea that's in my head.'

Mandy squeezed the phone as close to her ear as she could. God, she loved his voice. She had secretly saved some of the messages he had left, and replayed them in 'moments of weakness'. While Jake went on about needing them to meet she had her eyes closed, her lips forming a gentle smile. She was too tired to fight something that felt so good. She let Jake finish and then finally she spoke.

'OK, let's meet, but just this once. This is doing both our heads in for a reason. I've never known anything like it, but it's all a bit bizarre really, given that we've only met once.'

'Exactly!' laughed Jake. 'And for ten–fifteen minutes, if that.' He sounded relieved.

'It's probably nothing,' Mandy muttered, trying to convince herself as she spoke, 'so let's be grown-up, have a coffee and kill the mystery!' She found herself laughing out of nervousness.

'OK,' continued Jake. 'When is good for you?'

'Tonight?' Mandy blurted out. 'Might as well get it over with!'

Jake was quiet.

'Oh God,' sighed Mandy, 'that sounded really rude, sorry, I'm just— Well, I've never been in this kind of thing before, and I'm nervous, saying silly things, and it could all be nothing.'

Jake had been walking back home with papers and some French bread when he rang Mandy. He had imagined that as usual he would get her sweet, lovely voice message, but she had answered herself, and he was thrown. He found himself smiling.

'You've already said it could be nothing – noted and recorded,' he laughed. 'So I think we're both right in having no expectations. We'll just meet and, in your words, be grown-ups. And see what this is about – no pressure.'

'No pressure,' repeated Mandy.

'And it could be nothing.' He shrugged.

'Exactly,' she repeated again. 'So why don't I meet you outside the Natural History Museum around eightish this evening and we can decide where to go for a coffee from there.'

'Sounds fine to me. See you then!'

'Bye.' Mandy's voice softened.

'Bye – and oh by the way, I'm not a weirdo, I promise.'

Mandy was about to be miffed, but then she remembered what she had said earlier on.

'Oh, sorry! I thought it was my friend George being a prat, and I abuse him all the time. He's used to it.'

Jake stifled a chuckle. 'Maybe I should be worried about *you* being the crazy person,' he said warmly.

Mandy smiled softly: he had been kind, had not made her feel even more of a prat for being one in the first place.

'See you later,' she finally said.

'Bye.'

Click . . . and the line was dead.

Mandy felt as if she had been hit by a steamroller. She threw herself back on the pillow and covered her face with her arms.

'Don't think about it now, think about it later,' she told herself, and with that (and the Nytol) she gently fell back to sleep.

Tap-tap-tap-tap-tap, tap-tap-tap-tap.

The rain hit the little skylight in her bedroom with a gentle rhythm as she woke up. Christ, it was six in the evening! Had Jake called or was it all just a misty dream? Feeling delirious, Mandy checked her phone, her heart heavy. Yep, he called at nine in the morning, on a Sunday. Who does that? Jake, obviously.

Yesterday's visit to her sister had drained her emotionally, and she was overtired. She must have needed to sleep that long. She remembered her dad saying in his Irish brogue, 'If you didn't need sleep, you wouldn't sleep that long.' Also, 'Get it while you can – and that's not just the sleeping,' he'd chuckle. Dad always laughed at his own naff jokes; it must be where she got it from.

Mandy showered, exfoliated and moisturized. Standing in front of her closet, she couldn't really decide what was appropriate for the evening. 'Hmmm,' she pondered aloud. 'This is *not* a date, but he's also not "just a friend". Maybe I would regret it if I didn't knock him dead. Well, of course I would!'

She remembered George saying, 'Better to be overdressed and fabulous than underdressed and polite.'

Mandy grabbed a gorgeous silk vintage Pucci shift dress. Its yellow and brown swirling sixties print looked beautiful against her peaches-and-cream skin, and teamed with thick black tights and black Mary Jane patent heels it made her look effortlessly chic. The faithful Burberry mac went over the top and she kept her black wavy hair loose, with a centre parting. She kept her jewellery simple, just a long gold locket that her grandmother had given her. Her make-up was natural and her skin was glowing.

Grabbing her cream frilly umbrella, she went out, originally intending to walk the ten minutes to the museum, but her plans soon changed when the rain poured down so heavily that she slipped on the first step leading up from her flat to the street. Mandy stood back in the doorway and grabbed some things off the table to squash into her oversized black clutch bag. As always:

Car keys
Chanel perfume
Phone
Credit card
And of course the lippy!
Check, check, check, check, check!

She ran up to her car as carefully as she could. She would pick up Jake and they could decide where to go from there.

Mandy pulled up and parked despite the red lines outside the white floodlit museum. She put her hazard lights on, admiring the fairy lights that sparkled in the huge trees as she glanced up. Lots of people were leaving the ice rink that was there for the Christmas season. Suddenly, she felt nervous, jumpy and excited. She spotted Jake straight away, a little further down the road. The collar of his beautiful, tailored coat was up, in an attempt to protect his face from the rain. Mandy wanted to run towards him right there and then and fall into his arms. She fumbled with the lock and let herself out of the car.

At the same moment Jake saw her, so radiant and beautiful, and he already knew what he needed to know. He smiled and stopped walking for a moment. He waved; the rain was hitting his face hard.

Mandy felt stuck to the ground, and extremely self-conscious. She half waved back. Even though she hardly knew this man, he made her feel more special than anyone had in a long time. She wanted to run into his arms, and yet he hadn't even said a word. Suddenly, panic filled her body from head to toe, and various familiar happy faces started to flash in her head, one after another, and another: Olivia, Assia, her mum, Robyn, Milly. Mandy just wanted to be alone; she was so anxious she felt she was on the verge of passing out. She was already soaked from the rain and her hair was stuck to her face, exposing her childlike fear. She looked at Jake sadly and bolted for the car.

'Mandy, don't!' Jake shouted.

He ran towards the car, but it was too late. Mandy tried as hard as she could not to look at him as she drove past, but she couldn't help herself. He was the man that had turned her last few weeks upside down. Now he stood in the rain, looking lonely, hurt and broken.

Later that evening, a message was left for Jake:

'I'm sorry about tonight.' Mandy's voice was fragile. 'I just don't think this is for me, it's not meant to be, and I realize that now. Sorry again . . . I guess I'm just not built for it.' And with that she hung up.

Over the next couple of weeks, Mandy threw her heart and head into work, and it paid off tremendously. It was the festive season, so all the multinational companies were throwing their annual Christmas parties, some small-scale but most still huge, despite the credit crunch. Mandy had been nervous that all her hard work, socializing to the early hours and schmoozing with the foreign offices, would have been compromised as a result of the ever-declining economy. However, companies seemed to be going from one extreme to the other: some were really tightening their belts, but many were out to prove that everything was OK, and threw exactly the same kind of parties they always had. Certain clients had even chosen to splash out more than usual for what might be their last big Christmas bash for a few years. Mandy took one day at a time and embraced the varied expectations. She was a wiz at making something feel special despite a limited budget. Florists, entertainment agents and hotel managers had all become good friends. She adapted to different people to make *sure* that was the case.

Michael, her boss, had become a father figure to her, though he was so different from her real dad, and he encouraged her and believed in her completely. Mandy had been working for a boutique hotel agency for two years when she was assigned to plan every last detail of an important business trip for Michael to Switzerland. She had handled everything for him so impeccably that he had poached her from the company, offering over double her current wage, and a healthy bonus if other companies were brought to the table from Mandy direct. Mandy loved the vibe, loved the job, and loved Michael.

He was an older, very sexy, charismatic man, who smoked cigars, wore the most beautiful tailored suits and had the naughtiest sense of humour in the world. He had passion, though sometimes he lost clients by letting it get the better of him. Ultimately he was a good and decent man; he loved his life and he loved his wife, a thin blonde American called India with alabaster skin. She was by no means a raving beauty, but she was sophisticated and serene and acted as calm counterpart to Michael's boisterous ego. He was a larger-than-life character but India knew just how to handle him. Many women wanted to step into her shoes, but India was smart and dealt with them cleverly and graciously. At times she also worked with Michael; after all, she was an advertising account manager for some of the top luxury-goods labels.

Michael was not the richest man in the world, as he enjoyed a decadent lifestyle and saving and investing weren't his style, but he had become very popular on London's huge social scene. The love of his life before India had been a fiery, voluptuous Italian actress. They were often a fixture in *Vogue*, *Harper's* and *Vanity Fair*, but Claudia was too similar to Michael for it to ever last, and she left him broken-hearted. He had had many women fighting for his affections since then, and of course he dabbled along the way, but he spent many years steering clear of love until India came along. Nevertheless, his charm had not decreased and he still enjoyed teasing and tantalizing the women.

Even men mellowed in his company. His Jack Nicholson smile won him many admirers and his fiery temper and stubborn pig-headedness lost him just as many, but Mandy adored the way he challenged her, made her want to be the best version of herself that she could be. There were times when Michael swore like a trooper, but Mandy knew exactly where she stood with him at all times; with Michael what you saw was what you got, and you either loved him or loathed him. Mandy loved him.

The offices were *très chic*, exquisitely laid out within a large cream stucco house on the Fulham/Chelsea borders, situated just off the King's Road. Perspex-framed photographs and posters of Bond movies, rock stars and sportsmen were hung beautifully against the plain white walls. At the end of the hallway were two bronze statues of Buddha. Huge, sumptuous, rich purple sofas made the most discerning client feel at home. 'We are in the business of style and glamour,' Michael would say. 'Presentation is everything, darling!'

A breakfast buffet of croissants, lemon tarts and an array of savoury pastries was set up every day on a glass-topped table under a window. Still water and fresh organic orange juice were available in large crystal jugs, and the atmosphere was one of opulence, creativity and control. The team consisted of around twenty people, including the accounts department, most of whom Mandy liked. From day one, however, Michael's PA, Maggie, had rubbed Mandy up the wrong way. Maggie hated having a new girl on the block and was competitive and protective of Michael. If ever a row broke out, though, Michael would pop his head out of the door and bark and swear at everyone, and they would keep their heads down and get back to the job in hand.

This busy season had kept Mandy's mind off Jake for a bit. She had not had a message from him and she had not contacted him either. Deena told her she had done the right thing. George simply called her a wimp, and set her up on the most disastrous date ever.

'Get back out there, girl! Your tight arse and pretty face are going to waste.'

Mandy knew George's mind was elsewhere, probably wandering through rails and rails of beautiful clothes in Harrods.

The blind date was with a man called Freddie, who used to be a beautiful woman (he showed her a picture taken before the op) called Francine. He / she now wanted to settle down and adopt two Chinese babies. Mandy had spent the rest of the evening thinking of various ways to murder George.

What was he thinking of? Poor Freddie / Francine had been through enough! By the end of their date, Mandy had had a few Pinot Grigios too many and sobbed and sobbed about how desperately lonely she was. Poor bloody Freddie had had to bundle her into a taxi. Having waved goodbye sympathetically, surprisingly he never called her again.

Not good . . .

Mandy realized her social life was at an all-time low, but when Michael walked out and placed a request before her to throw a party for the Whitechapel Art Gallery in east London to celebrate the best of art and fashion, she felt her chance to achieve her dreams was on its way. Michael put his hand on his hip.

'Can you handle it? Last-minute, I know, so if you can't do it tell me now.'

Mandy couldn't say no, but as she scanned the email she saw it was only two weeks away.

'Of course.' She smiled calmly; meanwhile her pulse was going like the clappers. This was a chance for her to truly make her mark with Michael and maybe at last prove that she could, in time, also work for the firm over in the US with the big players.

She took a deep breath and was on the case within minutes. She organized a schedule, made calls and pulled in a few favours, lined up a designer for the invites, confirmed a guest list with the gallery, and booked press and photographers. The *Evening Standard* was covering the event: it would be a beautiful evening and Mandy couldn't wait for her big night.

Two weeks later, amazing pieces of art and fashion were hung on the walls at the gallery. The layout and the spaces in between sat right with Mandy's colleagues at the

Whitechapel. Everyone agreed that the star of the show should be the art and fashion itself. Some rooms were dedicated purely to fashion, vintage pieces from fifties Dior to contemporary designers, each lit like a star on show.

On the art side, Mandy had called Hannah, a dear friend of hers, whose family owned galleries in various countries, and her team took over the hanging for the various works of art so that each piece drew attention in its own right. The lighting of the whole gallery was edgy but inviting.

The staff were young and cool and whizzed expertly in and out of the crowds with trays of vodka shots, champagne and wine. Roland Mouret, Marc Jacobs and Giles Deacon all showed up, as did Gwyneth Paltrow and Agyness Deyn. When Kate Moss arrived, wearing vintage Chanel, the cameras went crazy. Mandy saw flashes of light for at least twenty minutes afterwards. Miniature fish and chips were served in newspaper, tying in with the gallery's location in the East End. The music was kicking, with the Ting Tings getting things started and later the DJ blasted out Blondie and the Clash till the next band arrived.

The party had only been going a couple of hours but was already in full swing. The turnout had been amazing so far, the night was going well, and still Mandy was petrified it wouldn't be long before *something* went wrong. She rushed to the door to check the guest list and see who was left to turn up. She looked pretty hot, wearing a black

Balmain dress with slashes of material cut away on one hip, and coloured rhinestones as embellishments. She looked as sexy as hell. Her hair was coiffed at the front, showing off her beautifully made-up, smoky black eyes. Her skin was luminous, with a pearly sheen to it, and her lips were sticky and shiny with lashings of gloss. Her short dress showed off her long legs in black opaque tights perfectly, and the highest silver-studded black Louboutin ankle boots made her strut confidently. Many a head was turned as she walked out to check the updates with Chantelle at the front.

George's sister Chantelle was dressed to impress the fashion crowd, with her lips bright red and wearing a black trilby hat and a full-length fake-fur coat to keep her warm. She was eccentric, tough, a party girl, but militant when it came to her guest list, and she was great with any kind of person. She was quickly becoming a favourite with Mandy, who trusted her.

'Hi, Mand,' said Chantelle, chewing gum. 'Just so you know, Jamie, Lily, Kelly and Alexa are on their way; they just called to check the vibe, and of course I told them, great, great, great! Kelly from the Stereophonics is still stuck in traffic, but wanted to know what the party was like and I told him, great, great, great! And the lead singer of the Killers is here with some friends, is LOVING the band music, and wants to get up and sing, can you believe it? So I of course said, "Brilliant!" Great, great, great!'

Mandy followed Chantelle's pen tracing down the list. She should have been ecstatic about the great names that were turning up to the event, but instead she was frozen.

'Um, who's this?' she tried to say as matter-of-factly as possible.

Chantelle checked her notes. 'That's Jake Chaplin – you know, of Chaplin Advertising. They do all the advertising for vodka, Orange Mobile and some of the major fashion houses. They also do sports brands – they're huge!'

'Oh, I see,' Mandy replied, holding her breath.

She walked away, trying to get her head around things. Obviously she knew she had no choice but to stay, as this was *her* night, *her* hard work, and no one, not even safely married Jake, was going to get in the way of that.

Michael and India approached Mandy. India looked elegant in a simple, long grey dress, her Jimmy Choo shoes peeping out. Michael was obviously feeling upbeat and happy.

'Well, I think tonight is going brilliantly. Well done, darling, I'm very proud of you,' he smiled. His eyes were twinkling as he looked around the room. 'What the *fuck* is this music, though?' He pulled a pained face. 'Sounds like a bag of spanners.'

'Ignore him,' laughed India. 'He's just old and bitter.'

'I know what's cool,' he bellowed. 'Don't have to fucking like it though, do I?'

Michael introduced Mandy to everyone that he knew.

More people were arriving by the minute and Mandy was chatting and laughing, working the room like a natural.

'Mandy,' India called, 'come and meet the Chaplin mob.'

Mandy spun round, and there right in front of her stood Jake with five other colleagues. One of them looked vaguely familiar.

'These lovely chaps were just saying what a great party this is,' trilled India. 'I told them that on this occasion it was all down to you.'

Mandy felt stunned. Jake was so close and she wasn't sure how to respond.

'Well I don't know about that,' Mandy stumbled. 'It was all down to me – and about ten other people as well.'

India shook her head. 'Don't be so modest, Mandy, otherwise Michael will take all the credit and you *know* it.' She winked. 'Sorry, where are my manners?' she continued. 'This is Mandy Sanderson, my husband's right-hand woman as far as I'm concerned, and, if he was honest, as far as he's concerned too.'

Mandy blushed.

India was being the perfect hostess. 'Sorry, but I'm afraid I don't know all your names. Please introduce yourselves.'

Two men called Bob and Chris came forward and shook Mandy's hand enthusiastically. Mandy turned to Jake and they stared intently at each other for several seconds, the electricity between them undeniable.

'Jake Chaplin,' Jake put his hand out to shake Mandy's.

She ignored it, but instantly felt she had been too quick to react emotionally; she was better than that.

Looking Jake directly in the eye, she said, 'I'm so sorry, what was your name again?'

He looked back at her in silence. 'Jake Chaplin, glad I made an impression.'

She shook his hand and smiled the sweetest smile.

'Lovely to meet you, Jake. I'm sorry, gentlemen, if I seem a bit distracted, but I have tour managers, celebrities and photographers waving at me from all different directions, all wanting me to sort something out.' She sighed. 'The show must go on, and apparently I'm the hostess with the mostest, so . . . lovely to meet you.' She felt Jake staring at her. 'Enjoy your evening, gentlemen.' She flashed one more killer smile, her heart pounding, and sashayed off as smoothly as she could, taking deep breaths and trying to remain in control.

The night was glorious. Everyone looked amazing, the champagne flowed, the celebrities sparkled, and everyone enjoyed themselves and let their hair down.

The photographer left at midnight, and by two-thirty it was time to end the party. The hard-core party girls all kissed and hugged Mandy as if she was a long-lost friend, some drunkenly exchanged incorrect phone numbers and others struggled to walk in a straight line, never mind get home. Most of all, everyone thanked Mandy for such a great night. She, too, would never forget it.

Mandy made her way outside, where Chantelle was smoking a cigarette, clearly a little the worse for wear. It was now nearly three o'clock, and there was a bitter chill. Other than some of the crew de-rigging the music stage, and security and cleaners, everyone had left.

Mandy's feet were killing her and, huddled up in her leopardskin coat, she sat on a step, pulled off her heels and rubbed her feet. Chantelle joined her.

'Great fucking party, Mand, everyone was raving about it as they left. They all said it was great, great, great, great!' Chantelle hiccupped. She started to laugh.

Mandy didn't know if it was the fresh air that had kicked in, but both girls sat on the step and giggled until their bellies hurt.

'I gotta go,' laughed Mandy, holding her stomach. 'I've got to be in the office tomorrow.'

'Poor you,' sighed Chantelle. 'I don't do daytime.'

Mandy made to get up and looked back at Chantelle.

'I'm going to get a taxi; need a lift?'

'Nah,' said Chantelle, still chewing her gum. 'I know a guy here called Lee, he's the great big security guard; he's giving me a lift home and he's bloody gorgeous.'

Mandy shook her head. 'Naughty girl,' she smiled.

Chantelle got up to stagger back inside. 'Shout me if you

have any trouble getting a cab, it's been murder trying to get them tonight.'

Mandy crossed her arms around her, shivering. Heels in hand, she looked left and right. It was still bloody dodgy round here, gallery or no gallery. Mandy suddenly felt unsure; she looked in her phone to dial a black cab.

'Sore feet?' said a voice behind her.

Mandy didn't need to turn round; she knew who it was. Her heart was beating so fast she couldn't speak.

Jake came over and stood next to her by the railing. He lit a cigarette and looked out to the deserted street before him. Mandy glanced at him from the corner of her eye; he always made her so nervous. It was so cold that she could see every mist of breath from his mouth; she wanted a better view and turned to take a good look at this man. Yes, he was beautiful.

'I can't find a taxi,' she said quietly.

Jake kept looking straight in front of him. 'Do you want me to take you home?'

'Yes, please.'

'OK.' He couldn't look at her. 'My car's just down here on the left.'

The two of them walked together in silence down the dimly lit edge of Whitechapel High Street. Neither of them said a word until half an hour later, when they were nearly at Mandy's flat.

'Sorry,' she whispered, 'I didn't even ask, this isn't out of your way, is it?'

'Not too far,' Jake assured her; he still couldn't look at her. 'I'm Notting Hill way, it'll take me ten minutes, tops, this time of night.'

The atmosphere felt sad and tense, their stifled emotions aching to come forward. Jake was being polite yet distant. Hardly surprising, really.

'I'm so sorry about that night,' Mandy said, suddenly looking directly at Jake. He sighed and continued to drive. The next few minutes passed in silence until Jake pulled over in Queensgate. Finally, he looked at Mandy. He took her in for an age before he finally spoke.

'This is obviously really difficult.' He paused. 'It doesn't sit right with you, or me either.' He shook his head. 'I hate not knowing what this is, but I'm not going to try and keep sorting it out when it's clear you simply don't want to know. It just makes me feel worse. I obviously got it all wrong and I'm sorry for that. With everything I've had going on in my head, I'd forgotten that we don't actually know one another, so again I'm sorry if I've scared you and I've been too full on.' He laughed, despite himself. 'You must think I'm a complete crank.'

Jake looked lovely when he laughed, Mandy thought.

He let himself out of the car and opened Mandy's door. She felt shocked at his tone, that it seemed so final. He was ready to walk her to her door and that was it, done. Finished.

The wind was blowing hard and the few remaining autumn leaves swirled around their feet as Jake led Mandy to the top of her stairs. She knew in her heart she hadn't abandoned him that Sunday evening because he was too full on; she had left because she was scared of herself and the intensity of her feelings whenever he was close.

She turned to face him. He was much taller than her. Her feet felt cold, but she tingled all over. She was trembling just being near him.

'Are you cold?' he asked gently.

Mandy looked up at him sadly and nodded.

He opened his coat to wrap her inside it and held her close for as long as he could. As she nuzzled into his warm chest, a voice in her head was pleading, Please don't go, stay here with me for ever. She finally looked up at him to find that he was gazing at her in a way that no one had done before. He cupped her face in his hands and there, in the early hours of a cold winter's morning, they held each other tightly and kissed, first tenderly and gently, and then with so much passion Mandy felt she would burst.

The wind was blowing her hair and as Jake stroked it back off her face he smiled.

'You're amazing.'

Mandy looked down shyly. She could taste him on her lips. It took her all the will in the world to say, 'I'd better go, and so should you. It's late and we'll catch our death up here.'

'I don't want to leave you,' he said. He smiled as if she was the most precious thing in the world. Suddenly the sparkle died in his eyes. Something else had kicked in. Mandy couldn't quite work out what it was but she knew it wasn't good. Jake released her gently and took one long last look at her before walking to his car and disappearing into the night. At that moment, Mandy knew her life would never be the same again.

FOUR

The Dance of Love

With Mandy's hand firmly wrapped in his, Jake led the way through the beautiful entrance of the Royal Opera House. He had phoned Mandy the morning after the party and said he had a surprise for her. Mandy was relieved: his departure had been so sudden and she had sensed he felt slightly afraid. As a result she'd been awake most of the night, her heart aching. She hadn't ever had to deal with anyone having doubts before, and the thought of Jake walking away made her realize just how much she cared about him. A deep, deep affection and God, it hurt. If anyone was going to run away, if anyone was going to protect themselves and stop it all, it would be her.

When morning arrived it was a relief, and when she saw on her phone that she had a missed call from Jake, she took a deep breath and listened to her voicemail. 'Hi, it's me, Jake . . . Sorry I left so suddenly last night, I . . .' His voice trailed off. 'Anyway, it's a lovely bright morning and I've already had a breakfast meeting, and,' with another deep breath, 'I also have a nice surprise for you tonight. I'll pick you up at six-thirty to be safe for time. Any probs with that, let me know and . . .' he stumbled, 'that's it.'

Mandy exhaled, giggled and felt a tiny pang of stubbornness all at the same time. She was thrilled he hadn't done a runner, thrilled he had to see her again so soon, but a bit pissed off he had just expected her to be free. She got on the phone to George.

'What bloody time d'you call this?' he moaned.

'Seven-thirty,' replied Mandy matter-of-factly.

'Fuck me, you've got me up with the crack of the sparrow's – and I didn't get laid last night. It had better be important,' said George tartly, who believed a start earlier than nine in the morning was just plain stupid.

'Well,' Mandy retorted, 'Jake has rung me and wants to take me out tonight.'

'What happened last night?' George was alert now.

'We kissed.'

'Fumbled?'

'A bit!'

'You dirty mare! And so what? What's your problem?'

'Well, he just expects me to be free tonight.'

George sighed. 'Well, are you?'

'Well, yes,' said Mandy stubbornly.

George was exasperated. 'So go! What the hell's wrong with you? Are you the fucking Virgin Mary in all this or are you Madonna? Look, you've clearly decided you like this man enough to cross the boundaries – the fact that he is married obviously doesn't bother you enough to refrain from seeing him – so playing the "Am I available?" game truly isn't an option now, darling.'

Mandy was waiting for a pang of guilt to hit her, but it didn't come. She had been in *such* turmoil all night that nothing and no one would stop her from seeing Jake again, not even her foolish pride.

'I'm waiting for it . . .' said George with a heavy sigh.

'What?'

'The "I feel so bad, seeing a married man, but . . ." routine.' George let out a large yawn.

Mandy scoffed. 'Well, Mr Roberts, you obviously have me down as a pretty predictable girl, and on this occasion you are wrong. Wrong, wrong, wrong, wrong!'

Mandy found one too many 'wrong's came out of her mouth. Who was she really trying to convince, George or herself? Could she really go through with this charade and come out unscathed? George knew Mandy well, and that ultimately, when it came to falling for someone, nothing was simple.

'Listen, darling,' he said, sounding a bit muffled – he had a flannel on his head – 'for your sake, I really hope this guy starts to act as a real pig pretty soon, so you can walk away with as little harm done as possible.'

'But—' Mandy tried to interrupt.

'No interruptions, pleeeze . . . Thank you. Or I truly

hope this man could be The One, because I'm telling you now, Mandy, I've never known you to be so ga-ga about someone so quick, and my God, it won't be easy. In fact, the more time passes and the more you fall for him, the harder it will become. He has a wife, babies and a whole history that you will never be a part of. Now if you think he's worth all the baggage, then go tonight, but if you have any doubts, get out now!' He emphasized the last three words.

Mandy's words just fell out. 'He's worth it.' And at that moment she knew she really meant it. She wanted to see Jake so badly that she felt she could overcome anything.

George went quiet. 'Oh dear,' he sighed. 'You really are up Shit Creek without a paddle, aren't you?'

'Thanks for the vote of confidence,' said Mandy, hanging up.

She felt a bit pissed off with George. She knew deep down that he only wanted to protect her, but she didn't want to delve deep down right now. Where she was in her head felt good and she had a sense of self, of hope and optimism. She would go all out for what she'd wanted all her life, even though she knew in her heart of hearts that this selfishness wouldn't last for long. If she didn't capitalize on it, the man she just couldn't get out of her head could disappear out of her life for ever.

*

That evening, as they walked into the opera house Jake pulled out two tickets and presented them to a front-of-house staff member, who ripped them efficiently.

'Great seats, sir!' she said with a smile. 'Just through these doors and you will be shown to your aisle.'

'Come on, Jake,' said Mandy excitedly, 'the suspense is bloody killing me. What are we watching?'

He turned to her and grinned. 'OK, you've waited long enough; it's the first night of *Swan Lake*.'

A wave of emotion came over her and her eyes glistened with tears.

'What's wrong, Mandy?' said Jake, holding her shoulders.

Mandy looked down to the ground. 'My dad brought me here,' she murmured. She felt her bottom lip tremble and tried not to lose control. She looked up again into Jake's concerned face. 'Thank you, thank you so much.'

Jake cupped her heart-shaped face in his hands. 'If you're not comfortable with this, we can leave, darling. You know it's not a problem, don't you?'

'No,' Mandy cut him off. 'I'll explain later, but nothing would make me happier than to watch it again with you.'

Jake inhaled her scent, taking her in. It was moments like this that completely consumed him. Mandy was so emotional, so raw, so *alive*, and, success or no success, he'd been like the walking dead for too long. He caressed her hand as they both sat on the red velvet seats to watch the first act. Not once did he let her hand go. Not once.

The ballet was breathtaking. As the audience jumped to their feet to applaud, both Jake and Mandy were wrapped up in the excitement, clapping and cheering. Their happiness was palpable. Mandy wiped a tear from her eye. 'Dad would have *loved* this,' she said, and Jake watched her as she applauded the principal dancers, now taking their bows and curtseying for the crowd.

'Fancy a drink somewhere?' Jake asked in a chirpy tone.

'Would love to,' Mandy smiled. They found the car and Jake drove back towards Kensington as Mandy flicked through all the pre-programmed radio stations on the dashboard. 'God, sounds like all the DJs want to kill themselves tonight – so depressing!'

'No, wait, I love this song,' Jake said. 'It's Gladys Knight and the Pips. I absolutely love her, saw her at the Royal Albert Hall a few years ago. Terrible seats, high up in the gods, but my, that woman could sing.' He pushed a volume button on the steering wheel and Gladys Knight's soulful voice belted out. 'Mind you, it wasn't really Gladys Knight and the Pips,' quipped Jake, 'as there was only one Pip.' Jake chuckled to himself, but Mandy wasn't listening. The lyrics to the song had really caught her attention.

> *I need somebody*
> *Who's consistent with me*
> *Someone already there*
> *When I need company,*

Cuz when I'm feelin' low
I don't wanna have to go out lookin'
For a part time love
And when the dreams and rainbows start to disappear
I don't want somebody up and runnin' out of here
Cus when you stop and start
Baby it's a just too hard upon my heart
For a part time kind of love

Mandy felt a hot flush of recognition. 'How apt,' she whispered under her breath, wound down the window and pretended to be fascinated by all the goings-on around her. She had a nagging feeling that wouldn't go away, as if she knew that, no matter what happened, Jake was already too special to be a part-time love. God, it was all moving so fast. If he wasn't true to her, would it be too much of a rollercoaster ride for her heart? In her mind's eye, she saw these great big doors slamming down on her every vulnerable emotion.

'Be strong now,' she muttered firmly to herself.

'Sorry?' said Jake, smiling. 'You know they say that talking to yourself is the first sign of madness?'

'In that case I'm a lunatic,' laughed Mandy. 'I've been chattering away to myself since I was a kid. My dad caught me at it all the time, apparently.' Her voice cracked unexpectedly.

Jake pulled over in a resident's parking bay and looked at Mandy gently. 'What exactly happened to your father?'

Mandy loved Jake's voice; it was warm and husky.

'He died,' she said simply. Pausing with her chin on her hand, she gazed out of the window for what felt like an eternity. 'He had cancer,' she added finally. Then she began to talk, to reveal her pain to Jake. 'He was so, so brilliant, always made people feel at ease. He could walk with kings nor lose the common touch. Do you know that Kipling poem? It was one of his favourite sayings. He was always much more tactile than my mum. I love her, but she's a bit of a cold fish sometimes. And my sister's just like her. I'm definitely my father's daughter.' Mandy's voice trailed off and she lost herself in looking out of the window again. 'I felt so sad for Mum. It was as if she didn't really realize how much she loved Dad until he died.'

Jake's eyes swept over Mandy's hair, pulled up elegantly with the odd dark curl hanging down artfully. Even though he couldn't see her face, he could sense the pain she was going through.

'Dad was so brave towards the end. He kept telling me he didn't want me to see him like that, so thin, so weak. He said to come back when he was better.' She laughed nervously. 'We both knew he wasn't going to get better. He cracked lots of jokes, made naughty innuendos with the nurses, and I would cringe sometimes but they all adored his wicked sense of humour. When Dad took me to the ballet, he absolutely loved it. He was such a big, manly man, but he was never afraid to show emotion. He could cry, you know? I remember we were in the royal box – my dad loved the fine things in life – and he thought we were the bee's knees up there. He even gave a royal wave to the stalls at one point, and even Mum, buttoned-up Mum, stifled a giggle. At the end of the performance he held my shoulders, just like you did earlier, and told me that the evening with the two of us watching *Swan Lake* would stay with him for ever. It was the only ballet we ever did see together, and he was so emotional. He said, "Remember that every moment we live, we are creating our history, and it's down to us to make our story as memorable and magical as possible. We are here for a good time, not necessarily a long time." Dad's eyes twinkled like diamonds, and . . . I never really found out for sure, but I think he already knew by then that he had lung cancer. Oh, Jake, I miss him so much.'

As the tears rolled down Mandy's cheeks, Jake couldn't sit back any longer. He pulled her to him and she sobbed into his chest. He wanted to take her pain away, but he knew there was nothing he or anyone else could do and that ultimately only time would help her. As Jake kissed Mandy's tear-stained face, stroking her hair back, he looked into her dark eyes and knew that to hold her just wasn't enough. It felt wrong, the wrong time and place, for he knew she was vulnerable.

And then there were Helen and the boys.

Mandy unbuttoned Jake's shirt a little bit further and

nestled her face in his chest. There it was, that special musky, perfumed smell, his skin mixed with aftershave, and she started to kiss his chest; he grabbed her hair, lifted her head and kissed her deeply, passionately. Jake felt as if he was going to erupt and pulled away, putting his head in his hands. This feeling was electric and he lusted after her so very much. He pulled his hands down away from his head and looked at the beautiful woman beside him. She looked completely ravishing: sad, vulnerable but with something intoxicating about her. Mandy bit her lip, raw with emotion. 'Take me home, Jake,' she whispered. Without a word Jake turned the key in the ignition and sped down Queensgate towards Mandy's flat.

In silence, Jake walked her to her door. He stood in the dimly lit doorway of her flat. Mandy looked at him, taking in his shape, his long firm legs. Even the way he stood, everything about him turned her on.

'I'm going to go,' he said, half nodding as if confirming to himself that it was the right thing to do. Mandy's heart plunged to the pit of her stomach. She knew there was madness in the air. Jake looked at her in a way she would never forget: intently, yearning, like she belonged to him and him only. He opened the door with her key and stood for a second, then leaned on the handle with one arm, as if in turmoil. 'Oh fuck!' he suddenly yelled. He slammed the door shut and walked purposefully towards Mandy, pushing her inside the flat. She was scared but excited, and as he lifted her off her feet she wrapped her legs tightly around his waist.

Jake carried her down the small hallway, searching for the bedroom. As soon as he found it he laid her down on the bed, his breathing becoming slower. He relished removing every last pin from her hair, allowing Mandy's curls to fall round her face. He pulled her dainty black dress straps over her shoulders and down below her breasts. He leaned down and kissed her pink nipples, gently, then more firmly, pulling her dress up to her waist, caressing the inside of her silky thighs with his fingers. He rubbed his body against her, kissing and gently biting her neck, and she could feel how aroused he was by her. Pulling his face towards hers, she responded, kissing him and gently biting his soft lips. She felt lust take over, and pulled herself up to face him so that they were both on their knees. She undressed him swiftly, revealing his taut, chiselled body. They could hardly take their eyes off each other and soon neither could take any more.

'I want you inside me,' Mandy whispered. 'But I want to please you too.' Mandy lowered her head towards Jake's stiff cock. He smelled wonderful and within minutes she sucked him into her mouth, twisting her tongue around him until he groaned loudly with the sheer pleasure of her foreplay. But it wasn't enough for Jake: all he wanted to do was to give her pleasure and show her how much he longed for her. Opening her thighs, he caressed and pleasured her with his mouth and fingers; watching Mandy's face in such an erotic state turned him on even more. She pulled him up on top of her and as she felt him enter her she experienced the union of two spirits, two bodies, a completeness she had never felt before. Everything flowed, and it seemed neither Mandy nor Jake had ever experienced so much love. Not a single part of their skin was left untouched. Their emotional bond deepened and they became one.

Jake curled up to Mandy. 'You're so beautiful, you know that?' he whispered, but Mandy was looking at a glow coming from his phone in his jacket pocket and knew that, at that moment, she had become 'the other woman'.

FIVE

The Craziness of Love

In the early-morning light, Jake watched Mandy sleeping peacefully. He hadn't slept a wink all night, knowing that he was already close to falling head over heels in love with her. What the fuck had happened? One minute every-thing was so simple, so clear; and now, as he gently stroked Mandy's face, he felt overwhelmed, scared at just how much he already really cared for her. He wasn't sure he felt comfortable with the unknown.

'I have to go, baby,' he whispered, but Mandy didn't stir. Quietly, he tiptoed out of the flat and into normality.

Mandy woke up later, feeling completely disorientated. Her lips tingled, her inside thighs ached, yet there was no Jake to be found. Her heart was in her mouth and Mandy didn't know whether to be sick with the upset and uncer-tainty that were churning around in her stomach or to accept a sense of happiness because she had been made love to by the man of her dreams. She *was* deliriously happy, but in a state of shock all at the same time. Alarm bells rang in her head. Had she been used? She looked around the room, trying to find some trace of Jake, but there was nothing. Her defence mechanism kicked in. 'The fucker's used me,' she snapped. 'Gone back to the wife and kids, no thought for me. I bet he got what he wanted and that's it.'

Feeling punch-drunk with too much emotion, Mandy threw on her soft cotton oversized white T-shirt and walked to her en suite bathroom. Looking in the mirror at her panda eyes as she brushed her teeth, she shouted, 'You stupid cow, you stupid, stupid, cow!' Peering at herself closely in the mirror, she mumbled, 'No wonder he's scarpered. You look like bloody Alice Cooper on a bad day.'

Mandy dragged her feet down the corridor to the kitchen, opened the fridge and saw nothing but some old smoked salmon and a bottle of champagne. 'Bugger, I'll have to get a Starbucks and a brownie on my way to work.' She imagined George telling her off: 'A minute on the lips, a lifetime on the hips,' he'd say drily. 'Sod you, George,' she muttered under her breath. 'I'm feeling vulnerable right now, OK?' She stumbled into her bedroom and pulled back her red satin duvet. There she saw a Post-it note that must have fallen off the pillow, saying simply *Missing you already* ☺

'Ahhh, that's rather lovely,' smiled Mandy. She sat and stared at the Post-it note for a good few minutes, memories of their love-making hitting her mind in flashes so that all her doubts and defences vanished instantly. 'Shit!' she shrieked suddenly, 'I'm going to be late for work!' She grabbed her wet wipes, stuck on her black skinny jeans, whacked on a black blazer and killer Sergio Rossi heels, and grabbed her big quilted Chanel bag from the night before.

Phone – check.
Keys – check.
Money – check.
Lip gloss – check.

By the time Mandy arrived at the office she had wet-wiped off her night-before make-up and, other than lip gloss and some cream blush, her face was feeling rather bare. She decided she would say that she was going for the natural look, but in reality she was gagging for some mascara and, despite getting a kick out of smelling Jake's scent on her, she felt pretty skanky.

Would other people know she'd had mad, passionate sex with a married man? Many times? As she walked into the offices, she saw her colleague Andrew sauntering like a complete jobsworth with a file under his arm. 'You look well today, Mandy, a bit rock-chicky,' he said as he walked by. Fuck me, thought Mandy, I didn't think Andrew would even know a rock chick if she hit him in the face. Not sure whether to take it as a compliment or not, she made her way to her desk. Maggie walked by with a large, black jug of coffee for Michael.

'Michael wants to see you in his office right away,' she said, looking smug.

'OK, Maggie, thanks,' responded Mandy, smiling sweetly. 'I'll check my messages and go on through.'

'Michael said right away,' Maggie repeated.

'Look, you concentrate on your coffee delivery and I'll concentrate on where and when I'll see Michael,' Mandy retorted, irritated. Maggie just pursed her lips and marched through to Michael's office as if she was delivering the Crown Jewels. Moments later, Michael popped his head outside his office door. 'Mandy, in my office ASAP.' Mandy was adjusting her make-up and nearly stuck the old mascara wand she'd found in her drawer right in her eye. She jumped out of her skin. He could have such a bark on him! 'Right-oh,' she quipped. As she passed Maggie, Mandy felt herself being scrutinized.

'You look different,' Maggie observed. 'Had a facial?'

'No.'

'Botox?'

Mandy cleared her throat and with a look of disdain: 'Overnight? No.'

'Hmm, something's changed. You actually look rather well.' Maggie trotted off; her short little legs never seemed to get her anywhere that quickly, despite her rapid pace. Mandy thought once more that she was such a pain in the arse.

'Come in, darling, quick, quick,' Michael urged. 'I have to leave in ten.' He sighed. 'Right. We have a big event coming up in Los Angeles, an engagement party for a big sports star and an actress at the Bel Air Hotel.' Michael turned in his big leather seat and flicked through an A4 memo. 'Dates keep changing due to their fluid schedules, but we need to be ready, no matter what.'

'We?' Mandy asked, raising a quizzical brow. 'But we're UK-based.'

'I know that, Einstein, but my good friend Margaret Walters is having a baby, and needs someone to help. I personally think you'll need to be out there in six to eight weeks' time, probably for two weeks max.'

'Me?'

'Yes, you! What the hell's the matter with you today?'

'I just can't believe it,' beamed Mandy. 'Am I right to think I'm doing this alone? It's just me and Margaret, right?'

'Well, yeah,' laughed Michael. 'And her assistant, and the assistant's assistant. You know what these Americans are like!' He picked up a *pain au chocolat* and took a big bite. 'Now, you,' he munched, 'go and do me proud. This will be great for us, if done properly. I've got shitloads on here, but do your best and we'll look into giving you that bonus.'

Mandy felt both proud and overwhelmed. 'I won't let you down,' she promised.

'You look smashing today, by the way. You've got a glow about you. What you been up to?'

Mandy blushed.

'Whatever it is, it suits you.' Michael smiled a warm smile. He was brash and bold, but utterly charming. He still, in his late fifties, had women fighting for his affections, despite them knowing he was married. Mandy had always thought these women, who she observed at their parties, should have more dignity, and yet now here she was, one of them herself. For the first time since making love to Jake, she felt a pang of guilt. It hadn't taken long.

'In the meantime, go and help sort out the première for that diabolical Christmas movie, will you?' puffed Michael, rubbing his chest with indigestion. 'They want dwarves, Elvis impersonators, elves and loads of bloody weird shit.'

'Michael!' shrieked Mandy. 'Don't be so mean! Dwarves are human beings, not weird shit!'

'I'm not talking about the fucking dwarves, darling, but what the fuck has Elvis got to do with Christmas? That's the weird shit!'

Mandy belly-laughed, and despite all the confusion in her love life, felt rich with happiness. Work was great, her friends adored her and she had truly been made love to by a man she was crazy about. And the marriage thing would sort itself out – wouldn't it?

That evening, George and Deena met Mandy at the Blue Elephant for dinner.

'Look, you can't just magic away his wife and kids,' stated George solemnly. He was looking especially dapper in a gorgeous grey cashmere roll-neck and slim-fitting Comme des Garçons trousers.

'Actually, she can,' laughed Deena. 'I've got some amazing witch spells and, I'm telling you now, they're pretty powerful.'

'Listen, you fruit-loop,' laughed George, sipping his piña colada, a little pink cocktail umbrella nearly poking his eye out, 'I don't care if you're the wicked witch of the south-west, you can't erase the Walton family just like that!'

'He only has *two* children, George, I'd hardly call that the Waltons.' Mandy smiled despite herself.

'Whatever!' said George, wafting his hand in the air. 'They are *very* much his kids, with *another* woman, and if you weren't already so much into this guy emotionally, I'd say go for it. What the wifey doesn't know won't hurt her.'

Deena frowned at him. 'You've got bad, bad, karma coming, George,' she sighed.

George simply ignored her. 'But, Mandy, you are *falling for* this guy big time, and I won't have you crying on my shoulder when you know it can't go anywhere.' He swallowed the cherry from his cocktail stick. 'Don't say I didn't warn you!'

'*Have* you fallen for him?' gasped Deena, wide-eyed.

Mandy felt herself grow hot and fumbled with her napkin. 'Why's it always so bloody steamy in this restaurant?'

'Because it's a replica of Thailand, sweetheart,' piped up

George. 'I'm wearing the wrong get-up really. With all this foliage, I should be wearing my khakis.'

Deena looked at Mandy through her big, kind blue eyes. 'Are you in love with him?' she persisted.

'No,' said Mandy, lowering her eyes to the table. She looked up at Deena. 'But I'm pretty close.'

George let out a heavy sigh, folded his arms and rolled his eyes.

'Look, I know all the reasons I shouldn't feel like this,' continued Mandy. 'Married men hardly ever leave their wives, and I'll always have to deal with playing second fiddle to a life I have nothing to do with and have no true knowledge of. I also know I could hurt innocent people, and I know I could really hurt myself, but I'm not in this alone. Who is to say I'm the home wrecker? His home life with his wife is obviously pretty damaged, otherwise he wouldn't have found me, would he?'

As her words hit the air, Mandy knew she sounded more ruthless than she actually was. She waited for a response from George and Deena, but there was silence. She found herself justifying her actions.

'And there is that something, you know? He's like a magnet, and the chemistry is mind-blowing. I almost feel like I don't have a choice, and I'm a slave to the emotion of this whole thing.' As her voice trailed off, she suddenly felt weary.

George looked at her. 'You slept with him, didn't you?'

Mandy looked downwards at the table again.

'Yes, I did. You know, he left me this Post-it note today.' She took out her diary from her handbag and put it on the table so her friends could see the note that had made her heart flip stuck on the front. 'But he hasn't called or texted me all day, and I keep looking at it, telling myself that he means it and that he will call any minute. Now it's seven-thirty and he left at the crack of dawn this morning. I thought I would have heard from him by now.'

Deena and George looked at the Post-it.

'Cute,' said George flatly, 'but not enough to keep me ticking after someone fucks me all night and then doesn't ring.' His voice was bitter.

'That's enough, George!' Deena said firmly.

'Forget it!' shouted Mandy. 'You're so fucking righteous sometimes, George, yet you're no angel – far from it. Who are you to judge me about the problems in my love life, when you can't even sort out your own? Who do you think you are? Just, just—' She felt herself well up. 'Just fuck off.' She pushed back her chair, ready to leave.

'Don't go,' Deena shouted out after her. 'He doesn't mean it.'

Mandy fumbled, picking up her bag, and turned to George.

'You're just bitter and twisted and jealous,' she spat.

'Of what exactly?' exclaimed George sarcastically.

'Of the fact that *I* know who I want now. Shame you don't know the same.' With that Mandy marched out.

She stomped a long way along the road before she found a taxi. Soaked from the rain, she let herself into her flat feeling shattered and extremely sad. She hadn't even had the chance to tell anyone about her exciting opportunity in LA; the whole conversation had been monopolized by talk of Jake. She checked her phone. One text message. 'Thank God,' she sighed.

SORRY FOR BEING A WANKER. LOVE YOU, G.

Mandy's heart fell and she lay back on her pillow and pulled her duvet up to her chin. She could smell Jake and felt a tugging in her heart. Part of her wanted to pull the duvet to her and hug it all night; the other wanted to change the sheets and shower, to prove she was stronger than this, that she didn't need him on her bedsheets or her. She did the latter, scrubbing every last bit of Jake off her, changing her sheets and spraying the fresh ones with Chanel No. 5. For that night, she cried herself to sleep, feeling a fool for giving her heart away. There was *no excuse* for him not texting, *no excuse* for not leaving a voice message, and Mandy herself had *no excuse* for becoming what she had already become: a mistress.

SIX

All Shook Up

The roof of the Aston Martin convertible had been opened and Mandy threw her head back, laughing. She was all wrapped up to protect her from the wind as the Aston sped along the motorway. Mandy looked at Jake driving fast and singing at the top of his voice, badly: 'I've got you under my skin.' Not a patch on Frank Sinatra.

'Oh God,' yelled Mandy, 'I'm turning Frank up. This is hell!'

Jake chuckled. 'I taught the man everything he knows!'

'He's dead!' Mandy shot back.

Jake smiled. 'OK, smartarse.' He loved it when Mandy was cheeky.

Everything had been wonderful. Christmas was in three days' time and the last few weeks had been some of the best ever in Mandy and Jake's lives. Eventful, but wonderful. Evenings out and shopping trips had been fantastic: every-thing from fancy Christmas-tree baubles to little black dresses had been bought and unpacked in Mandy's little flat. They had both become tipsy decorating the tree and ended up passionately making love on the floor beside it. They tried to continue as they were both feeling extremely horny, but in the end the stabbing of stray pine needles getting in places they shouldn't became too much and they gave in.

Suddenly, Jake had winced in pain. Mandy moved to roll over on him but Jake winced again. 'Please don't touch down there,' he murmured, pulling a pained face. He was cupping his privates with his hand, gasping for breath.

'What the hell is wrong, Jake?'

Jake could hardly breathe, never mind speak. The poor man looked like he was going to pass out at any moment. Mandy shook some pine needles off her body on to the floor, and quickly got dressed in her skinny jeans and navy roll-neck. Whacking her knee-high boots on as fast as she could, she tried to pull Jake back to his feet. Now he was howling and making a right old fuss, and Mandy was increasingly worried. Pulling his jeans up from around his ankles, she bent to do up the zipper.

'No!' Jake screamed in panic. Mandy had finally got him into her car and whisked him to the emergency surgery in Wimpole Street. Her Dr Dawkin was the best, could solve anything and everything – at a price, obviously. Mandy pulled the hobbling Jake into the surgery. He still wasn't able to sit without screaming the place down.

In time, the doctor had come out and seen Jake doubled

over. 'I think I'd better see you next.' Poor Jake, who still couldn't sit down due to the pain, had Dr Dawkin on his knees looking straight at his willy. The doctor prodded Jake's privates, knocking his penis to the left and then to the right, and basically seemed to be slapping it about a bit, until finally Jake laughed and cried all at the same time, tears rolling down his cheeks. 'What is it, doctor? Whatever it is please sort it out, I'm dying here.' The doctor picked up some medical tweezers, and quickly extracted something.

'Looks like someone has been taking loving Christmas to a whole new level!' he chuckled. 'It's a pine needle,' he continued. 'It lodged itself in the place that normally you would urinate from.' The doctor looked more serious. 'No wonder you were in so much pain.'

Jake looked bewildered.

'It's made quite a hole,' the doctor said. 'I don't think you'll need a stitch, but you need to keep it incredibly clean so there is no infection.'

'Well, of course,' stammered Jake. 'I always wash it with Imperial Leather.'

Mandy burst out laughing: this whole situation was outrageous. Dr Dawkin was very sweet and ignored Mandy cackling in the background.

'Just warm water is best,' he said in a sympathetic tone. 'Bathe it gently and you'll be back on form in no time.'

*

the Mistress

Now, a fresh cold breeze hitting Mandy's face, she smiled at the memory and looked down at Jake's crotch as he turned the Aston into a lovely quiet country road.

'How's your willy, darling?' she whispered mischievously in his ear. 'Does it need me to kiss it better again?'

Jake's face lit up. 'Well, you know it helps heal him,' he said as seriously as he could.

Mandy tore open his flies and started to pleasure him. Jake gasped and pulled over in a dusty little road with hedges everywhere so that they weren't seen and he wouldn't crash.

He tilted his pelvis up, pushing as hard as he could from his feet near the pedals of the car; he and Mandy had the perfect rhythm. Mandy looked up at him, her eyes gleaming. She had never enjoyed satisfying a man so much, and she couldn't ever get enough. She wanted him, every bit of him, and when she had him in her sexual power she felt sometimes that it was the only way she could ever feel she had Jake completely.

Afterwards Jake bit his lip and sighed, 'God, you're crazy and I love it.' He smiled at her and shook his head, looking around the empty road. 'You just don't give a fuck, do you?'

Mandy grabbed his face and kissed him. 'No, I don't,' she said softly. 'Not if it means I can have you.' As Mandy's words hit the air she felt her heart tug. She also worried that her words sounded too strong, too much like pressure. The truth of how she felt had come out, but maybe it was

89

too much, too soon. Lately she was feeling brave, more wrapped up in the affair as every day passed. At that moment Jake knew that Mandy was falling for him, just as he had fallen for her. They both felt over-emotional, but he simply kissed her, started the car and drove off to the beautiful weekend retreat that awaited them.

A huge cast-iron gate opened slowly to reveal the elegant listed house adorned with white shutters and covered in ivy. Mandy gasped, it was so beautiful. She stepped out of the car on to the gravelled drive. Wide stone steps led up to a large front door. 'Come on,' smiled Jake. 'I'll get the bags in a bit, but let's get in, warm up and then make a plan for tonight.'

Excitedly, Mandy ran up the steps to join Jake and held his hand as he opened the door and let her into the lobby of the hotel.

Beautifully arranged flowers had been placed atop a huge circular mahogany table. A large lantern hung from the ceiling and the scent of tuberose filled the air, thanks to the lovely Louise Bradley candles that twinkled all over the house. Dark wooden floors added to the richness of the decor, and a huge Christmas tree sparkled at the bottom of a swirling staircase with rich, dark red carpet that followed the stairs all the way up to the balcony that overlooked the lobby. Antique paintings hung on the walls. Logs glowed and crackled in an imposing fireplace.

Jake sighed. 'Perfect,' he smiled. 'So cosy, and so warm.' He grabbed Mandy's face and kissed her. 'I know you like everything to look like a picture postcard, so how did I do?'

Mandy gazed at him. Could this really be true? Had this wonderful man really planned all this just for her? She blinked for a few seconds, trying to take it all in. 'You did great. It's amazing, I'm so lucky.' She tried to stop her bottom lip from trembling, not because she was overwhelmed by how much effort had been put into the place but because she also knew they only had one night together. She was already missing him and felt sad about it all ending before it had even begun properly.

She had actually been booked to see George and her other friends for their annual Christmas dinner at the Ivy. She always loved it there and every year without fail they would all, as soberly as possible, stumble out of the restaurant following a stellar dinner.

Mandy felt guilty that she had cancelled her dear friends at the last minute. Jake had planned a surprise and she had only discovered it that morning. When he had called he'd announced, 'Wrap up warm, I'm taking you somewhere gorgeous for the next two days, and you will love it!'

Mandy protested, but not as hard as she could have. He had only been gone two days and she missed him like crazy, plus he sounded so excited. She just couldn't say no. The phone call to George had not been easy.

'Hi, George.'

'Oh, hello stranger. Long time no see or speak,' he said drily.

'Um, I know,' Mandy had stammered. 'I'm sorry but I can't make tonight. Something has come up.'

'Hmm, now I wonder what that could be?'

Mandy tried to keep calm. 'Don't be like that, George.'

'Like what?' he snapped. 'I have had this dinner booked in for the last four months, and now you cancel?'

Mandy swallowed hard. She loved George, and hated hurting him.

'George, I will make it up to you, I promise.'

'Oh save it, Mandy. I don't need you to make anything up to me, cos you know what? We'll go ahead with the dinner, with or without you. And you know what else?' George could feel his chest well up with anger. 'We're so used to you not showing up these days that I doubt anyone will notice.'

That had stabbed Mandy in the heart: she had only ever cancelled once before. Or was it twice? It had been some time since she had seen her friends properly. With Jake and work, things were pretty difficult to fit in, but she knew she was wrong. They normally caught up very regularly, even if it wasn't all of them. Yes! Actually George had cancelled in the past too! They all had! Why did *she* always have to be Miss Perfect?

'George, *you* have cancelled in the past,' she finally answered.

There was silence for a few seconds.

'Whatever,' was the reply. 'Have a lovely time with what's-his-face, and maybe see you next year.' With that the line went dead. Oh no, George was NOT happy.

Jake brought some bags in and led Mandy up to the bedroom. It was stunning.

'Thank God,' he sighed. 'I did all this via the internet, and it was so beautiful online that, to be honest, I thought that any place available at this time of year with such short notice must have something wrong with it, but it's gorgeous.'

Mandy looked at the polished four-poster mahogany bed, draped with beautiful crisp white cotton-and-lace curtains. It was so fresh and pretty.

A huge dressing table stood in the corner. The room was softly candlelit and the white-marble en suite bathroom was luxurious yet elegant. Mandy looked at the double basin and saw a small envelope tucked behind the old-fashioned taps. Another note from Jake, she thought, unfolding the paper inside.

Hello, my name is Joan.
    If you have any requests or questions you can contact me on this number or knock on the little red door at the back of the house.
    Enjoy your stay.

*PS Please note that we have a problem with the
plumbing and the electrics. The sink taps work but please
use the outside toilet only.*
Thanks,
Joan

Fuck!!

Jake walked in, very proud of himself, and winked at
Mandy. 'How wonderful is this, eh?' He smiled his arrogant smile.

Mandy handed him the note and waited for a reply as
she rubbed her arms in the freezing cold room. The snow
fell slowly and gently landed on the window panes of the
bedroom. All Jake could muster was 'Ah.' He bit his lip and
pondered for a moment. 'Let's pop out, eh? I don't know
about you but I'm dying for the loo . . .'

Wonderful.

Leaving the house, driving carefully and slowly down the
lanes, Mandy finally twigged where they actually were. She
cleared her throat. 'I know I didn't actually ask you exactly
where you were taking me, but . . .'

'We're in Surrey. I'm taking you ice skating. Thought it
would be wiser to come out this way so we don't have to
worry so much.'

Mandy felt a cocktail of emotions. Mum and Olivia didn't
live far away, but surely they wouldn't be ice skating tonight.

Mandy also knew what he meant about not worrying, but didn't like it that he had to bring it up. She had to ask him:

'Worry about what?'

Jake suddenly looked awkward. 'Well, you know, being seen together. Neither of us needs that.'

Mandy's blood started to boil; he'd never said anything like that before. She had always tried to be responsible where Jake was concerned, and had always been discreet, more so than him at times, but suddenly it all felt a bit cheap. She'd only ever felt gloriously happy with Jake when she was with him; until now. It upset her, hearing him say out loud that he wanted to hide her, hide them and their feelings for each other. Yet she had always known the score, hadn't she? So what did she expect?

As Jake pulled up in the car park at Hampton Court he looked at Mandy. 'You OK?'

All she could manage was 'Fine.' She felt far from it as she looked out of the window, but as they walked towards the ice rink Hampton Court looked magnificent. Mandy's doubts and fears were soon brushed away when Jake had his arms wrapped around her, trying to keep her from falling over on the ice. She was a terrible skater!

Hundreds of fairy lights glittered in the trees, and Christmas carols blared out of speakers all round the rink. Children and adults alike skated, and giggled as they fell over. It was one of the funniest and best times Mandy had shared with Jake.

He had a way of changing her emotions in an instant. She would never forget how he had failed to call after they had made love for the first time. Then, she had been so vulnerable – devastated. The whole situation was bizarre. Any rules that normally worked successfully for Mandy in life seemed to be tossed away when it came to Jake. She knew the reality of the situation, she was a clever woman, yet now she was so highly strung, changing by the minute. Jake was concerned; he had waited a day, then called and called. It was only twenty-four hours before she just *had* to answer.

'I just wanted to check you were OK, that I haven't frightened you off?'

Mandy had felt confused. He couldn't be more wrong; how could he even think that? She had done everything but tear her hair out so as not to call him, and here he was asking if she was going to do a runner. It seemed there had been a misunderstanding: she, as a woman, had expected a million calls as reassurance on the same day she had made love to him. Jake on the other hand, as a man, had played it cool and decided to give her space – for precisely the same reason.

Words were exchanged, tears were cried and within hours Jake had Mandy in his arms again. So much for Mandy's vow never to see him again. She would chuck yet another rule out of the window – and God, it felt great!

Mandy was like Bambi on ice, and her darling Jake had her tight in his grasp so she didn't fall over again. She felt like a child. She experienced one of those very rare moments that you never forget, where absolutely everything in the world is perfect, as it should be. The crisp air hit her face and she could smell roasting chestnuts. Jake's body was like an oven, keeping her warm and safe. She leaned back as he continued holding her while skating beautifully around the rink.

'Mandy! Maaanndy!'

Mandy's bubble burst.

She felt bewildered, not being able to work out where the voice calling her name was coming from. There were so many people, but as Jake took her around the ice rink another time she knew for sure a familiar voice was calling. There on the sidelines of the rink were Olivia, Robbie, Robyn, Milly and her mother, all taking a breather. Milly was trying to get her skate off in the middle of the damp floor, much to the annoyance of the other skaters. Mandy froze. She had no rehearsed answers to the questions she knew were forthcoming. She had practised, but everything just flew out of her head.

They were all waving now, frantically, looking like the Muppets, all arms and legs. Mandy wanted to dash over but, forgetting she was on ice with skates rather than on dry land with Louboutins, found her legs sliding in different directions like a giraffe. The girls were giggling at her now and Jake was trying to lift her up, but with such a slippery base it was tricky. Everyone started to look at her and Mandy's inside thighs were starting to throb. It had been a long time since she had done the splits. Time was ticking and Jake was trying his best to help her up. Two teacher skaters came and helped; they got an arm each and hoisted Mandy back up to an upright position. She wanted to die.

Jake was crying with laughter. 'I tried to get you up,' he gasped, 'but I was laughing so hard I lost my strength!' Mandy was so humiliated she didn't want to laugh, but Jake's giggling was contagious. She'd never seen him laugh so hard that he couldn't speak; tears were streaming down his face. OK, credit where credit was due, it *was* funny, really funny! 'Come on,' he said, getting his breath back. 'Let's get you to dry land, and for fuck's sake hold on to me.' Mandy giggled and let him steer her home to the safe shores of a wooden bench.

Robyn and Milly ran over to her and hugged her, laughing. 'You were so funny, Aunty Mandy,' said Robyn, shaking her head.

Mandy, finally safe, looked up to Jake. He looked a bit uncomfortable. 'Aunty Mandy?' he questioned.

Olivia, Robbie, Valerie and the girls all now stood round them. 'That's right,' said Milly. 'She's our Aunty Mandy, silly.'

Jake was the perfect gentleman in an instant, greeting everyone and introducing himself as Jake, Mandy's 'friend'.

Mandy understood, but her heart sank. Olivia looked rather excited for Mandy. 'We're popping to Carluccio's in Esher for some food; I can't be bothered to cook tonight,' she smiled.

'Oh, OK,' nodded Mandy, trying to think of something to get herself and Jake away.

Robbie nudged Olivia. 'Oh sorry, forgot my manners,' smiled Olivia, blushing with embarrassment. 'Why don't you come with us?'

'Oh, we would but, but . . .' Mandy was stumped. Why the hell couldn't she and Jake join them for dinner? She had to think of a good reason, and fast.

Jake put his arm around Mandy. 'I've got to get back into town actually, and Mandy has kindly offered me a lift as she's meeting friends there. Thanks so much, though.'

'No worries!' Olivia was putting on her Miss Perfect voice, clearly impressed with the looks and charisma of this gorgeous new man in Mandy's life. She always flattered men and tried to charm them, whether she wanted them or not. Mandy actually enjoyed seeing her sister with a gleam of excitement in her eyes. Shame it didn't exist for her own husband.

The family all said their goodbyes and hobbled off in their socks, ready to swap their skates for their shoes. As they did so, Mandy felt relieved but guilty. Jake's own guilt had obviously kicked in about his boys.

Just as they were leaving, Mandy noticed various photos

of that evening's Hampton Court skaters for sale in naff Christmas cardboard frames.

There they were – her and Jake laughing their heads off while trying to stay upright on the ice rink. They looked so in love and happy. Her guilt was soon wiped away with the huge smile on Jake's face. 'Oh my God,' he laughed, 'we truly looked as ridiculous as I felt.' He handed the man some cash and took a copy of the photo. Looking in Mandy's eyes, he shrugged. 'I can't help but adore you, you make me laugh so much!'

Mandy felt herself blush. Statements like that just *got* her in her heart.

Jake put his arm around Mandy and held her tightly as he walked her back to the car. She felt like they were beaming so much that everyone's eyes were on them and at that moment she didn't care who saw; she felt high on love and never wanted that feeling to leave her.

Maggie watched them go, paid for a copy of the same photo of the happy couple and then promptly left.

The country house seemed cold and was still in darkness apart from the various candles lit all around the building. They illuminated the bedroom beautifully.

Huddled together and wrapped up in bed that evening, things could easily have been awkward for Jake and Mandy, but it seemed they were falling for each other more, not less.

Facing each other with their bodies entwined, they

shivered as they tried to keep warm. Jake laughed. 'I wish someone could take a picture of this. In fact,' he paused, 'that's not true. I will keep this photo in my head for ever.' He smiled warmly.

Mandy was baffled. 'Why?'

'Well,' said Jake, rubbing his foot on his leg, trying to keep warm, 'here we are in a beautiful house with no plumbing, no working lights and no heat apart from all the candles round us – and body heat!' He kissed Mandy on her forehead. 'And to top it all off, I'm in bed with a nutcase,' he laughed.

'Oh no, I'm not that bad,' Mandy said.

'Look at you, though!' exclaimed Jake. 'You want to keep warm, yet all you have on is a woolly hat and socks!'

Mandy looked down under the duvet and said matter-of-factly, 'To keep warm, they say you need to keep your head and feet warm. I'm doing that, aren't I?'

Jake shook his head at her, laughing out loud.

'I'm glad you've kept the rest of you clothes-free.' His hand touched her breasts and skimmed over her hard nipples. 'Are you cold, or just pleased to see me?' he joked.

Pulling his hands down to her moist and warm pussy, Mandy whispered, 'I'm definitely just pleased to see you.'

His hand continued to caress her. His touch was electric and the way he kissed Mandy was unbelievable. She honestly believed that just by kissing him alone she would be able to orgasm. The two of them wrapped themselves round each other and made love for hours, playing, stroking and keeping each other warm and happy for as long as they could.

Later, just as Mandy was about to close her eyes and sleep, Jake spoke.

'I love you, Mandy.'

Mandy's heart jumped. She looked at him and sighed. With the melting twinkling candles all around him, his green eyes burned through her and looked utterly beautiful.

'I know I shouldn't, but I can't help it.'

Mandy wanted to cry. She bit her lip and, stroking his face, she smiled.

Neither of them wanted to give in to sleep, but it finally won. Jake closed his eyes and Mandy drifted off with her hand on his gorgeous face. Neither of them stirred once, not once, till morning.

SEVEN

Christmas Eve

'Brrrrrr.'

Mandy's teeth were chattering, and she was shivering all over. She had three jumpers on and felt like the Michelin man, all huge and padded up. Her face, hands and hair were full of glitter as she finished off wrapping some last-minute pressies for Robyn and Milly in bright 'Dorothy' red-glitter paper. She looked around her little one-bedroom basement flat and at that moment felt rather childlike herself, almost like a teenager who needed to grow up. Since Mandy had met Jake he had made her feel so much more like a woman, more sophisticated and grown-up.

He had been teaching her about various wines, as well as different works of art from Rembrandt to Banksy. His passion was contagious. Mandy had loved the instant education and admired the fact he could teach her so much. It was sexy, and next time she worked on an art event she would *really* know her basics rather than bluffing it.

She looked at the little white shelf that framed her fireplace. Instead of having a warm working fire she had filled the space with church candles of varying sizes. It looked pretty but, despite the central heating, the room was cold. On her shelf was a photo that Jake had given her of the two of them laughing, tucked away in a corner at the fabulous little restaurant called Ffiona's in Kensington Church Street. Jake had quickly stretched his arm out and taken a picture of them both feeling rather merry; he looked so handsome, and the candlelit restaurant was cosy and homely. Ffiona, the owner, was always discreet with them, tucking them round the corner away from prying eyes. Her chicken Kiev and colcannon mash were famous, and both Mandy and Jake adored Ffiona, who was feisty, funny and full of heart.

Mandy gulped as a sudden wave of emotion rushed over her. Jake had also given her the frame, a beautiful, silver Tiffany number – oh yes, Jake had good taste, and the fact that he was so generous with his gifts made him even more attractive. However, he was meant to have popped in to see Mandy tonight for a drink so that the two of them could give each other their presents. Christmas Day and Boxing Day were off limits as Jake and his wife were with his family on one day and hers on another, so when he had asked if he could call in and see Mandy on Christmas Eve she had found herself nodding, seeing it as a bonus. But when she had returned with a handful of shopping bags, her neighbour Diva had popped her head out of the main front door to the flats.

'A nicely dressed gentleman called by earlier,' Diva croaked.

'Lucky you,' replied Mandy promptly, smiling.

'Oh, he wasn't here to see me,' giggled Diva mischievously. 'Mind you, I wish he was, he was devilishly handsome.' She smiled gleefully. 'He was knocking and knocking on your door and, you know me, I heard it through my front window and went to see what the banging noise was. Anyway, he left this for you, told me to tell you it's from Jake – or was it Jack?'

Mandy smiled as Diva handed her a medium-sized white velvet box with a big silver and crystal bow on the front.

'It's definitely Jake,' Mandy grinned.

'He also told me to tell you to check your phone, he's left you a message to explain he can't come this evening.' Diva was really concentrating to get the details right. She was so lovely, and tonight she was dressed in a cream satin blouse with pussy-cat bow, smart trousers and pearls. Her grey hair was back in a bun and she wore red lipstick. She looked extremely chic.

'So what are you doing for Christmas, Diva?' asked Mandy softly, hiding her disappointment as she huddled in her coat.

'Well, I'm off to see the family later on tonight, and the driver is coming at eight. As it's only seven now, why don't you come in for a little orange squash and some biscuits?'

Diva was so polite and quaint, Mandy wished there were more like her.

'I would love that,' smiled Mandy as she followed Diva into her raised-ground-floor flat. She hadn't been inside before, and she couldn't believe the size of it; it had huge high ceilings, beautiful cornicing and large twinkling chandeliers. Diva had placed freesias in glass vases, and old mahogany and walnut furniture graced the living area, while bookcases were filled with classics such as the Brontës, Dickens and of course Shakespeare. The flat was very old-fashioned and smelled of Rich Tea biscuits and powdery flowers, yet there was something comforting about it.

'Take a seat on the sofa, dear.' Diva hobbled off, keeping her wooden walking stick tightly in her grasp the whole time. She was so elegant but so frail. Mandy sat on the green and floral-print damask sofa and looked around. There were lots of photos everywhere, black and white and faded colour. She could see clearly how beautiful Diva had been in her youth. Dark hair with green eyes – just like Ava Gardner.

There was one photo in particular that grabbed Mandy's attention, of a very young Diva wearing a glamorous, off-the-shoulder, long, dark dress. She wore a tiara, her lips were glossy and her skin appeared flawless. She looked so graceful and regal, she certainly caught Mandy's imagination.

Within minutes Diva came through with orange squash

poured into a lovely heavy crystal glass. She disappeared then returned, bringing her own glass of squash and a silver tray of Rich Tea biscuits and custard creams. No interfering or help from Mandy was accepted – she was certainly independent, and rather theatrical too. Mandy loved it.

'I love that photo,' said Mandy, looking at the regal Diva in all her splendour.

'Ah,' smiled Diva, nodding her head. 'That was a fun time in my life; I actually did the whole thing for a joke really.'

'What do you mean?' Mandy wasn't quite sure where she was coming from.

'Oh my darling, it's a long story and I shan't bore you, but I was a very vivacious girl in those days and how I didn't land myself in more trouble than I did, I don't know!'

Mandy was dying to know more. 'You can't leave it there, Diva. I'm desperate to know what trouble you got into, you minx!'

Diva looked as if she was bursting to tell her story, but she took a delicate bite of her custard cream and sipped her orange juice very daintily.

'Come on,' coaxed Mandy. 'I've always known you would have great stories.'

Diva wiped a falling crumb with her napkin, expertly avoiding her red lipstick.

'That, my dear, is indeed correct.' She looked at Mandy. 'I've hardly shared this story with anyone other than family and a couple of friends.' Diva smiled and said, 'But it's Christmas, and it was all so long ago now that I doubt anyone would really care or bat an eyelid these days.'

Mandy put her hand on Diva's. 'Don't worry if it's something you'd rather keep private. I'm useless at taking the hint, sorry!' she laughed, but Diva was staring at the picture that had captured Mandy's imagination and seemed swept away with her own thoughts.

'I was a dancer,' she explained, looking quite misty at the memory. 'I enjoyed tap and ballet, but I ended up working in a burlesque club when I was around twenty. Gosh, I had an amazing time! I met so many wonderful people, and the outfits were tiny but oh-so-glamorous!'

Mandy chuckled. 'So what decade was this?'

Diva shot Mandy a knowing look. 'Well, that would be giving my age away, but what the hell, we're talking early fifties.' Diva winked. 'Maybe extremely late forties, early fifties.' She sipped her orange squash again and played with the glass as she spoke; her nails were long and lacquered in a rich red.

'Anyway, a lovely chap would always come in and tip us girls very generously. He was never interfering or anything like that, in fact sometimes he looked rather bored. However, he would bring various men in and discuss business with them in between and sometimes during each girl's act, depending on how good they were!' Diva shot Mandy another telling look. 'I would like to add that no business whatsoever was discussed while *I* was on stage: I always had the audience's full attention.'

Mandy tried not to laugh.

'So,' continued Diva, 'this gentleman was called Frederick and darling Freddie changed my life for ever. To this day I'm not sure whether to look up to heaven and thank him for it or punch him when I get there.' Diva knocked back the rest of her drink.

'Freddie was asked to talent-scout some girls for beauty pageants, so he approached me and my dear friends Iris, Patricia and Betty. When we realized the money that could be earned we jumped at the chance. Betty was nervous, as she had a husband (who thought she was a waitress) and young baby, but her body was amazing. The lengths we went to in order to tuck her head of red curls into a blonde wig were hilarious, but the wig, combined with using her full name, Elizabeth, worked for ages and she won many competitions and pageants without anyone realizing it was her. Iris was quiet, a simple girl, brunette with big breasts, and she went on dancing for years. Patricia was a gorgeous long-legged blonde. Everyone said she was like Betty Grable. But she was a tough cookie, a loose cannon so to speak; she loved a drink back then and we got into *all* sorts of trouble. Then there was me. I was rather naïve, but full of life, and found the whole journey one long exciting adventure, that's for sure.'

'And you were probably the most beautiful,' added Mandy.

'Actually, if I do say so myself I had to beat the opposite sex off with a stick.' Diva giggled, then added naughtily, 'Although sometimes I'd have much rather they stayed . . .' Diva smiled fondly at the memory of her youth.

'So Freddie was very upper-class and articulate, and everyone was his friend. The people that came up to him to say hello at parties were unbelievable – movie stars, politicians, you name it – and nearly all of them would go to the burlesque clubs with him. In those days they were rather naughty, but the more famous and successful these people were, the crazier they seemed to be.

'By now I was around twenty-two, and after being spotted singing in a pageant for one of my talent pieces I was asked to be a magician's assistant.' Diva started to laugh at herself. 'I know it sounds so ridiculous now, but the magician had worked in Vegas and all over the world and was quite a coup. He was gay, and so I always felt safe travelling everywhere with him. We even stayed in the same bed while touring in certain rougher areas. My goodness, we had a ball! I travelled the world and all expenses were paid.

'We were asked to put on a special performance for the royal family, a big affair booked through Freddie. He was managing us, taking a cut of our money. The stars they had singing and performing that evening were quite something. While coffee was being served we had to go on and do our magic act. I remember I was wearing a pink and black leotard with fishnets and high black heels. I had feathers in my hair and some were also attached to the bustle at the back of my outfit. It was proper old-fashioned glamour. The first part of our act went very well but, but—' Diva's voice faltered and her face twitched, as if she didn't know whether she wanted to laugh or cry.

'But what?' urged Mandy after twenty seconds or so.

'But unfortunately in the next part we had a rabbit in a hat and, and – I can't bring myself to say it.'

Mandy bit her lip, trying hard not to laugh, as Diva tried to carry on.

'Unfortunately the rabbit was very old and had died in the hat so the act was completely ruined; in fact without Ronnie we had no other finale ready.'

'Ronnie?' Mandy choked.

'Yes,' said Diva solemnly. 'Ronnie the rabbit. Everyone could see what had happened. I came forward to apologize. Freddie then rushed up and whispered in my ear, desperate for me to do something. I just started singing "We'll Meet Again". Vera Lynn! Do you remember her?'

Mandy nodded, and Diva began to sing. As she did her voice was clear, smooth and simply stunning.

'Wow, you are wonderful, Diva,' whispered Mandy in disbelief.

'I was better in my twenties,' winked Diva, smiling. 'Later on that evening I had changed into a beautiful red gown and Freddie introduced me to someone who would change my life for ever.' She looked down and smiled sadly. 'He was the love of my life. Unfortunately he was the love of someone else's too, and to top it all off he was – how shall I put this delicately? – linked with the royal family.'

Mandy was dumbstruck. Had all this mistress malarkey been going on since the dawn of time? She'd felt she was in it all alone, as if she was the only woman in the world ruled by selfishness and an intoxicating spell cast on her by a man who already belonged to someone else. Diva laughed in spite of herself.

'I fell for him hook, line and sinker. We secretly walked out for many, many years – and they were the best years of my life.' Diva's voice trembled as if she would cry. Mandy couldn't bear it.

'Oh don't cry, Diva – please.' Mandy grabbed Diva's hands and held them tight. 'At least you truly loved. Some people never have that.' Mandy found herself reassuring herself as well as Diva, who squeezed Mandy's hands hard.

'Yes, I have loved.' She looked Mandy right in the eye. 'But, my God, the pain of losing him twice was unbearable.'

'Twice?' Mandy whispered. She was baffled.

'Yes, dear, twice. You see, one guarantee in life is that things change, and that certainly happened for us. Our feelings didn't change, in fact we fell more in love every day, but the way the royal family and their inner circle were investigated so much meant we had to be extremely careful and in the end we were not careful enough.' Diva shook her head sadly. 'A so-called close friend had pictures of us and demanded a huge, huge sum of money as blackmail. We had to come clean with the family and ask for financial help and guidance. In those days, seeing another woman was so catastrophic it wouldn't have been just gossip or newspaper fodder, it could have torn down the monarchy.'

'Oh God, that's just awful,' said Mandy

Diva wiped her eyes with a pretty little cotton hankie. 'They helped, and did all they could to protect themselves from scandal. I'll never forget him telling me they called us "that scandal", for it felt so wrong. We were so in love, and I felt so hurt, but I suppose it was true. Blue blood falling for a burlesque dancer is hardly respectable, it *is* scandalous. I can even understand that to many it seemed ridiculous, but for me it was the case that when it comes to love the rules are: there are no rules.'

Silence fell like a heavy blanket for a moment or so.

'There was only one condition to them helping and protecting him, and that was that he would never ever see me again.'

Mandy felt her heart break for Diva; it was so desperately tragic and sad, almost too much so to be real. It made Mandy realize just how much this kind of situation must be going on and how true it was that rules and regulations and love do not go hand in hand.

Diva continued: 'By then he had bought me this flat. It

was where we always met alone and that's why I never left. I love it here. All the same people who condemned us and told him never to see me again sat at that very same dinner table and laughed and drank with us. They were my friends too, aware of our situation but keeping it swept under the carpet, if you know what I mean. Their friendship soon changed once it all went wrong. The invitations stopped, as did the phone calls, and it was just hideous; so much of my life went out of the window.'

Mandy couldn't help herself. 'But what about his wife? What did she make of it all? It can't have been easy for her either.'

Diva shook her head and sighed. 'It's a strange thing to say but I will be honest with you. She always knew, from the beginning, I think. I avoided her and she avoided me. We were never friends, but at social gatherings occasionally our paths would cross and we would be polite; but nothing of substance was ever said, not till he died anyway.'

'What did she say when he died?' asked Mandy. She felt wary of asking such a personal question but curiosity was taking over.

Diva sighed heavily.

'She came here pretty late on the day of his funeral – I believe it was late in the evening. I couldn't go to the funeral, for obvious reasons, and the most respectful thing was to stay away. I lit a candle for him earlier in the day in church and I came back and played "Unforgettable" by Nat King

Cole, over and over.' Diva smiled, blushing ever so slightly.
'His wife arrived, looking very pale in black, and seemed
broken. She came into my flat and saw all my photos of
us together. It must have been so hard to see, but I've always
had them up; it was the only way of keeping him with me
no matter where he was. She gave me a package tied with
a blue ribbon. "I believe these are for you," she said, clearing
her throat afterwards. "I know he wrote to you every week
of every year. It kept him going," she continued rather
calmly. "He became too ill to post them and did not trust
anyone else to do it, so he put all of these letters under his
bed until more and more of them mounted up. When I
last spoke to him he told me how much he loved me, and
thanked me for being me, but he also knew deep down
that I knew about the letters. Just before he died, he made
me promise to give them to you, so here they are – twelve
months' worth.'''

Diva walked over to her cabinet and opened the door
with a small old key. 'He reminisced a lot. In the end, all
these envelopes contain pretty much the diary of my life.'

Mandy looked at them. 'So what was the outcome of
the conversation between you and his wife?'

'She thanked me, actually,' said Diva in disbelief. 'I
honestly thought she was coming to the house to give me
some home truths but she was so gracious, grown-up and
kind, I'm sure she did it for him. They had their own story
and that was something I never wanted to take away. She

knew how passionately in love we were, and despite many women being ruthless and making demands, I had never done anything like that. Since he was instructed to never come near me I had never seen my darling man. Even once little Henry arrived, I just got on as best I could, and dear old Freddie would give us an allowance. There was never a week till the day he died that Freddie didn't pop by to make sure we were looked after.'

'I'm sorry, who is Henry?' Mandy felt that she must have missed a vital part of the conversation.

'He is my son. He is *our* son.' Diva sounded comforted just saying it.

'Oh my goodness.' Mandy shook her head in disbelief. 'So you and he . . . ?'

Diva nodded. 'Yes, my dear, everything you're thinking is correct.'

'So all this time you had to bring him up alone,' Mandy said, and Diva nodded sadly.

'Look, darling, I had to take the rough with the smooth. Despite our only contact being letters for many, many years, I was sent a document to sign, promising nothing would ever be revealed about our relationship by me, and of course, I understood. It was my own fault really. I loved someone in the public eye, someone unavailable. You play with fire, you get burned. But we got through, and I never did anything to bring the family down. I kept my mouth shut and my head held high and did the best I could. I think his wife and the family were grateful for that. She also gave me his favourite cufflinks, his watch and, most amazingly, a letter stating that this flat and a house in Belgravia would be left for Henry. At least I know he got something from his father other than old photos and recounted memories from me.' Diva sighed with relief.

'You may find it hard to understand – many would – but his wife and I chatted about him that evening, for hours. We talked about things as you only can to someone who has also been close to the person you loved so deeply. We still speak occasionally on the phone. I don't have her round for tea and we will never be close, but there's a mutual respect and understanding despite all the sadness and the madness. Anyway, I prefer my afternoon teas and cocktail evenings with my old friends Patricia, Iris and Betty.'

'Oh my God,' exclaimed Mandy, 'so *they're* the ladies you have round for tea?'

'They rallied round me when I lost my man. In some ways *they* have been the loves of my life too, they have witnessed so much.'

And with that Diva offered Mandy another orange squash with a little something from her hip flask.

'Is that vodka?' asked Mandy in shock.

'Keeps me warm in the winter,' said Diva with a twinkle in her eye.

'You little devil,' laughed Mandy.

A bell rang. 'Gosh that must be my car already,' Diva said, shaking her head at how quickly time had flown.

'I've had *such* fun, Mandy darling.' She hugged Mandy tightly. 'You are a delightful, special girl and very patient with my stories.' She smiled apologetically.

'My pleasure,' Mandy said sincerely. 'I'm honoured you told me something so precious.'

Diva showed Mandy out and watched her skip down the stairs, clutching her beautifully wrapped present.

'Listen, my dear. Listen and learn.' Diva smiled sadly.

Back in her tiny flat, Mandy felt lonely. She missed Jake already. How was she going to get through Christmas? He had only dropped her at home the day before, yet her heart ached for him.

Oh dear. She knew at that moment, in her heart, that something had shifted. It hit her like a ton of bricks, slamming away any self-preservation.

She had fallen in love, truly and completely, for sure, and she knew that on Christmas Day she would be without Jake, who would be where he should be, at home with his wife.

EIGHT

Christmas and New Year

George banged on Mandy's door. 'Open up, my little Christmas fairy!' he shouted. Mandy opened the door and she was thrilled. There was George, looking very dapper in a smart chocolate-brown corduroy jacket, long stripy scarf, cream roll-neck and slim-fitting jeans. In his arms was a big white box with a gigantic red bow.

Mandy squealed with delight. 'George! Thank you!'

'No, thank *you*,' he smiled. 'Bloody bitch of a sister of mine has met a man for all of five minutes and is snuggled up with this so-called love of her life, in some place I've never heard of in the country. As you know, Mum and Dad have gone on a cruise and left me to keep an eye on Chantelle. Now that clearly hasn't worked, thanks for letting me join in your day so last-minute. The little cow only told me last night that she wasn't even coming home!'

'No worries, darling.' Mandy gave him a hug. 'Let me grab my coat and we can leave.'

'Well, maybe you should open this first?'

Mandy couldn't contain herself. 'OK! Let's unwrap this little beauty.'

Sitting on her white linen sofa, Mandy opened the box as George looked on excitedly. She took the lid off and unwrapped layers of tissue. 'Oh my,' she sighed as she held the beautiful cream Chloe coat. It was encrusted with a sprinkling of stones and crystals and was simply stunning.

'Do you like it, darling?' George was holding his breath and peeping dramatically through his fingers, hiding his eyes. 'If you hate it, I can change it and sneakily swap it for another sample in the Chloe press office.'

'Don't you dare. I love it!' Mandy hugged and kissed George. He unbuttoned the coat and put it over Mandy's pretty black Temperley dress. The dress was so well cut and she always felt great in it. Today she had teamed it with black opaque tights and suede Louboutin heels with a slight platform. She looked both cool and sophisticated – her hair was swept back in a sleek ponytail, showing off her beautiful jawline; her make-up was pretty and simple, with lashings of beige lip gloss perfectly highlighting her full lips – and putting the coat on made her feel a million dollars. The fabric was exquisite.

'It must have cost a fortune, George, I can't believe it's mine.' She spun round for George and with one hand on her hip and one on the side of head she pouted seductively. 'What do you think?'

George took her in. She looked so beautiful.

'You look like a bloody page-three girl with that pose,' he laughed. 'More fitting for a bikini shoot than for Chloe. And please don't worry,' he continued conspiratorially, 'I got one of the girls at a fashion PR company completely smashed, and made her nod in agreement three times that this little number got lost on a shoot in Milan. You see?' He smiled knowingly. 'A gay guy truly is a classy girl's best friend!'

Mandy jumped up and down, clapping her hands. This was truly hers, thousands of pounds worth of coat was *hers* for always, how fabulous! They made their way to leave.

'Wait,' said George, 'aren't you going to open those pressies by the tree? The one with the crystal bow looks divine.' The wonderful coat had taken any thought of Jake out of Mandy's mind. She had checked his voicemail last thing the night before, and he'd explained that his wife, Helen, had asked some friends over for drinks. The minute Jake had known he had called Mandy, hoping to see her earlier. But she had been shopping in a part of Harrods with no phone signal and didn't hear the message until she had left Diva. 'Helen, eh?' she mumbled under her breath, feeling slightly hurt and angry. Suddenly the other woman in her life had a name. She was *real*. Until then she had been referred to simply as 'my wife', and for obvious reasons they hardly ever mentioned her. A simple thing, but a name had hurt Mandy so much, like a stab in the stomach. She had used the anger to her advantage and punched a text back:

NO WORRIES, HAVE A GREAT CHRISTMAS. M. X PS DIVA
GAVE YOUR PRESENT TO ME, THANK YOU. SHAME I DID
NOT GET A CHANCE TO GIVE YOU YOURS. X

With that she had promptly wrapped the rest of her presents and packed the ones for the family in the back of the car. She did not check her phone again and slept like a baby. Her upset gave her the energy to switch off. She turned it into a positive and in a way felt stronger and stress-free again. It was simple – empty but simple – and she needed some simplicity in her life at the moment.

This morning she had woken very early. Her natural instinct had been to reach for the phone without even opening her eyes. It read 2 TEXT MESSAGES. The first one was from George.

THE BITCH HAS MET THE SHAG OF HER LIFE. I AM LEFT
STRANDED AND ALONE FOR CRIMBO, SUCH A WASTE OF A
FINE MAN! CAN I JOIN YOU FOR CHRISTMAS? NO WORRIES
IF YOU ARE TRAPPED UNDER SOMETHING HEAVY . . . G. X
PS I FORGIVE YOU . . . PRETTY PLEASE CAN I COME TO
YOU AROUND 9 OR IS THAT TOO EARLY?

Mandy had giggled to herself. God, he must be lonely, wanting to be up at that hour! She checked the next text message.

SO SAD I MISSED YOU AND SO SORRY I WILL TRY AND
CALL YOU WHEN I GET A MOMENT LATER. I LOVE U. J X
PS I HOPE YOU LOVE YOUR PRESSIE

Bang! Just like that a million emotions exploded in her heart. Her chest felt tight. 'I hate that you can do this to me,' she mumbled to herself as she brushed her hair off her face with her hands and rubbed her eyes. 'Thank God for George,' she whispered as she texted him straight back.

OF COURSE YOU CAN COME. OFF TO SISTER'S EARLY,
THE LITTLE FRAGGLES ARE DESPERATE TO SEE ME AND
TO OPEN THEIR PRESSIES SO GET TO ME ASAP X

And as for Jake, she just had to wait and see if and when he would ring.

'Yoo-hoooo, wakey wakey,' said George now, clicking his fingers. 'And you're back in the room!' He giggled – he absolutely loved Paul McKenna.

Mandy stood motionless, wearing her beautiful coat in her little living room.

'I'm not sure what to do, George.' She pondered a moment, and folded her arms. 'Jake brought me the pressie with the beautiful crystal bow.'

George raised an eyebrow. 'Wow, well done Jake, not bad for a straight guy.'

Mandy stood staring at the present. 'I'm feeling quite emotional. I miss him and I feel sad opening it without him, but I don't even know when I'm seeing him again. The children kept him really busy yesterday.'

'And you kept him pretty busy leading up to it, I hear,' smiled George.

Mandy shot him a quizzical look. George laughed. 'Deena told me about the Christmas-tree incident.'

Both of them burst into fits of giggles.

'Sod it!' said George. 'You will never have Jake a hundred per cent. At least enjoy the bits you do have! If you won't open that beautiful present, I will!' He went to dash for the gift but Mandy moved even faster, knocking George out of the way with her elbow and pushing him on to the sofa as she grabbed the beautiful present from under the tree.

'What about the others?' asked George, recovering from the elbow in the ribs.

'Oh, one's for Jake, and *this* one is for you.' She handed it to George and sat next to him on the sofa. George smelled her powdery perfume, so feminine, so . . . Mandy.

'OK, you go first,' Mandy said, nudging him. He opened his gift and put his hand over his mouth, astonished.

'They are the most beautiful cufflinks ever.' He smiled. 'Wish I had a shirt on so I could wear them right now.' He examined them and started to get emotional. 'You've had my initials engraved on them,' he said excitedly, his eyes welling up, 'and I *love* the little diamonds on each link, so chic.' He hugged Mandy tight and then pulled away and held her face gently. 'They are so beautiful, and you are just *too* thoughtful. I've missed you, babe.'

As Mandy looked up, she caught him looking at her in a way she hadn't noticed before. He pulled her to him with his big strong arms and gently kissed her cheek. His breath was warm and it brushed faintly past her lips. George always smelled so heavenly. Mandy pulled away and looked down at her present. She felt so overwhelmed, she must be going crazy; her emotions were all over the place at the moment. She was sure that what she had just sensed must be completely wrong. She lifted the lid off the velvet box and found a smaller box within it, then as she opened the next lid she found another, then another, until she reached a final small box. She looked inside and gasped.

'A Tiffany blue bag!'

'A Tiffany blue bag!'

Both she and George giggled at their outburst in unison.

'Quick, open it!' rushed George.

Within the pale blue bag was a Tiffany blue box, and within *that* box was a beautiful black suede box. Mandy gently pulled the top part of the box back. Two large glittering diamond studs sat before her. Nestled beautifully against satin, they sparkled brilliantly.

'Ahh,' was all George could muster. Then after a few seconds of taking them in he said, 'Wow, put them on! Put them on!'

Mandy crossed to the art deco mirror that hung on the

shelf above her fireplace; she put both studs in her earlobes. She instantly looked more beautiful.

'They light up your face,' smiled George. Mandy looked down at the photo on the shelf of her and Jake, then she picked it up and kissed it.

'Wherever you are, whatever you're doing, I miss you, and thank you.'

George looked down at the floor. He loved her so much, seeing her have such a touching moment with a man who wasn't even there left him feeling frustrated, and even more determined to show her a great time this Christmas.

Sometimes it was tough for George; he had moments where he almost felt he was in love with Mandy, and until recently he could let those emotions come and go. But Jake had made him question certain things: how did he truly feel about letting another man be closer to Mandy than him? He knew that as a gay man he could never give Mandy the stability that she craved, deserved; yet Jake was hardly in a position to give her the best either. Diamonds maybe, but support and a truly equal relationship? No.

Early on, the love of George's life had been a woman. He was only nineteen at the time, and homosexuality was something he put down to a vivid imagination. Her name was Lana. Occasionally when George got drunk he would tell Mandy all about her. He had adored her completely, and in his eyes they bonded like no one else. The only person who had ever come close, male or female, was Mandy.

George had shown Mandy photos and yes, Lana was stunning. She looked like Halle Berry, but with green eyes, and was an intriguing cocktail of Bajan and Irish. They met at fashion college, became best friends and fell in love. Apparently the sex was good, and George had put that down to them having such a connection emotionally. They kept in touch to this very day.

Lana had always sensed that there was something missing with George, but they were both so in love that they almost felt that if they ignored that sense of something missing, it would go away. But George's 'vivid imagination' in being attracted to men became more of a reality. He met Dominic on a fashion shoot. Dominic had been telling the girls and George at lunch about his new, first-ever boyfriend, whom he had just met. He said so many things that George identified with, and George had felt uneasy, full of guilt. That night the whole team had gone to a local pub for drinks and after a few too many George found himself confiding many inner demons to Dominic, a man he hardly knew. In a way that made it easier.

That night as he walked home he had cried and cried. Being true to himself was going to lose him the very thing he loved most: how was that fair? It was confusing, messy and heart-wrenching but George had admitted too many fundamental truths to himself that would never enable him to go back to his relationship with Lana. He knew he had to move forwards to a life that would be difficult and challenging, but true to the core of who he really was. He let himself into their north London flat and watched Lana sleep peacefully. He stroked her hair and after she'd woken he made love to her. Ironically it was the most beautiful sex of their relationship together; neither would forget it. As they faced each other and looked deep into each other's eyes, a sad but very brave conversation took place. Lana was amazing, and she knew now what was missing. She loved George so much and so unconditionally that she could only support his decision to be truthful to her and himself. She smiled, stroked his dirty-blond hair back and gently whispered:

'At least this way we'll *never* break up totally. This way I'll have you for ever.' George nestled into her neck and wept at such maturity from this amazing young woman. He knew that she was right: in some ways they would *always* have each other. He was just sad and angry that it could never be completely.

As he looked at Mandy now, uncomfortable feelings from the past came flying back.

'Come on, we'd better get going,' he sighed.

Mandy put her beloved picture of Jake back on the shelf and grabbed her keys. She linked her arm through George's and they skipped up the stairs and into Christmas Day.

'HAPPY NEW YEAR!' Champagne flutes clinked and dear old friends whooped and cheered with delight. Mandy kissed and hugged all her friends. Assia blew air kisses in order to keep her red lipstick in check, George pinched everyone's bum and tipsy Deena hugged everyone as tightly as possible, telling them what their individual star signs indicated for the year ahead.

'Right, Mystic Meg, it's time to send off the bottle,' said George, wrapping his scarf around his neck and downing his champagne. 'Come on, everyone!' he yelled over lots of chatter and a band playing loud celebration music. 'Wrap up, it's freezing out there.' All the girls grabbed their coats from the bespoke white Italian leather chairs. They had met at Gaucho on the river in Richmond and it had all been completely delightful so far. The glass-walled frontage of the restaurant meant they had a perfect view of the firework display, which had looked truly magical.

'Have you all written your dreams down for the new year?' George asked, grabbing the empty Laurent Perrier bottle off the dinner table. 'Ye-ess,' chorused all the girls as they rushed outside to the bank of the river and huddled up. George rolled the paper into a tube and pushed it into the bottle, pressing the cork in as hard as he could. He stood a couple of steps back and said, 'OK, girls, here's to all our dreams coming true this year, and lots of fabulous sex!' And with that he threw the bottle into the river, to the accompaniment of cheering from 'his' girls. Everyone seemed so hopeful, and as Mandy watched it float away she thought about what she'd asked for.

Her note had read:

May this year bring me and all my loved ones health, wealth and happiness, but most of all may I be guided to make the right choices and fulfil my true destiny.
Thank you
Mandy x

She thought of Jake. She was meant to see him for lunch between Christmas and New Year, of course, but Helen had surprised him with a gift of a skiing trip for two weeks. Fabulous – not. He was due back on 10 January, and Mandy was pretending that she no longer really cared. She was extremely busy and simply didn't have the time to miss him, but he had been gone three days and she'd only had one text from him. Oh, who was she kidding? She missed him so much, and she was tired of missing him – and this was just the beginning. As she stood by the river, looking out over the twinkling ripples of the water, she almost wanted a reason not to love him any more, for the relief if nothing else.

Being a mistress was not what it had been cracked up to be. Assia had been right about one thing, though: to be a mistress you had to be tough, strong and extremely independent. That was fair enough for everyday relationships, but with her soulmate? Mandy wanted to feel that she could be anything she wanted to be, and maybe she wasn't really cut out for this after all. Only time would tell.

NINE

Caught in the Act

Mandy pulled Figgy in to the petrol station on the King's Road just in time. As she pulled up in front of the pump the car completely cut out from lack of fuel. Mandy raised her eyes to the heavens and mouthed, 'Thank God.' The car could so easily have stopped dead right on the King's Road and caused a major traffic jam! She looked for her purse, ready to fill Figgy up so that she could continue her little trip down the A3 to see Mum, Olivia and the girls. Robbie was away in Denmark for work for a couple of days, so they were having a girly night in. Mandy had been rather taken aback by the invite. She had been sent a warm and sweet text from Olivia and it really touched her.

HI MAND ME AND MUM WERE TALKING, DIDN'T REALLY
GET ANY QUALITY TIME WITH YOU OVER CHRISTMAS,
TOO FRANTIC WITH THE KIDS! WOULD LOVE FOR YOU TO
COME OVER FOR A PYJAMA PARTY, JUST ME YOU MUM
AND THE FRAGGLES. I MISS YOU, OLIVE X

Mandy had smiled and texted back straight away to arrange details. She jumped at the chance to see her sister, who hadn't called herself Olive in years. Mandy had given her that nickname when they were kids, as Olivia had thick horn-rimmed glasses till she was fourteen; she was always breaking them and constantly had a plaster keeping the arm attached. She'd been told she looked just like their dinner lady, Olive. Even Olivia laughed when Mandy first blurted it out, and it was lovely to be reminded now of something so funny about her sister.

Mandy filled Figgy up, grabbed water and an apple to keep her ticking on her journey and skipped back to the car, ready to put some Rolling Stones on the stereo. Putting the key in the ignition, she couldn't quite believe what was in front of her. She didn't know whether to duck and hide, scream or run over there. But instead she sat motionless, wondering why her eyes would play such a cruel trick on her as she watched Robbie walk out of his beloved 1980s silver Porsche and turn back to a red-haired woman who sat in his passenger seat. He smiled, and Mandy saw in the wing mirror that she flashed him a suggestive, toothy smile back as he disappeared into the garage to pay.

Mandy could not help herself: she had to check out this woman some more. She was wearing a light fur coat, her red curly hair had been teased to perfection and her blue eyes had the perfect set of full false lashes. She reached for a lip gloss and without looking for a mirror expertly applied lashings of the sticky gloss to her full, dark-pink lips. On closer scrutiny, Mandy could see she was older than Olivia but extremely well groomed, and her alabaster skin had a soft dusting of subtle pink blush over her high and chiselled cheekbones. She was very thin, maybe an ex-model. Mandy felt herself holding her breath as she leaned at various angles trying to get a good view of the mystery woman.

Robbie walked out suddenly and Mandy pretended to look down and be extremely interested in her old-fashioned radio dial. There was no need to worry: Robbie was oblivious to her as he beamed at the redhead. He walked back to the car with a bottle of wine under his arm and once he was inside the woman grabbed his face and kissed him passionately. He kissed her back just as hard. Mandy took a sharp intake of breath, seeing that they couldn't keep their hands off each other. It was a Friday, 6 p.m. According to Olivia he had left for Denmark the day before. The redhead opened her eyes after a long lingering kiss and looked Mandy in the eye. At that moment Mandy wanted to smack her as hard as possible in the face. She was furious for her sister, knowing that, despite everything, Olivia's pain was hers too. Jake's voice came into her head.

Helen has the family over . . . Helen has booked a skiing trip . . . Helen is worried about this . . . Helen is worried about that . . . Helen, Helen, Helen, Helen! The voice got louder and louder in Mandy's head until she could take no more. Huge waves of guilt slammed over her body like breakers hitting the shore. She hated feeling like this; she hated herself.

She put her foot on the accelerator and made it to her sister's house in record time. Once there she sat, stuck to her seat: all this anger, energy and emotion consumed her, but what would she actually *say*? Nothing was going to sound good or make anything any better. 'Don't think about the exact words now,' she mumbled to herself. She took a deep breath and checked her eyes in the rear-view mirror. She had cried throughout her journey and could not work out why something so awful would bring out so much rekindled love for her sister. Wiping away any remnants of her watered-down mascara, she took another deep breath, grabbed her bag and walked up to the front door of her sister's perfect house.

Valerie opened the door and knew something was wrong instantly. Mandy covered as best she could, aware she wasn't seeming herself.

'Hi, Mum. God, it's cold today.'

In actual fact it was rather mild, and both of them knew she was talking nonsense.

'Hi, Mand,' Olivia shouted down. 'I'm just drying my hair.' Olivia popped her head over the banisters – she was wearing a pair of men's pyjamas. Her caramel hair with its highlights was half dry and hanging wildly around her face.

'I won't be long,' and she darted back to her bedroom to switch on the hairdryer.

Mandy walked through to the living room and placed her bag by the side of the sofa. Mum had been cooking again, this time home-made pizza with a lovely big salad.

'We've got popcorn and ice-cream later,' said Valerie, smiling. 'Can't believe it, but Olivia wanted to be naughty with her food tonight!' Mandy half laughed. Her emotions were sitting on her chest, crushing her like a baby elephant, and she was finding it hard to swallow.

'Mum, what would *you* do if you knew someone should know something, but it would devastate them to know the truth? How would you go about dealing with it?'

Valerie shot her a look. 'What's going on, Mandy? It's not like you to ask me my advice on things.'

Mandy looked down at her tightly clasped hands, the knuckles white. She was literally trying to hold it together.

'Mandy, what's wrong? What do you know?' her mum went on.

'It all feels a bit like a dream, Mum.'

Valerie walked over to Mandy and sat next to her on the sofa. The house was undeniably beautiful but there was an emptiness to the place, unusual considering there were children living here. But it seemed to lack soul, and Mandy felt cold.

'Oh, Mum, why me? Why do *I* have to be the fucking bearer of bad news?'

'For God's sake, Mandy, what is it? Unless you give me some kind of clue, I can't help.' Valerie looked sincerely at Mandy and grabbed her hands. 'Is this about you, or someone else?'

Mandy found herself unable to speak. There was no halfway house with any of this, and Valerie drew a sharp intake of breath. 'It's Robbie, isn't it?'

Mandy looked up to her Mum. How the hell had she known?

'It's *Robbie*, isn't it?' she repeated emphatically.

Mandy nodded sadly. 'I saw him at the petrol station just now with another woman, a redhead, older – they were all over each other, Mum.'

Valerie put her hand to her mouth in shock. Suspecting it was one thing; having it confirmed was another.

'Did they see you?' Valerie's voice cracked unexpectedly.

'No. The woman did, but obviously didn't really register me as I could have been anyone.' Silence hung in the air.

'Bastard, what a fucking bastard!' Valerie was seething. 'If you're not happy in a relationship, fine, get out, but don't do this, it's the lowest of the low.'

Mandy found herself nodding and crying.

Valerie was angry but trying to keep a lid on her emotions. 'And those babies, those *poor* babies. Where's the thought for them?' Her mum hugged her tight. 'You are such a good girl, darling, we'll get her through this. Between us she will be OK, I know it.'

Mandy felt completely choked.

'I'm not a good girl, Mum, I'm awful, just terrible. I've done something so, so bad and I can't believe I've put myself in this position.' Mandy struggled to find the right way to confess what was going on between her and Jake. She hugged her mum, clinging to her olive-green jumper and giving way to tears.

'Listen,' said Valerie, holding Mandy close like she had never done before, 'you aren't awful, you've just seen something terrible. That's not your fault at all, it's not your doing.'

Mandy closed her eyes tight and knew this wasn't going to be easy. It felt like the wrong time and place to talk about her own problems, and a childlike part of her was enjoying being comforted by her mother. She could not remember them ever being like this.

'What's the matter, Aunty Mandy?' A small voice came from the doorway of the living room and there stood little Milly. Mandy dried her eyes and pulled away from her mother's embrace.

'Oh, nothing, darling. I just ate something that's given me a bad tummy. My tummy still hurts.'

Milly looked at her blankly for a moment and then quipped, 'Get Granny to rub it, she always makes mine better.' With that she dashed up the stairs, shouting, 'Aunty

Mandy is here! And she's crying because she's got a bad belly!'

'Right,' said Valerie, taking control. 'You need to tell Olivia now. It's only fair she knows. Enough is enough.' She shook her head. 'It's just a shame that glimmers of the old Olivia were coming back to try and save the marriage, and now it's just too late.'

Mandy hoped to God there could be some way out of all this mess, although what that would be, she had no idea. 'I'll go up, Mum,' she sighed. 'I want to get this done for everyone's sake.' Mandy swallowed hard with dread, and her mum leaned over, her head on Mandy's shoulder.

'Do you want me to come with you?'

'No, Mum, but thanks. Just be here for when we come down. Can you keep an eye on the girls, just keep them busy for half an hour or so?'

'Of course,' nodded Valerie. 'I'll go and get them now. You talk to Olivia in her bedroom.'

Mandy opened the door gently and sat on the end of her sister's perfect, pristine bed.

'Darling, I need to talk to you. Something's happened and I, and . . .' Mandy's voice trailed off, knowing the news would break Olivia's heart. She hated Robbie for doing this to his beautiful family, for putting *her* in this position, and most of all at that moment she hated herself more than words could ever explain. She looked at her sister's expectant face. She looked twelve years old in her baggy white cotton pyjamas, her hair fluffy from the dryer.

Unexpectedly Olivia's face drained of colour and her brown eyes filled with tears. Her hands were shaking as she placed them to her chest. Finally she said, 'It's Robbie, isn't it?' Mandy sat motionless on the bed and nodded, dumbstruck.

'How did you know?' she asked.

Olivia bit her lip and looked around the room as if she was disorientated. She stood up and her toes gripped to the carpet as she tried to keep her composure, but her body was swaying ever so slightly.

'I think a woman knows these things,' she whispered gently, half to Mandy, half to herself. 'I know when Robbie is sad, happy, feeling creative or frustrated. I know his everything.' She smiled, forgetting for a moment that this wasn't her usual chit-chat to someone at a party about how much she loved her husband. Her face suddenly fell and her eyes seemed full of darkness. 'What did you see?'

Mandy took a deep breath.

'I was in the petrol garage.'

'Where?' fired Olivia.

'Chelsea,' muttered Mandy gently. 'King's Road. Robbie came into the garage after I'd paid, and as I got back into the car I saw him walking back to a woman.'

'And?'

'And, and . . .' Mandy's lip began to tremble and tears

fell again. She tried to tell her sister what she saw as kindly as she could. 'And he embraced her, kissed her.' This was terrible, she felt so awkward. 'And she kissed him back. They clearly knew each other well, put it that way.'

Olivia cleared her throat, a nervous reaction she'd had since she was a child. A tear ran down her face and she brushed it away angrily as soon as it had landed on her cheek.

'What did she look like, Mand? And don't be nice to me – tell me the truth. Was she beautiful, perfect?'

Mandy looked at her sister. 'She was an older woman.'

'How old?' blurted Olivia.

'I'm not sure, maybe forty-three, forty-four?'

Another question was fired. 'What does she look like?'

Mandy concentrated as hard as she could to get the details just right. 'Red, longish hair, blue eyes. I think she was wearing a fur coat – oh, and fake eyelashes.' Mandy kept concentrating. 'She had lots of lip gloss on, and she appeared to be very thin.'

'Thin?' murmured Olivia. 'How thin?'

'Very thin, as far as I could see,' said Mandy solemnly.

'Thinner than me?' asked Olivia, looking even more vulnerable.

'Oh, don't be silly, Olivia. Does it really matter?'

Olivia put her head angrily in her hands and looked like she would squeeze her skull so tightly that she would crush it. She looked up with so much raging pain in her eyes that for a split second Mandy felt shocked and slightly scared.

'Yes, it fucking does matter!' she yelled at the top of her voice. 'All I've ever tried to do is be every fucking thing *he* wants me to be! Everything, *everyone* wants me to be! I look after the house, the children and *myself* better than anyone I know! I entertain his friends and pretend that I'm interested in yet another fucking building that looks exactly like the last one!'

Mandy had never seen so much anger and upset in her sister, never seen her lose so much control. Olivia was now crying as she was screaming.

'It was the same with Dad! I was like a pathetic little clown trying to come up with something new and special. I was trying to perform better and better tricks, and none of it was ever good enough, was it?' she yelled at Mandy, getting closer and closer to her face. 'Was it?!' she repeated, yelling at the top of her voice. 'There's always someone else or something to turn their heads away from me, someone better in some way.' She laughed bitterly. 'And it's so effortlessly done too! With Dad it was Mum or you. And I was always the fucking afterthought! With other men I was only worth having when I was fun or a pick-me-up – and God forbid I ever needed something from them! I could never just fucking relax and be *me*. And now,' she stumbled, 'now the man I tried the *hardest* with doesn't think I'm enough either.'

Olivia fell to her knees, sobbing, and covered her face with her arms. 'What's wrong with me, Mand?' She was crying so hard the words were spluttering out, and Mandy could hardly understand what she was saying. 'What's wrong with me?'

Mandy knelt down by the bed and hugged Olivia tight. Her sister fell into her arms and Mandy rocked forward and back cradling her.

'You are beautiful just the way you are,' she whispered gently as she brushed Olivia's hair back off her face. 'You always have been, you lucky cow. You just need to believe it, and stop trying to tick *every* box, just tick the ones that really matter to *you*. The people that don't want you as you are are arseholes, so fuck them! They obviously aren't what the real you deserves in your life, it's energy wasted on the wrong people.'

Olivia sobbed in Mandy's arms for what seemed a good ten minutes. Mandy wished with all her heart that things were different, that she could make things better for her sister.

The pain that Robbie and this other woman were causing was horrific. Realization began to creep in completely that the 'other woman' was *her* equivalent, just with someone else's family. Mandy felt sick with disbelief. How could she have done something so, so wrong?

The really sad thing about Olivia and Robbie was that, once, he had truly loved the real Olivia, and so had their father. Everyone did, but somewhere along the line Olivia had felt unloved, and the person she really was got lost along the way. She had become uptight, materialistic, controlling and paranoid. Mandy had noticed it herself for the last few years and Robbie must have too. Olivia had become drastically different and in truth rather difficult to live with. Ironically, trying to be perfect made her unattractive and soulless, yet Olivia was naturally so full of soul, laughter and passion. What the hell *had* happened along the way? True love was meant to see you through good, bad and ugly, wasn't it? Robbie had been tempted by another woman, and yet Mandy knew how much he loved Olivia. Had he fallen out of love with Olivia because she wasn't the same woman he married any more? And, if so, whose fault was that? People change. Was anyone to blame really?

'Oh questions, questions,' sighed Mandy. 'So many are going through my head, God knows how you feel, darling.' Mandy kissed Olivia on the head. Out of nowhere Olivia started to laugh . . . and couldn't stop. She laughed and laughed.

'What the hell are you laughing at?' said Mandy, bewildered, half laughing herself with the madness in the air. Olivia clutched her stomach and truly belly-laughed.

'Only *you* would notice fake eyelashes!' she giggled. 'I love you, Mand. You're a one-off!' They both fell about laughing, then Olivia hugged Mandy as tightly as she could.

At that moment Mandy knew she had a huge part of her sister back.

At home later that evening, racked with guilt and feeling like shit, Mandy had rung her darling George, who in turn rang the moral Deena, who in turn contacted the tough-talking Assia.

They all sat on Mandy's bed and said, 'Do it, just do it.'

When the three of them had arrived at the flat earlier, Mandy had looked horrific, with pink swollen eyes from crying. Talking to George had been the closest thing to a Catholic confession for Mandy. The day's events poured out of her, along with all the built-up emotion from the last few months. It all came tumbling out at once and it didn't stop for a good three-quarters of an hour. Poor George, he was truly worried. But once she started sobbing she couldn't stop. This messy situation with Jake, mixed with the heartache she had witnessed at her sister's, became too much for her to bear. George had never heard her so upset; she was clearly in a terrible way, unable to cope, and he was deeply concerned.

Mandy was a blubbering wreck as bit by bit she re-counted her day to her wonderful friends: her guilt, her helplessness with her sister and her sadness in now know-ing what she had to do to sort out this sorry mess. Mandy threw caution to the wind and rang Jake, knowing he would probably be with his wife and children. She had no idea of his exact location and as a result no idea of the time difference; all she knew was that they were on a skiing holiday.

She needed support, and fast.

With a stiff vodka to hand, she waited for a response.

'Voicemail,' she whispered sadly as she cleared her throat ready to make her big speech. The three friends looked at each other, trying to think of something they could do to make it all better, but just being there was all they could think of.

'Hi, Jake, it's Mandy.'

Mandy looked down at her feet to concentrate on what she was saying and take her mind off the fact that her friends were hanging on her every word.

'I am really sorry for calling you. You know I wouldn't unless I needed to – and I *do* need to . . .' She trailed off, and George grabbed her other hand and squeezed it to reassure her. 'You see, something happened today. My sister's husband is seeing someone else, and I caught them, saw them . . .' Mandy knew what had to come next and swallowed. This was all so hard and sad. 'So I've seen how devastated my sister is – and it's absolutely killed me.' A tear rolled down Mandy's cheek, and then another and another tracked down her tired, flushed face.

'I feel so, so bad, so sick with myself for what we've done. And it's brought it all home . . .' Mandy started to cry properly. 'What we've done is *so* wrong, Jake, and after tonight I can't possibly carry this on. I feel sick in my stomach – God knows how you must feel when you're with your own family.'

George motioned to Mandy to wrap it up: she was getting too upset to be understood completely.

'So I was just . . . calling to say goodbye, I suppose. I'm so sorry I didn't get to talk to you properly, but I can't even risk ringing you again . . .' Mandy broke down but tried to finish with one last thing.

'Please don't ring me. Thanks for the most amazing time ever, I'll never forget it, but this relationship – affair, whatever you want to call it – also makes me feel awful, and with all this stuff happening with my own family I just can't do it any more. Be happy . . .' Mandy held her breath for a few seconds. 'I love you, bye.' She ended the call and fell into George's arms.

'I didn't want to say goodbye, George – but I had to, didn't I?' she sobbed.

George cradled her and gently stroked her hair. 'It was going one way, darling – down. You were never going to get a good outcome with this situation, and as much as I love the diamonds they don't keep you warm at night. Someone, somewhere along the line was going to get hurt. You've done the right thing, I promise.' He shot a look towards the girls, who sat helplessly and feeling a tad emotional themselves now. 'Don't you think, girls?' he said, eyeballing them so they could only agree with him.

'Of course,' agreed Assia as softly as she could muster. 'Dharrling Mandy, as the other woman, it's OK if you fuck with their head, they kind of like it, but when they start fucking with yours you get out! And all this stuff with your sister, it's too much for you, you are too sensitive. It's *too* much.'

Deena got up and walked round to Mandy, kneeling down in front of her. She took hold of her hands. 'This whole thing, this whole situation, Mand. It's not you. You are a hopeless romantic, and romantics always end up getting hurt. Look at me: we're not built for all this.' Mandy wiped her eyes and held Deena's hands again, trying to smile. Deena went on, 'I know you all think I'm just a dippy hippie, but I truly do believe in certain things – I believe that our destiny is our destiny no matter what. I definitely believe in karma, and what goes around comes around. So treat others how you want to be treated. I believe you can make this journey of life as complicated or as simple as you like. If you truly follow your gut instincts, you will make the right decisions. Life is like school: we have lessons to learn, and some we find easy and others are too hard for us to comprehend. But the more challenges we have, the better, richer souls we become.'

'Oh pleeeze,' said Assia, rolling her eyes. 'Life is a bastard and then you marry one.'

'Listen, you!' said Deena, raising her voice ever so slightly.

'Stop belittling what I say just because you're too bloody ignorant to get your head around it.'

'Oh shut up,' snapped Assia.

'You shut up,' retorted Deena defiantly.

Mandy looked bemused; this was most unlike Deena, who was normally the first to back down, especially with Assia.

Assia looked slightly taken aback. 'Who's rattled your cages?'

'You mean my cage?' said Deena, enjoying putting Assia right. 'No one has rattled *my cage* but you and your lack of depth. It isn't the only way to live life, Assia. Just because you don't understand anything that isn't dipped in jewels doesn't mean that it's wrong or it has to be a big joke.'

'Oh what do you know?' scowled Assia. 'You're about as real as your boobs!'

Deena gasped in shock. 'How dare you? You don't know what you're talking about!'

'Whatever,' smiled Assia sweetly. 'I have it on good authority from a friend who had the same surgeon that you had them done in the last year, and you didn't tell a soul, not even us, your friends. I'm sure God *really* wanted you to fulfil that part of your destiny.'

'You are evil, you know that?' yelled Deena. 'You don't even know what the hell you're talking about half the time, and maybe you should learn when to speak out.'

'Well, did you or didn't you?' barked Assia determinedly.

Silence ensued.

'See, you are no better than me, Deena, you are *just* as shallow and materialistic and vain, except I am honest about those traits and you, dharrling, are not.'

Mandy's own problems disappeared under the heavy atmosphere. George twiddled his fingers and pulled a Kenneth Williams face as if to say, 'Ooh, it's all kicking off, isn't it?' Something was going on and Mandy wasn't sure exactly what it was, but was grateful for the respite.

'Well, don't just stare at me as if I'm crazy,' said Assia nervously. 'Say something!'

Deena never took her gaze off Assia. As she spoke, tears filled her eyes.

'Yes, I had surgery on my breasts.' Deena bit the inside of her mouth to try and control her emotion. 'I had the surgery because I had breast cancer, OK? By the time they had finished cutting me up I had hardly anything left – and yes, I had reconstructive surgery, and yes, my tits look great. But most of all I'm glad I only confided in George because you've shown your true colours. And let me tell you, yes, I turned to healers, Tarot cards, fortune tellers, precious stones and homeopaths – you name it! And I'm so glad I did, because it gave me hope and strength of mind, and an insight to a world that I believe saved my sanity and my life.'

Assia moved to speak, but Deena was having none of it. 'So save your bullshit for someone who wants to hear it!

Me *and* the tits are off!' Deena grabbed her belongings and stood to face her three friends as she draped her expensive velvet coat over her shoulders. 'I am a survivor, Assia. I dealt with cancer and heartbreak *alone*. When have you ever been strong enough to do anything on your own?'

Assia was speechless, as were George and Mandy. Deena inhaled deeply through her nose yoga-style. 'Now, I would rather *live* my precious life, with positive happy people round me. That means without *you* in it, you twisted old goat.' Assia's eyes widened with horror. 'So go back to your wrinkly old husband and your dirty dreams of Federer. My breasts may be fake but at least my life isn't.'

And with that Deena strutted proudly out of the flat and upstairs into Queensgate.

'Bravo!' cheered George. 'Bravo, Deena!' he laughed, clapping his hands with delight. 'You must admit, Assia, you had that coming to you!' he chortled as Assia sat on the bed, completely bewildered.

Mandy spotted the vodka shot glass in George's hand. 'Just how many of those have you had?' she asked.

'Just the six,' said George.

'Bloody hell, George. When did you get those down your neck?'

'Mmmm, not sure, but feel grreat!' He started doing a silly little dance.

Mandy walked over to Assia and sat on the bed. 'Are you OK?'

Assia nodded. 'I think so. I'm just a bit shocked, you know?'

Mandy thought Assia looked sad and lonely. 'It certainly puts things into perspective though, doesn't it?' she offered. 'I feel all my dramas are nothing compared to that really.'

Assia continued to seem a bit distant. 'I can't believe she didn't tell us, Mandy.'

Mandy had never seen Assia so deep in thought, or gentle, come to think of it.

'My mother died of cancer,' Assia said softly. Mandy wanted to put her arm around Assia's slight shoulders but didn't feel comfortable doing it. Assia had never been very touchy-feely. Air kisses were about as tactile as she ever got.

'I'm so sorry,' said Mandy quietly. 'Did Deena know about your mother?'

'No, no – I very rarely talk about things like that, dharrling.' Assia shook her head sadly.

Mandy smiled. 'Seems silly, doesn't it? All these secrets that no one wants to discuss. It's a shame. If only people could speak up more, they would probably find help, or at least feel better.'

Assia nodded and sighed. 'Secrets are bad for the soul, dharrling . . . and they never stay secret for ever.'

Mandy looked at Assia's fragile, perfectly made-up face. She hoped to God she was wrong.

TEN

A Woman Knows . . .

Jake flew down the stairs of his four-storey Notting Hill house with the phone charger in his hand, desperate to find a plug socket. Helen was putting the boys to bed. They had had such a great trip skiing; the boys were becoming so good, faster than their dad. At times they would whoosh past him giggling, and little James, who was only five, was a natural: he had loved showing his dad his latest moves. His brother Alexander was seven and was the spitting image of his father. He was less boisterous than James, more gentle and sensitive – too sensitive for his own good at times. Jake often worried about him being tough enough for this world. He was a gentle soul and battled with asthma most days. James was very funny, such a little entertainer, very articulate for his age and was very much a mummy's boy, but Alexander had a bond with his dad – secrets, problems at school or with friends: only Jake would do as a confidant. He loved his father so much because Jake made him believe he could be anything he wanted to be. His dad was his hero; no one could ever top him, not even Superman!

Jake sat on the bottom step of his stairs, near the large front door of the house. He could just about see the socket thanks to the large lantern that hung outside and shone through the glass panel above the door. Turning the phone on, he quickly switched the setting to silent. For some reason he had not been able to access his voice messages abroad. It was ridiculous, he thought, a VIP customer and yet he couldn't even retrieve his voicemails! He would give the network a call first thing tomorrow, he could've missed something urgent to do with his work. He wouldn't bother to mention that in fact all of his work colleagues had been able to contact him via email on his BlackBerry. He wanted to make sure that he could access his voicemail no matter what, for one reason only: to hear Mandy's voice. He had missed her desperately – there had been so many times he wanted to say or show something to her. He had also had moments that had made him want to end the whole thing. He would feel overwhelming guilt over his boys, then randomly he would decide that all he wanted to do was fly her out to meet him. These crazy notions surprised and scared him. Occasionally he could recall her smell, and his heart would flip over, almost as if she was standing right next to him. It was very disconcerting; he would look around feeling nervous in case Helen could sense his anxiety. He would have vivid flashbacks of their love-making, and God, he wanted her naked; her skin against his was the best feeling in the world, something he daydreamed of often.

Helen and Jake had not made love for nearly a year, and when they had attempted it everything felt wrong and clumsy. It wasn't Helen's fault, but Jake knew in his heart that it wasn't his either. He loved Helen – she was a wonderful mother, so together, so elegant and beautiful – but the relationship was lacking spark. He had felt guilty even admitting it, and until Mandy had swept into his life he had successfully put it to the back of his mind. Denial was a full-time role.

When he was working it was easy to switch off; his career was so demanding yet also so rewarding that it could take his mind off anything. But it was definitely tougher when he was at home, especially when the boys were asleep and he and Helen were left alone. Luckily, as the last few years had gone by and Jake's success had reached an all-time high, dinner parties and social gatherings had become a regular fixture, and Helen thrived on them. Jake's power was her turn-on, above anything else. The decadent life that went with it was something she was very much accustomed to.

Jake and his father-in-law did not see eye-to-eye. Jake had never been good enough in Alastair's view. He was a formidable and extremely rich businessman and his daughter was his darling, his world, his only child. When she brought this handsome working-class boy from Shepherd's Bush home, Alastair had been far from impressed. Jake had found

Helen fascinating; her life seemed so perfect, so clean and effortless. She was also intelligent and cultured, living the life Jake wanted. Helen looked at Jake as a novelty at first; she loved his naughty, brash humour and, most of all, the way he kissed. He was confident and passionate, women always noticed him and he certainly possessed a sexiness and a happy-go-lucky attitude that both infuriated and inspired her. Helen had always been Daddy's perfect little girl, and young men had always been daunted talking to her. One brave young man had unfortunately been caught touching her breasts under her pretty blouse at their country home in Hampshire and he was promptly chased out of the house by Alastair, running with a shotgun and screaming, 'I'll blow your bloody bollocks off!'

Jake, however, wasn't afraid. He would do anything to her; he loved messing up her perfect hair and seeing Miss Prim-and-Proper lose control when he went down on her. He loved watching this uptight, posh girl get drunk and lose her head – she could be so much fun. And she was *much* more of a challenge than most of the easy girls he dated in Shepherd's Bush.

One day at lunch Helen had explained Jake's idea for a brand-new advertising company to her father. Alastair promptly insisted on putting up the money for the idea, providing he would always have a minimum share of 40 per cent of the business. The deal was that the arrangement would stand for as long as the business existed. Jake was confident that his new slant on advertising and his ideas and people skills would be a success no matter who backed him, but Alastair was the only rich person he knew. Jake figured that, despite Alastair's strictures, the pay-off would still be worth it. Jake sat down in his future father-in-law's sitting room and was told by Alastair that he would give him the contacts, the full finance, but the rest was up to him. If he didn't make a success of it and a substantial turnover within two years, his deal would be over, completely finished, and that included Helen.

Jake thrived under pressure. He had always wanted to build an empire. He had a hunger to *be someone*. His dad was a musician, never around, and his mum's life consisted of looking after his nan full-time in a two-up, two-down. Jake wanted so much more. Helen wanted him to do well too, and he loved that, but felt some of her desire was about her own little power trip with her father. Alastair was so dominant and Helen was two very different people – one with Jake, and another in the company of her father. Helen could never make a decision without consulting her family.

The business grew, and with it so did Jake's confidence. He became a fine, powerful man with a mixture of strength and humility (something Alastair lacked). The more Alastair was shown that Jake could pass any test, the more difficult he became to work with. He had started to poke his nose in where it wasn't needed and on occasion tried deliberately to sabotage a deal, just to then come in and look as if he'd saved the day. Alastair's strange behaviour only surfaced once in a blue moon, but became worse once Helen got pregnant.

But Jake and Helen worked: completely aware of each other's flaws and attributes, they embraced the high-flying life with gusto. Jake's success had been Helen's success. She was, in her way, just as controlling and manipulative as her father. She felt she had sculpted Jake into the man he was, the powerful player. Because of her father's huge financial involvement in Jake's company she knew she had a hold on him for ever. Helen and Jake had one common goal, to show the world, and Alastair, that Jake could make it. That had been proved and now what was left? The excitement of 'making it together' had long ago faded. The children were born and their dynamic team relationship had been channelled into being great parents.

Jake sat on the steps in his grey T-shirt and white boxer shorts, pondering the fact that they had been in love with the challenge, and were now in love with the children. But had they ever been in love with each other? Were they enough for each other on their own? Jake would be lying if he said he found Helen anything less than beautiful; she was naturally fair-haired, light skinned and long-limbed. She had always been the perfect clothes-horse. Lanvin and Stella McCartney hung beautifully on her small-breasted, fine-boned frame, but Helen only seemed to be in love with Jake when there was an audience, when someone else was looking. It was almost as if their love was all for show, playing to a gallery. The sad thing was that when she turned that switch on, the coldness in her melted away and she became luminous, warm, and so feminine. That was when Jake loved her most, when she wasn't her true self.

The computerized voice of his phone interrupted his thoughts: 'You have seventeen new messages.'

'Good grief,' mumbled Jake as he skipped through each message as fast as he could, desperate to hear *her* voice at last. When he did his heart felt stretched like a piece of rubber, pulling in every direction. He couldn't bear to hear her so hurt. Putting his head in his hands, he tried as hard as he could not to cry. The house was now silent, and he couldn't afford to be heard, but before he knew it he was dialling her number. Helen was on the top floor, she wouldn't hear: she was probably showering or something. His heart was pounding when he got the voicemail.

'Hi, it's Mandy, leave me a gorgeous message and I'll call you straight back.'

Jake sighed and whispered, 'Hi, it's me. Please don't do this. We have to talk – please. Please don't leave me, Mand, I've just fucking found you. Please, let's just talk together before anything is final. Call me, or I'll try you again tomorrow – I've missed you so much.'

He sighed, feeling useless, and hung up. He pulled the phone out of the socket and made his way upstairs. He felt moisture on his right cheek and realized a tear had fallen.

He was shocked, both at the tear and at the fact he felt so broken at the thought of losing her.

From over the banister, Helen watched Jake walk slowly, solemnly up the stairs. As he reached the top floor she stood back against the wall and saw him wipe away tears from his face. She had never seen him look so sad. He seemed oblivious to everything around him, including her.

'Everything all right?' she said quietly.

Jake took a sharp intake of breath, as if he'd seen a ghost emerge from the shadows.

'Fuck, Helen! Sorry, you startled me. I'm fine, just tired.'

Their eyes locked for an instant as he walked away, and at that moment Helen knew for sure what intuition had already whispered.

Mandy tapped away on her keyboard at an alarming rate. She was together, efficient, organized – and miserable. Work was going well – ish. She had been without Jake for two months and was keeping herself busy with everything and anything she could, even things that didn't concern her, much to her colleagues' annoyance. Maggie was more furious with Mandy than ever.

'You don't need to take the coffee in to Michael, that's *my* job. Now let me do it,' said Maggie with gritted teeth. The two girls had the jug of coffee between them and were yanking at it as if it was a tug-of-war competition.

'It's fine, I have to talk to Michael anyway,' said Mandy, smiling with clenched teeth, yanking it even harder.

'What's got into you, you power freak!' Maggie retorted, struggling with all her might to yank the jug back.

'What did you call me?' Mandy gasped, releasing her grip ever so slightly.

'What you are! A power freak!' Maggie tugged with frustration. 'You're driving everyone nuts! Go and get laid or something, and calm the fuck down!' Maggie was losing her rag.

'You bitch!' yelled Mandy.

'You fat bitch!' yelled Maggie, still tugging at the glass jar as if it was the most important thing in the world.

Ouch! That comment hurt Mandy. Food and alcohol had been a great help most evenings, and since breaking up with Jake, yes, her jeans felt a little tight, but this little cow was taking it too far! Mandy felt her rage pumping her heart fast and her cheeks filling with pink colour. 'I can lose a few pounds. Shame you can't grow, you stunted little midget!'

'Fuck you!'

'Fuck *off*!'

'What the hell is going on?' bellowed Michael, coming out of his office. 'It's like a fucking circus in here.'

At that point Maggie, still tugging at the jug, tumbled backwards with the full jug of black coffee. It splashed and stained her crisp white Gap shirt and the front of her cropped beige Capri trousers. Maggie saw red, her eyes flashed with a madness and she launched herself at Mandy.

Mandy tried to shake her off, spinning around the office trying to chuck Maggie, who now had her legs clenched tightly around Mandy's waist and looked like she was trying to bite her. The growling noises coming from Maggie were bizarre. As the girls wrestled quite an audience gathered.

Michael decided enough was enough. 'Maggie, you're like a crazed banshee! Get off Mandy right this second!'

Andrew and the rest of the office were all standing around watching the show; their faces looked shocked but then a nervous laughter filled the air.

Maggie slowly climbed down from a rather dishevelled Mandy and put her straying red hair behind her ears as she tried to comprehend what the hell had just happened. Years of resentment had just exploded and now there was no denying it.

'Michael, I'm sorry, I don't know what came over me, but *she* has become overwhelming, unbearable actually. She's trying to take my job away from me.' She shot Mandy a look of hatred.

'Maggie, Mandy, I want you both in my office, now!' Michael barked, and marched off to his glass-walled, sound-proof office. The two girls scuttled behind him. Andrew saw but couldn't hear the shouting from Michael. At the end of a twenty-minute roasting the girls shook hands and smiled as if they were the best colleagues in the world. The glass door opened and the girls left quietly and walked back to their desks. Maggie whispered with a sweet smile:

'I'm going to make your life hell, Mandy Sanderson.'

Mandy gritted her teeth in a fixed smile. 'Just try it and see what happens, you troll.'

Mandy sat at her table looking tired, sad and puffy.

Andrew adored Mandy and would often fantasize about her lying naked on the work breakfast table with strawberry tarts on her breasts and an iced finger on her fanny. One of his favourite bits of his fantasy was when Mandy ordered him to eat and lick them off her body; if he didn't, she would whisper seductively that she would tell Michael. He pushed his glasses up his nose and stared at Mandy, licking his lips – she was such a luscious woman! He would kill just to kiss her beautiful plump lips, but all she ever went on about was some guy who constantly let her down because of his job. Andrew sensed that there was more to it than that, but he didn't care, he just loved her talking to him. She was way out of his league, but if she was a fraction of the woman he saw in his fantasies, she was the lushest woman in the universe.

'What are you staring at?' said Mandy, hanging up from a call.

Andrew blushed. 'Oh, just you,' he laughed nervously, thinking on his feet. 'You and Maggie were crazy this morning!'

Mandy sighed. 'She's a lunatic, and she'd better be careful from now on.'

Andrew giggled. 'You are so funny!' He laughed far more than the comments deserved, then gazed at Mandy for a bit too long.

Mandy shifted uncomfortably in her seat. 'Don't you have something to be working on?' Everyone around her was starting to freak her out. She had been so looking forward to Los Angeles but the engagement and the party for the football star and his actress girlfriend had been called off. The assignment made her think of Jake, and her stomach ached. God, she missed him so much. He had called her mobile many times but she had already said all she needed to say. Now she was desperate to get away. Los Angeles would have been the perfect escape from London, Jake and her own ever-analysing mind. Why hadn't he truly fought for her? Yes, Jake had rung, but had he knocked her door down? No. Had he left a note or written her a letter? No. Had he at least turned up at her flat *trying* to see her? No. A handful of phone calls was all she had been worth to him; therefore she had done the right thing.

Out of the blue an email popped up from Olivia.

THE BASTARD HAS MOVED INTO A FLAT IN PIMLICO, AND THE REDHEAD IS STILL IN THE PICTURE — CALL ME. X

God, the first couple of months of the new year had been shit. Valentine's Day had come and gone and all Mandy had got was a card from Andrew. He honestly thought she didn't have a clue that it was from him, but it had been in his top drawer for two weeks before he sent it and his handwriting was distinctive and a complete give-away. From Jake there had been nothing.

Mandy had spent Valentine's night with Deena in Groucho's in Soho, sipping herbal tea with a stinking cold. They were miserable, ill and sneezing alone – alone, alone, alone, alone. A gorgeous independent film director had come over to chat up Deena, but she spotted the wedding ring and scared him off within minutes.

She sighed. 'What are these men like?' she said, rolling her eyes and sneezing into her tissue. 'Why do they even bother being married, when they know that all they really want to do is chase every piece of skirt under the sun? It's Valentine's night! It's so depressing! I mean, where is his wife? When you're single you're worried that the man you fall for is married and taken, and then when you're married you worry he's going to be taken by someone else!'

'Well, we've never been married so we don't actually know, do we?' mumbled Mandy.

Deena continued: 'Either way, do we ever have the chance of feeling safe or comfortable in a relationship? Does The One really exist? Just because it feels good, does the label really fit that? I mean, look at you and Jake – everything feels right, but morally it's all wrong. Does The One mean every box has to be ticked? Because if that's the case, I don't think he does exist.' Deena looked down at her cup and saucer sadly. 'There's something very optimistic about marriage, if nothing else,' she sighed. 'I wish someone wanted me enough to be positive and want a future with me.'

'Oh pull yourself together, woman, you're talking nonsense!' blurted Mandy. 'Optimism isn't always the *truth* of a situation or relationship. You cross your fingers and toes and hope for the best when you marry someone, because life moves on and the only guarantee is change. I know people that aren't married and are so in love. The most important thing is not ticking boxes or what looks good on paper, it's pure love and respect in the *truth* of a situation, good, bad and ugly. I don't believe you can have love without truth.'

Deena looked confused. 'You've lost me. Sometimes your loved one lies to you to protect you, don't they?'

Mandy felt just as confused herself now. 'Ah, but are they protecting you? Or themselves? Because they don't want to admit they fucked up?' Mandy looked at Deena, all dressed-up and looking stunning despite her red nose, and she looked down at her own gorgeous high heels. Here they were, all made-up and with only each other for company – on Valentine's night. 'Oh, what do I know?' half laughed Mandy. 'I've got a crazy female hippie as a date on Valentine's!'

Going home that night, sitting in the back of a taxi, all Mandy could think about was Jake. Everywhere she looked, she saw couples. One woman looked particularly beautiful, holding a red heart-shaped balloon as she walked beside a very handsome man. He had his arm tightly round her waist and they were laughing.

Every time Mandy was tempted to text or call Jake she thought of Olivia and the devastation Robbie had caused the whole family. Mandy had been at the house when Robbie had gone to pick up some of his clothes. Olivia had needed the support, and it turned out to be one of the worst nights of Mandy's life. It felt almost too personal for her to witness.

Robyn and Milly had been asleep. Robbie was trying to carry his suitcase down the stairs but dropped it, and as it fell into the hall it hit the girls' bikes by the door. They in turn fell on the floor and made such a racket that the girls woke up. They had thought their dad was still on a business trip and cried and sobbed with confusion when he was near the door and about to leave again with his case. It was heartbreaking.

'Tell him, Mummy!' Milly had screamed, crying. 'Tell him to stay home, Mummy, I don't want him to go to work any more.'

Robyn was crying quietly, trying to get her little sister off their dad's leg as he attempted to leave the house. Although Robyn was older and very bright, she didn't understand the full ins and outs. But she did know her dad wasn't leaving for work again. She had heard her mum crying most nights, and crawled into bed with her to cuddle her and make her better. Olivia was trying to hold it all together, but seeing Robbie for the first time since confronting him about the affair, she was shaking. Trying to keep her story straight that Daddy had another trip away and would be back soon was no mean feat. It was dreadfully sad, and none of it made sense. All Mandy knew for sure was that the pain it had caused everyone, including beautiful innocent children, was too much to bear.

The memory of that night kept her strong and on the right track. She would keep away from Jake.

ELEVEN

The Blind Date

After a day at the office with the ginger troll looking daggers and Andrew licking his lips and staring at her breasts, Mandy made her way over to her sister's house to check on her before she got ready for a date set up by Assia. She was dreading it, but was determined to start again. God knew what kind of man she was meeting.

'He's a great catch, dharrling,' Assia had purred with delight in her heavy accent, 'so powerful and rich.'

Mandy felt like a carthorse, with various bags of clothes, lotions and potions draped over her as she struggled through the door. Olivia gasped. 'Strewth, are you staying here for a few months?!'

What once would have felt so difficult for Mandy to say came tumbling out from nowhere. Mandy was so random at the moment that she couldn't predict what the hell she would do or say next. Knocking Olivia's bedroom door open with her bags, dropping them to the floor and collapsing on the bed, Mandy brushed her fringe back and confessed.

'No, I'm not staying, all right? I'm going to tell you something and I don't want you to interrupt me until I've finished, OK? OK?'

Olivia nodded, bewildered.

'I'm like a bloody packhorse because I'm trying to keep busy – I'm hardly ever home and I'm staying out and as booked up as I can because I'm heartbroken. I don't want a day, hour, minute or second to think about him because when I do I feel devastated – not just because I'm desperately in love with him but because I feel so fucking guilty. He's married, has two children just like you and Robbie, and I'm no better than Robbie. I'm just a home wrecker, and I could have caused so much misery and heartache. That's assuming I haven't already. When you do something bad, God always gets you back, you know. So I'm doing my best to not think about it.'

Mandy's eyes filled up with tears. 'Because I feel that God's way of getting me back has been to hurt you, and I'm so, so sorry, Olivia. I feel like all of this has come to show me what a bitch I am. Now I'm getting what I deserve, but *you* don't deserve any of it and I'm so sorry, I'm so, so, sorry . . .'

There was a silence while Olivia looked at her. 'Can I speak now?'

Mandy nodded, wiping away bucketloads of tears.

'I know, you silly cow!'

Mandy gasped. 'What do you mean, you *know*?'

'Mandy, do you know Mum at all? Do you honestly think Mum ever misses a trick? She's the eyes and ears of Surrey, for God's sake.'

Mandy wiped away more tears, extremely confused. 'The man at the ice rink? For starters, Mum saw you drive in with him to a friend's house on her way to pick up Milly from ballet class. Secondly, he had a wedding ring on when we met you both, and thirdly, you looked at each other like you wanted to rip each other's clothes off!'

Mandy was lost for words. Olivia sat next to her on the bed.

'It doesn't take a genius, Mand. Why on earth did you come to Surrey for an illicit affair, of all the stupid things?'

'He booked it as a surprise, he had no idea my family lived here. How come you didn't say anything?' retorted Mandy, trying to get her head round it.

'Mum was hoping it would go away, I think. You know what she's like.'

Mandy and Olivia sat on the bed in silence for a moment. Olivia grabbed a tissue from her bedside table and gave it to her little sister. As she blew her nose Mandy said, 'Do you hate me, Olive?'

'No, but I think you're heading for trouble,' her sister replied firmly.

'Why? I've left him.'

'Yes, but look at you: you're lost without him! It's not over yet, is it?'

'I've promised myself I won't go back, Olivia. You know me. I've always been confident, a go-getter. I'm old enough now to be clear on what I want, no excuse. And yet he challenges everything I thought I knew.' Mandy twiddled with her tissue as flashes of Jake, their chemistry and their love-making washed over her – she loved and hated it all at the same time. 'I never knew I could feel this way about someone,' said Mandy, 'and I don't know if I like it. I was never the type of woman to settle for second best, and let's face it, that's what I am. I was never going to be someone's silver when I should be their gold. I never dreamt I would be the mistress. What the hell happened to me, Olivia?'

Olivia looked at her sister in surprise and unexpectedly felt sorry for her.

'Look, your life is your life. No, I don't agree with what you have done or what you may do, I think it's wrong.' Mandy felt a stab in her heart. 'But we're all grown-ups and have to live our own lives. *No one* knows what goes on between two people except for them. You, and only you, have to live with the consequences of how you lead your life, but don't you feel you're better than being someone's bit on the side, Mandy? Because *I* do. You're such a beautiful girl, an amazing catch, and whoever you end up with is lucky to have you.'

Mandy grabbed her sister and hugged her tight. 'God, you're brilliant. I've missed you so much, Olive.'

Olivia pulled away sadly and said something strange, a
sudden revelation appearing like a light bulb switched on
in her head: 'I've missed me too.'

Mandy was all dressed up like a dog's dinner, in order to
compensate for her tiredness. She was in Fifty, the casino
in St James's, close to Piccadilly. It was a magnificent place,
with wealthy clientèle and many glamorous, elegant women.
Frederico, the owner of the bar within Fifty, was fabulous;
he was very fond of Mandy and always treated her like a
movie star when she arrived. He had a real knack of making
people feel special, as if they were the only person in the
room. His cocktails were amazing, and his crazy, colourful
friends were a never-ending source of fascination. Mandy
had met him on her first trip to the Lanesborough Hotel.
She had never seen a place so grand and opulent; she
hadn't known where to sit, what to order or how to behave.
Frederico took to her instantly: seeing someone so awed
and excited by his everyday surroundings was refreshing.
He had made her laugh and feel at ease within minutes.
She was then working for the luxury travel company,
and she was meeting a top client about his holiday. In truth,
she felt out of her depth but she got through the meeting
brilliantly. Whenever Mandy had a problem about what to
order, or even what she should tip the valet-parking guy,
Frederico had been on hand to see her through. Thank
God!

Mandy was like many other people in London, a player, a pretender, and Frederico had made things run as seamlessly as possible. 'Don't-a worry,' Frederico would say with his strong Italian accent, 'you are so beautiful that people will forgive you everything!' He was charming and sweet, intelligent but always modest; his guests were the stars of his bar. He looked exactly like Peter Sellers in the Pink Panther movies: his suits were beautifully made, and he was passionate about life – a true Italian. After many successful years at the Lanesborough, Frederico had decided to set up his own bar at Fifty. He had had many successful books published on his own fabulous way of making cocktails as well – plus recipes for potent hangover cures. In his own way, he had become a famous fixture on the London social scene. He worked very hard to look after his family, and always wanted to provide his loyal clientèle with a touch of magic and glamour from an era long forgotten. He had succeeded: the bar was undeniably grand and very beautiful. But the best bit of all was that success hadn't gone to Frederico's head: he was always the same, and there was something very comforting about that.

Mandy's date was a disaster. God only knew what Assia was thinking of. Frederico's eyes kept flicking to Mandy to check she was OK, because this guy was undoubtedly creepy. He was foreign, but Mandy couldn't quite put her finger on the accent. He seemed to believe that his huge personal wealth gave him the right to be rude to everyone, and that he could buy whoever and whatever he wanted. He kept scratching his balls; Mandy tried not to look but couldn't help herself – was this man really being that brazen? This was hardly the time or the place! Finally, when he left to go for, in his words, 'a pees', Frederico came over to check on her.

'Mandy, are you OK, my darling?'

'Yes, thanks,' said Mandy, trying to stifle a yawn. 'I'm about to hear about his palace and his third jet.'

Frederico stifled a laugh. 'As long as you're OK. Any problems, you call me, yes?'

'Of course,' smiled Mandy thankfully.

Her date came back, wiping his nose to the point of almost picking it. He had clearly decided to do coke to boost his stories even further, and to reinforce his belief that he was a living legend. 'So, where was I?' he said, animated. There was a trace of white powder clinging around the rim of his nostril.

'Um, I think you were telling me about one of your jets,' said Mandy, desperately trying not to be distracted by his nose, which was now running. He clearly couldn't feel it, but licked his lips. What a waste, thought Mandy. All that money for cocaine, and none of it had even hit his brain.

He was clearly older than her, and yet all Mandy wanted to do was wipe his nose with a tissue, just like she did for Milly when she had a sniffle. Mandy was very much of the live-and-let-live school; however, this man with a runny nose and millions in the bank just looked rather sad and pathetic, a walking cliché. His big hairy hand slid underneath her little black dress and squeezed the top of her thigh, so hard it hurt. Mandy felt grateful she was wearing her black opaque tights.

'Ah yes, the jet,' he smiled, taking a swig of his whisky. 'Why don't you come on it with me? I'll take you to places you've only dreamed of.' His hand squeezed even tighter on her leg, to the point where she could stand no more and had to say something.

'You're actually really hurting me,' she said, pushing his hand away.

'You like it rough, no?' he smiled, but his eyes looked dead.

'No, I don't.' Mandy was aware of the people milling around and she didn't want to cause a fuss. 'I'm just going to the ladies' room, excuse me.'

Mandy stood up sharply, and pushed through the people as fast as she could. The bar was very busy and noisy and she wished her friends were with her now. She made her way past the lovely receptionists and over to the cloakroom. Damn, there were around eight people waiting to check their coats in.

The atmosphere was exciting, strong expensive perfumes filled the air, and yet Mandy's heart was now pounding with fear. Call it women's intuition but she sensed that if she stayed any longer there would be trouble. All she wanted to do was to leave one of her favourite places, because of the pig of a date. Wait until she saw Assia, she would kill her! She decided to quickly use the ladies' room before she left, then grab her coat and get out of there. As she made her way past various doors and downstairs, she felt a hand cover her mouth, and an arm pull her and slam her into a wall. Facing the wall, she started to shake. She felt the full bodyweight of someone heavy crushing her against it. A hand tugged her hair to one side and a voice whispered, spittle hitting her ear, 'You wanted me to come and get you, didn't you, you dirty girl? You dirty, *dirty* bitch.'

The right side of Mandy's face was now being pushed against the wall so hard she thought her jawbone would be crushed. She tried to move her arms but couldn't; her collarbone felt bruised. She thought she heard a couple walk past, clearly tipsy and giggling, unaware that Mandy was being physically hurt by this man. He took his hand from her mouth, reached down and tore her tights with his fingers. He pulled her knickers roughly to one side. Mandy managed somehow to pull her head back from the wall and scream. With every ounce of her strength she pushed herself back, turned around and kneed the bastard in the balls. Before she could even think straight, Frederico was there. He had a huge security guy with him.

'What the hell do you think you are doing?' he yelled. 'Mandy darling, are you OK?'

Mick, the big security guy, put his arm around the culprit's shoulder, ready to crush him. 'Did anything happen, Mandy?' He had a very deep voice. 'Just tell me and I swear to God, I'll sort him out.'

Mandy looked at her tormentor's dark eyes. 'Please just get him away from me.' Her knees suddenly went weak and she felt herself fall into Frederico's arms.

'Come, Mandy, come, let's get you some tea.' Frederico hugged Mandy and tried to pull her to her feet. There were now a few people watching. 'Come on, it's all right now, they've got him.' Frederico was such a sweet, sweet man. 'I tried to getta to you sooner,' he said anxiously. 'I just knew he was coming to find you, but it was so busy, and I was trying to getta through the crowd as quickly as I could.'

Mandy looked up at the man's sorry eyes. 'Don't be silly, Frederico, you got to me when it mattered. I'll never forget it, thank you.

'Can you get me a car, please? I just want to go home,' she pleaded.

'Not alone, darling. Do you 'ave someone to meet you?' Frederico's kind face looked at Mandy with real concern.

'Yes,' she lied. 'I have someone to meet me.'

Frederico put her into a chauffeur-driven Mercedes with one of Fifty's best drivers.

'You take good care of her, OK?' Frederico closed the door.

As the car was about to take off, Mandy wound down the window: 'Thank you so much, Frederico, you are my angel.'

The car pulled away and took a left past the Ritz. Mandy felt so alone, so vulnerable. As her shock melted away, she started to cry.

The driver looked at her, slightly embarrassed, not sure what to say. 'Are you OK, madam?'

'Yes, sorry, just had a very difficult night.'

'I know, madam. Frederico and Mick told me about it and wanted me to stay outside your flat tonight, just in case he showed up. Although by the time Mick has finished warning him off, I don't think you'd need worry, madam.'

The driver had kind eyes, and Mandy felt better. Not all men were arseholes.

'If you need anything, you just let me know,' he smiled. 'Frederico wanted me to check. Do you want me to inform the police or anything?'

Mandy thought for a moment. 'No thanks.' She smiled gratefully. 'I think Mick will scare him more than anything.'

All Mandy wanted right at that moment was her father to hug her and tell her everything would be all right. She felt she needed reassurance with absolutely everything. 'Give me a sign, Dad, please,' she whispered to herself as she looked at the bustle of London life through her window. 'Just show me you're around or something, show me there's a heaven, *please.*' A tear ran down her face and she wiped it away with her sleeve. She decided to be brave; she was made of stronger stuff.

At that moment, she could smell Jake's aftershave. She thought of how he looked at her as if she were the most magical thing in the world. It sounded simple to say but she just knew, in her heart, how much he loved her. She instinctively felt it at various times of the day and night, and for her it didn't need explaining. There was no other man like Jake, and there never would be. At that moment her phone rang. She knew who it was; there was only one person that in tune with her. Her heart leaped and all rules were forgotten. Nothing else mattered at that moment.

The Mercedes pulled up outside Queensgate and there he stood. Mandy ran into his arms and he held her as if his life depended on it. He cupped her angelic face, brushed her hair back and kissed her cheeks, her forehead, her cute little nose and finally her lips with overwhelming passion. Tears ran down her face. Mandy looked fragile, but she was laughing and smiling. Jake kissed her again, even more passionately.

'Don't ever shut me out. Let's never be like that again.'
Mandy smiled and nodded.

'You promise?' Jake said it with such urgency that Mandy felt nothing would ever be wrong again.

She nodded, tears still streaming down her face.

Jake grabbed her shoulders, 'Say it. Say it – say, "I promise."'

'I promise.'

Jake smiled, wrapped her in his arms and squeezed her tightly, never wanting to let her go.

'Let's get inside,' Mandy murmured, pulling back to look at her lost lover's face.

He put his arm around her waist and held her close as they walked down the stairs. Mandy opened the front door and as Jake went through into the flat, she looked up to the sky. It was midnight blue and scattered with stars.

'Thanks, Dad. I don't know if it's you, but if it is, thank you,' she said gently. She smiled, and with that she walked into her flat and closed the door on a night she would never forget.

TWELVE

Happy Times

The next six months were just like heaven. Mandy was sure she would count them as some of the happiest days in her life. Unable to be apart from each other, she and Jake grabbed every possible moment they could.

They had celebrated Jake's birthday – he was a Pisces – and on 15 March Mandy, clad in La Perla underwear and naughty spiky heels, certainly gave him a birthday present he would never forget.

Unusually, Jake adored shopping, and the more he got to know the real Mandy, the better and more fabulous her presents became. Many weekends away were booked, as being anonymous proved more and more difficult in London. Between them they knew so many people, and they would often have to pretend that they were out with a client for work purposes.

One day at work, Maggie had even made a snide remark about how it was a *very* small world, and had hinted that she knew something about Mandy's love life. She looked at Mandy viciously. 'I believe India is very good friends with Helen Chapman, and I hear the Chapmans' marriage is on the rocks. It's all very hush-hush but I wonder what's going on there.'

Mandy glared back at her as her heart nearly jumped through the ceiling. At that moment Maggie pulled open a drawer to reveal the photo of Mandy and Jakc holding on to each other at the ice rink in Hampton Court.

Mandy had sighed and tried to keep her composure. 'Are you truly this desperate, Maggie? And do you honestly believe that you are the only one in this place with secrets?'

Maggie folded her arms smugly. She knew Mandy felt extremely vulnerable.

Mandy continued, keeping her eye on the photo as she spoke, 'Maybe you should be focusing on your own love life, Maggie? Maybe once someone other than Andrew actually wants to shag you, you will find you have no time or energy to poke your ugly nose where it doesn't belong, or to start vicious rumours.'

Maggie was furious and dumbfounded. 'How . . . how did you know about me and Andrew?' she stammered.

'CCTV,' replied Mandy promptly. 'I always bring Dave a coffee and cake in the mornings. Lovely man. It's amazing what these security men get to see . . . little trolls having sex with Andrew on the desks, on the floor of Michael's office, in the toilets – every little grubby space they can get their mitts on, really. Just terrible, isn't it?'

Maggie's face was nearly purple with anger and humiliation. 'I didn't realize we had CCTV *in* the building as well as outside,' she faltered.

'Well clearly,' said Mandy, reaching for the photo and ripping it into small pieces. 'Now, let's just keep our business between us? I would hate either of us to be the laughing stock of this office.'

Mandy grabbed her papers and went to chat with Michael in his office. God, that was close! There *was* no CCTV in the building – just gossiping colleagues who had laughed their heads off when the cleaner had revealed she had caught Maggie and Andrew at it after hours on more than one occasion. Maggie had rattled Mandy's cage, but Mandy had kept it together. She hoped to God Michael and India knew nothing of her relationship with Jake – her work meant so very much and couldn't be compromised, no matter what.

The thought of being caught did, rightly or wrongly, at times add to the thrill, but the most amazing times they ever shared were simple, pure and private. Jake loved nothing more than seeing Mandy snuggled in one of his baggy jumpers. She was so feminine and pretty that she looked extremely sexy in anything masculine. His favourite thing in the world was to have his hair played with while lying in Mandy's arms watching a funny comedy or a romantic classic on DVD. Ice-cream was a must, cuddles a necessity, and talks of happy plans kept them hopeful for a starry future.

Fitting work in proved simple for Jake and Mandy. She was like a different person now he was back in her life: upbeat, confident and easygoing. Andrew still glanced at her from time to time as if she were good enough to eat, but Mandy took it in good heart. Even when the sugar doughnuts arrived with her morning coffee and Andrew started licking his lips, she found herself stifling a giggle.

It was a wonderful spring day and, after juggling a few meetings around, Jake and Mandy found themselves walking in the spring sunshine at Hampton Court. The crocuses and daffodils were in full bloom, and although there was a slight nip in the air the sun shone, its warm rays heating the winter chill that had run through their bodies. Holding hands as they walked, Mandy knew the silence between them was a comfortable one. There were times when neither had to say anything.

Suddenly Jake spoke out. 'Let's be brave and go to Harvey Nicks for a coffee and a bite to eat. Walking and this fresh air has left me hungry.'

Mandy thought for a second. She knew the risks, but today her happiness seemed worth it. 'Yes, let's.'

All the shops in town displayed the Easter theme. Large bunnies filled shop windows, along with enormous golden eggs, yellow chicks and bright, sometimes outrageous, displays.

'I'd love you as my Easter bunny,' smiled Jake.

Mandy giggled. 'You're terrible at times, Jake Chaplin, but I love your forward thinking.'

After coffee and a panini with side salad in the café, the lovers wandered the store, browsing. They then made their way to Harrods, where Jake spoiled Mandy rotten. 'Let's get you some new dresses. I want to take you somewhere special over Easter, and only a new dress will do.'

Mandy was in no mood to say no; how could she? The day had been magical and their time together was wonderful.

Jake had his own ideas on what looked fabulous on Mandy. They purchased a slinky, tight-fitting black Alaïa that would match beautifully with her new diamanté Jimmy Choos, and a dark bottle-green Azzaro off-the-shoulder number that emphasized her beautiful shoulderline and pert bosom. She looked and felt a million dollars. Mandy wasn't idle herself: she excused herself to the ladies' and called Angels and Bermans to order in a Playboy bunny outfit. She had her surprises for Jake too! She loved being with someone who enjoyed all her fabulous fantasies with her.

Later that evening Jake needed to go home. After deep sensual love-making back at Queensgate, as the sun started to go down Jake knew he had to leave. Mandy never liked these moments, but was now confident and happy with Jake and she had no jealousy inside her.

'Don't forget, baby,' he said, 'I'm taking you away for a few days. Pack the black dress, your passport and your accessories and be ready when I call for you the day after tomorrow.'

Mandy felt a surge of excitement run through her. 'Where are we going? What is it, is it something special?'

Placing his fingers on her lips, he whispered quietly in her ear. 'It's no surprise if I tell you! Just be ready for pick-up at ten-thirty on Saturday, sharp!'

After one more passionate kiss, he skipped up the stairs and Mandy walked back into her bedroom, ecstatic. Nothing would change the way she felt. Her heart pounded with love and satisfaction; she was on cloud nine.

Mandy called Olivia. 'Hi, babe, how's things?'

'Robbie called in today to see Milly and Robyn. It was difficult,' she said with a sigh.

'Do you need me to pop over?' Mandy asked.

'Thanks, Mandy, but right now I just need to be alone with the girls. I'm slowly getting there, but it's hard, Mand. Still, Mum is never far away, and right now I just want to snuggle up with the children, eat pizza and watch *Sleeping Beauty* for the fifth time.'

'OK, Olive, no worries. I'm away at the weekend, but I'll get down soon. Love to the girls, and to you.'

Mandy clicked off her phone, and thought about the whole situation once again. It always seemed to come back and haunt her; it made her feel guilty, but the pain never lasted long. How could loving Jake like she did ever feel bad for longer than a minute or two? In any case, she was in a great place at the moment, more happy and contented than she had ever been in her life.

As they arrived at the opera in Verona, Mandy was breathless with awe. She looked stunning in her new black Alaïa dress, beautiful shoes and with her jet-stone clutch bag. She had applied subtle, simple make-up and had piled up her hair in pins to hold the waves in place. Around her shoulders was a fur wrap. Jake held her arm in his, looking immaculate in his tuxedo. They both knew they looked good, a pair who turned virtually every head.

The opera was amazing, *Romeo and Juliet* performed in Italian. That made no difference to their enjoyment of the story of the star-crossed lovers. Both Mandy and Jake had tears in their eyes as the curtain fell.

Back in their luxurious hotel, Jake ordered Laurent Perrier pink champagne, stripped off and lay on the bed, waiting for his Juliet.

A smile spread across his face as a provocative Mandy made her entrance in her bunny outfit. She strutted across the floor, twirled three times for him and wriggled her fluffy white tail virtually in his face.

She passed him his champagne, got her own and raised her glass to announce a small toast. 'To Italy, the opera, and the naughty bunny that can't be satisfied!'

Jake howled with laughter as her floppy ears dangled

all over the place. 'You little minx, when did you plan all this?'

'Drink your champagne, my darling, and let's see what the Easter bunny has in store for you.'

Throwing caution to the wind and with no inhibitions, Mandy took the lead and pleasured Jake in a naughty but exciting way. She used every trick in the book, from her furry ears to her bunny tail, and after hours of passionate and sometimes bizarre sex, the two lay exhausted together, drinking and giggling like six-year-olds. 'It's true what they say about rabbits,' said Mandy and Jake just burst out laughing. What a wonderful weekend, what a fabulous romantic evening, and what a wicked, glorious night!

The months crept on and soon it was summer with its golden sunshine, early mornings and sultry late nights. At last things seemed to be going smoothly, with no emotional hiccups.

Jake had planned another trip, this time nearer home.

Ever since he was a child, he had loved the holidays he had shared with his family in Cornwall. He described the area to Mandy, and she was keen to go with Jake and relive some of his youth. She wanted to get an even deeper understanding of the man she loved.

St Ives was beautiful. Their hotel was right on the seafront, and the views of the bay were stunning. Seafood restaurants stretched on to the beaches. Mandy loved it.

Jake was happy seeing her in casual jeans and a plain white cotton shirt, her hair blowing in the wind, wild and untamed.

During the day, he took her to places he remembered and loved. One in particular was what he recalled as 'the land of the giants', a barren hilltop with enormous boulders scattered around. How they got there, no one knew, but pagan myth and the legends of the Cornish people still held that giants had ruled the hilltops, and would often fight over patches of land, throwing stones at each other, scattering them around. The Cornish believed that was how the landscape in the land of the giants had been formed. Jake loved the story and so did Mandy.

On one particular, burning hot day, the two made their way to Carbis Bay, a small inlet cut into the coast, offering sandy beaches and a small rippling tide of water that stretched out to the sea. As Mandy lay full-length on a towel Jake thought of how much he loved her. She looked more stunning than ever with her tan deepening in the hot sun, making her olive skin glow. Her hair shone in the sunlight, whipping around her face in the slight breeze. To him, she had never looked lovelier.

Lying next to her and stroking her arm lovingly, he made a sudden and unexpected announcement. 'Mandy, I think it's time I met some of your friends. I know that it might prove difficult, but at the end of the day, they know about me. I've heard so much about them, and I want to know who they are, because they are such a part of you. What do you think?'

After a very short pause, Mandy answered, 'Why not?' She would start with Assia, Deena and George and then, maybe a little further down the line, the family. 'I think it's a great idea. I'll make some plans when we get back.'

Jake nestled up close to her and the two soaked up the sun for the rest of the day. As the sun started to go down, they walked hand in hand along the beach, saying nothing, taking in the golden colours and the salty air.

In the evening they visited a small local seafood restaurant, and chatted away. Mandy spoke of her friends and how much they meant to her. It had been a glorious time together, and only emphasized how precious their trips together were.

Jake thought deeply as she spoke.

Back in London in late July, and after all her wonderful experiences with Jake, Mandy found herself needing to contact her friends, as well as Olivia and the family. She didn't feel guilty, for her time with Jake had bonded them together more than ever, but she had neglected the others a bit. It was the perfect time to ring the gang and get together. And for the first time she would include Jake.

Mandy thought about things rather carefully and picked what she decided would be the best place. High Road House in Chiswick was perfect for Sunday-afternoon drinks and nibbles. With its wonderful jade-green colours and muted music, it was a calming and peaceful place to meet. They would go to the upstairs bar and have drinks together, and sit in the cool area.

Mandy arrived on the dot of two-thirty, and as she made her way upstairs with Jake on her arm she felt her legs wobble a bit, but then she breathed in deeply and her courage and resolve returned. She glanced at Jake. Even on such a hot day, he looked cool and confident. He felt privileged to be taken into her world, her friends, her domain. He knew this was a special day.

As she entered the bar, the Golden Girls were waiting. They were all friends again and had turned up early to have a few drinks to get them relaxed.

'My darling, you look fantastic,' said George enthusiastically. 'You're glowing, full of radiance. I take it that you're the one to make this wonderful change in her,' he added to Jake, eyeing him up and down. 'I'm George, the poof, and this is the lovely Assia and the delightful Deena.'

Jake smiled, shook hands with George and kissed the girls hello. He wanted to break the ice immediately, and the girls seemed charmed by him.

'So, dharrling,' Assia purred, 'it's been a long time, waiting to meet you, but I can see why Mandy has kept you locked away from us.'

Jake smiled. 'I've been looking forward to meeting you all for a long time. With work and Mandy, it's been hard to pin time down and get together, but I'm glad the chance has finally come.'

'And of course, there's your wife and children!'

'Assia,' snapped George, with a warning glance.

There was a slight pause and an uncomfortable moment.

'Oh, dharrling, I didn't mean to be so rude, it just slipped out,' Assia teased.

George focused his attention on Jake. 'Ignore her,' he whispered. 'She can be a witch, but her mouth speaks before her brain. Hardly the tactful type, but harmless really.'

Jake just laughed. 'It's OK, George, don't worry. Let's get some drinks and relax.'

Before long the ice had been broken. Assia was spilling the beans on her marriage to Marius, Deena was already predicting Jake's star sign and what the future held, and George was pumped up and ready to tell them about the new love in his life, Pedro. Shushing them all, he demanded to be heard.

'Now, I know you and Assia are up to date with all my romantic news,' he said, looking at Deena, 'but Mandy and Jake don't know anything. So sit there bored or go away and amuse yourselves for ten minutes while I fill in the details of *my* wonderful love life for these two.'

Taking a deep breath, George began. He could never resist being in charge.

'Well, a few weeks back I was bored shitless, and wanted to do something. I went to the local tapas bar – you know,

Mandy, the one in the Fulham Road. I sat at the bar sipping a piña colada, when out of the corner of my eye I saw a tall, bronzed Adonis looking my way. Not one to pass up the possibility of a good night out fucking, I swept my hair from my face, pursed my lips, looked at him and said hi, brazen as ever. Lame, I know, but I felt really mesmerized by him. He almost walked into my body, as I felt his eyes take all of me in. And, darlings, I mean *all* of me! Well, my face just blushed crimson. I mean, when have I ever blushed at anyone or anything? You know me, Mandy, never one to be flustered! We started talking, had a few drinks, ended up at my place, shagged all night, and he hasn't left since. So, that's me and Pedro!' Giggling, George looked at the two with their mouths open, waiting for more.

He raised his arms, slapped his legs and announced, 'I'm fucking loved-up! How fab is that?'

Mandy could see an inner glow in George that she related to. He was in love. She jumped out of her seat and hugged him. 'I'm so thrilled for you, my darling.'

Jake went off to the bar to order more drinks. George looked her in the eyes.

'And I for you, bar the small problem of marriage. But he's made for you, and you are made for each other.'

She hugged George again with the suggestion that all was well with them and their friendship.

'Gosh, I need the loo,' said Deena. 'Anyone else?'

'I'll join you, babe,' replied Mandy.

George looked at the unusually quiet Assia.

'What's up with you, sourpuss?'

'Nothing, dharrling, just feeling a little subdued. Things are not working with Marius and me and I'm contemplating my future. Well, I look at Mandy and she's so young. I don't want to see her with a relationship that won't have a happy ending.'

Leaning forward and almost whispering, George said, 'Assia, not everyone is in the same situation. Yes, you're older and yes, of course you're thoughtful for the future. Time doesn't stand still for anyone, but you can't just blurt out rude and hurtful remarks, however well intentioned you mean to be.'

Assia placed her hand on George's. 'Dharrling, you know I love Mandy with all my heart. The remark slipped out and I'm sorry. I didn't mean to hurt anyone or make them feel ill at ease.'

'I know,' replied George, 'but you don't have to be loud pushy Assia to get noticed. You are a beautiful woman, and you have a beautiful heart. Just be softer, and think before you speak. Jake's on his way back, so let's just enjoy the rest of our time here, and we can play catch-up once they are gone.'

In the ladies' loo, Deena was simply gushing over Jake.

'My God,' she said, 'I wouldn't care if he was Henry VIII and had six wives, I'd still like a night to play with him. And a Pisces too, the most lustful, naughty, sexual star sign, what fun it must be! He would turn Mother Teresa into Mary Magdalen in five minutes flat!' Deena burst out laughing, adding, 'He's simply divine, darling.'

'I know, and I love him, Deena, so much. I want everyone to be happy for me. What's up with Assia?'

'I'm not really sure, but the stars are not good for her at the moment. There's change, big change, coming, but we haven't really found out everything yet. I'm sure when we all get together again soon she'll spill the beans. You know Assia. When it's about her, she'll want our full attention. Now let's get back to that man of yours!'

The rest of the afternoon went off wonderfully. Assia brightened up, Deena waffled on more about how Mandy and Jake were so compatible, and George was just as saucy and naughty as ever.

On the way home, Jake cuddled Mandy in the back of the cab.

'I thought that all went rather well, don't you?'

Mandy pondered. 'Assia was quiet and not herself. Deena mentioned in the toilets that something was wrong, but other than that, yes, I thought it went brilliantly, and everyone will end up loving you as much as I do.'

The taxi arrived at Queensgate and Mandy knew she would be leaving Jake as he had to get home to Helen and the boys for Sunday dinner. Jake kissed Mandy passionately and held on tighter than usual. Mandy knew he didn't want to leave, but circumstances gave them both no choice.

'I'll call you, sweetheart.'

At that Mandy was out of the taxi and down the steps to her own front door. She didn't mind Jake going, though of course she had wanted him to stay. Yet she was realistic and knew he had to go. She had some clearing up to do, some well overdue paperwork to sort out for work the next day. So she pushed herself into organizing the things that had been abandoned for some time. Soon the flat was sparkling and the paperwork filed and ready for the office, and after a long soak in the bath Mandy went to bed, tired and worn out. It was good to get an early night.

Helen pulled the envelope out of her handbag for the seventh time and looked at the torn pieces of a photo of Jake and a mystery brunette. She laid them out on the lime-stone kitchen counter to piece them together. He was laughing and looked so happy. She felt overwhelmed with anger and humiliation. There had been no note with the photograph, nor any clear postage markings. She had no idea who had sent this information, but she was thankful. She would not give up her life because of some passing fancy. Nothing truly unsettled Helen too much, and nor would this. That was her decision as she tried to catch her breath. She was a strong woman, a bright, sexy, formidable woman, and she would do anything it took to get life as she knew it back on track. As she heard the front door open she quickly swept the tiny pieces of the photograph back into her bag, flicked her hair and licked her lips.

Jake would be hers again and that was final.

THIRTEEN

Summer Loving

The summer days went by, interspersed with the arrival of flowers and perfume, little pressies and cards. Each time, Mandy was surprised at how diverse and clever Jake could be.

It had been on her mind that now he had met her friends, it was time to prepare him for her family. This was something that unnerved her because of the situation with Olivia, but on a rare day alone Mandy made the trip down to see her mum and sister.

Olivia's girls were playing happily in their paddling pool, looking like two little Smurfs, smothered in thick white high-protection sun cream. Olivia was in the kitchen making a lovely fresh chicken Caesar salad and pouring sparkling rosé into crystal glasses. Lunch was perfect and everyone seemed light and happy, the weather coaxing them all outside into the warm sunshine. Sitting there relaxing, Mandy knew this was her opportunity to pose the question of them finally meeting Jake.

Mandy took a deep breath and said, rather coolly, 'Guys, I've thought about something and I've come to the conclusion that it's time for you to meet Jake. I know this may be bad timing, but I'm desperate for you to meet him, and to see that I'm happy and content with the situation. Love him or loathe him, it won't change anything, but if I'm honest, I want to be open with those I love, and I need you to meet him.'

Mandy held her breath, looked at her mum and Olivia and, for what seemed like an age, waited with her heart in her mouth for their response. Valerie piped up first.

'Darling, we've seen him already, so we know what to expect looks-wise. He's drop-dead gorgeous, and besides, if the difference in you has been brought about by him, then I can't see any harm in meeting him properly.'

'He's in your life permanently now, isn't he?' Olivia said. 'Of course we'd all like to meet him. How about here, a small informal dinner and a chance for him to meet the girls and for us to get to know him better?'

Mandy was elated but tried to play it down; she felt it only fair, considering all the heartache her sister had been through. At last Jake was not just becoming a part of her, but a part of her world too.

After a few more drinks and some hearty laughter, Mandy bathed the girls, tucked them into bed and made her preparations to leave.

Olivia walked her to the car. 'Don't worry, Mandy, I'm OK about all of this. I can cope; there are no real similarities with you and Jake, and me and Robbie. We all have our own lives, and even though Jake's married, he loves you and causes you no pain, so I'm more than happy to welcome him into my home and to meet my children. Let's make it soon, eh?'

Mandy hugged Olivia, content, and felt closer to her than ever before. She set off in Figgy.

On the drive home her phone went. She instinctively knew it would be Jake, so pulled over and answered the call.

'Hi, baby, where are you?'

'Hi, Jake, just on my way back from the family. Should be home in ten.'

'Great, honey, I'll meet you at yours. Got a little surprise for you.'

She knew that despite her pleas he would tell her nothing, so she finished the call, got straight back on the road and made it home well in time.

Jake had let himself into her flat, and as Mandy entered the room was full of flowers. Champagne was on ice, and he looked smug and happy.

'How about a lovely weekend in a classy hotel where they do painting, pottery and, for the *non*-artistic, general spa treatments?' Mandy nodded excitedly. Jake continued, 'I'd love a go at the painting, and if you want you can take in the mineral waters, enjoy a lovely massage, and then we can make love all night!'

Mandy jumped on to his lap.

'That's a fantastic idea, I'd simply love to. But, for your information, I got three gold stars for my paintings in secondary school, so be prepared for me to whip your arse!'

Jake laughed. 'Don't tempt me, OK? It's all booked for this weekend, and personally I can't wait. How was the family?'

Mandy thought for a moment. 'They were great, and – they would love you to come to dinner, sometime soon. I'd love it, Jake, please say yes.'

'For you, anything. Let's sort it out for sometime next week. Helen is off to a summer camp thing with the boys. I've never gone, so it won't be a problem.'

Mandy faltered slightly. Helen and the boys hadn't been mentioned for some time, and it struck Mandy that while Jake would meet all those in her life close to her and dear to her, there was a part of his life that she would never really know.

'Hey, baby, what's wrong?'

'Nothing, just silly mad thoughts, that's all. Do you truly love me, Jake?'

'More than anything, you know that,' he responded, staring at her. 'Tell me, what silly mad thoughts?'

'I know it seems so crazy, and I am so happy, but the mention of Helen and the boys just makes me think about your other family. Something I'm not part of.' Mandy looked at the floor.

Jake took a deep breath. 'It's funny, but I was never one of those men who had high romantic expectations. When I met Helen, we seemed to tick every box, it was almost as if it was a given that we would be married. Most of the family didn't seem against it, all except one! The only one against the whole idea, who couldn't bear the thought of losing his little girl, was her father. Maybe it had something to do with the fact that Helen was an only child. Over-loved, over-spoiled and basically given everything she could ever want. Maybe it was his way of compensating for the lack of love in his own childhood. His own mother died in childbirth and Helen believes it really affected him. I also felt he would have preferred someone from a better family. Anyway, he had built an empire in the world of advertising as well as many other ventures, and what an empire he created. He was already a wealthy, powerful man, with virtually everyone in his pocket – no one crossed Alastair Brightman – but times were changing. He knew that, and so did I. A fresh finger on the pulse was needed, and that's where I came into play.'

Mandy poured another glass of champagne, and urged Jake to speak on. She needed this talk, to get a picture of Jake's other life. Jake sipped his champagne and looked at Mandy, clearly wanting her to understand.

'The wedding went ahead. I loved and still love Helen,

in my own way, but you must understand, Mandy, that it is so different from what I have with you. Helen was there from the beginning and persuaded her father to invest in me. With Helen behind me things went well and eventually I proved to her father that I was worthy of my partner status, and the business expanded. With Helen as my support, my friend and my rock, I made it to where I am today. Without her, I'm not sure that would have happened. After the thrill of proving to all that I, with Helen behind me, could surpass both our dreams, I realized our passion was for the thrill of the chase, not necessarily each other. The boys came along fairly quickly and with Helen and his two grandsons Alastair felt he always had to cut me down. But I stood my ground: I know my work inside-out and there is little he can find fault in now.'

Mandy was listening intently. 'Where does all this leave you now, Jake, and how do I fit in? You clearly love Helen and your boys, but where am *I* in all of this?'

Jake drank down the glass of champagne, then refilled his glass.

'You, my darling, my beautiful, sweet girl, have opened up a whole new world for me. I never believed that a man could love two women, but I have to accept it does happen. I'm finding it harder and harder to be away from you, but the respect I have for Helen and my love for the boys keep me grounded. Why a man would want all this heartache and confusion out of choice, I truly don't know. Helen and

I have no real passion, no urges, no lust, and no desperate want for each other. Sometimes I feel like I am a great father to my kids and more a sibling to my wife. We are a great team, but are more like brother and sister – we seem to drift through time, not wanting or asking any more of each other. There's a history with Helen, but I now feel that I could have a new history, with you.'

Jake looked down sadly. 'I hate this situation, Mandy. I want you to know that. It's not like I'm having a *ménage à trois*, for Christ's sake, but this situation brought me you, and that's something I would never wish away.'

Mandy walked slowly over to him, sat on his lap and wrapped her arms around him. She knew in her heart then that she would stay the mistress, and that there could be no expectations on her part, just a deep meaningful love that grew stronger every day. No one else would understand it, they would probably cheapen and demean it, but she could never give Jake up, and she knew Jake couldn't go on without her either.

The weekend away was blissful, and as usual Jake was loved tenderly by Mandy; he felt complete in her arms. Their love-making was instinctive and unselfconscious. Everything was spontaneous and wonderful: it was an area of their lives that needed no change; they worked perfectly and in unison.

The painting class was hysterical, and in their group they

were possibly the worst painters ever seen by their tutor. They didn't care, though: it was fun and they loved every second of trying to be creative, and making each other laugh.

They indulged themselves in absolute luxury, having massages, spa treatments and reflexology. Mandy was amazed that Jake loved it. She was discovering more and more about his likes and dislikes.

As usual the weekend whizzed past and soon it was time to leave. On the drive back to London they laughed and joked about their adventure, and Jake took the opportunity to test Mandy on her new-found knowledge. He'd spent the evening before telling her about different wines.

'I'm amazed by you,' Jake said. 'You absorb everything like a sponge. I love you so much.'

'Ditto,' replied Mandy, smiling.

It now seemed an ideal time to bring up the dinner invitation from Olivia again. Mandy wanted it to happen soon. She was so proud of her man, so loved and protected, and she was eager to show him off. She had accepted the situation with Helen and now she knew more history, something inside her had settled down. When Helen's name was mentioned she didn't feel the same crazy waves of near-hysteria, but felt content that she was someone significant in Jake's life. Nothing, not Helen or anyone else, could stop him loving Mandy as he did.

By the time they arrived at Queensgate, Mandy knew

the routine. Jake would return to his family and she would busy herself with all the catching up she needed to do. They had fixed a date for the following Sunday to have dinner with Olivia and the rest of the family. Jake appeared to take it all in his stride, and as soon as she got in she called Olivia to confirm.

Olivia was excited and eager to get arrangements sorted out. She wanted to make it special for Mandy and Jake.

Mandy put down the phone and pondered for a while. Olivia sounded great, but there was something slightly amiss. She couldn't put her finger on it, but she sensed it.

The week went by quickly. Mandy was full on at work and despite Maggie still being a pain and Andrew still salivating over her, all was well. Mandy was creative, even shocking Michael with some great innovative ideas and suggestions. Things couldn't be better.

As they arrived at Olivia's house in Esher, Jake held two bouquets of flowers and some champagne. Mandy smiled to herself: he certainly knew the game – Mum and Olivia would be thrilled. He had even thought of the two girls; Milly had a fairy costume with gossamer wings, and for Robyn there was a case full of children's make-up. Despite having two boys, he was spot-on with the girls' presents; Mandy knew they would love them. As they were greeted at the door, the girls were screaming for Aunty Mandy, but they drew back slightly as they saw Jake. Mandy put it down to initial nerves: they were not used to male visitors these days, as their father seemed to stay for less and less time on every visit. Trips out had been cancelled and visits to the house were few and far between. He had started to let the girls down, and Mandy thought that this was possibly the reason she had sensed a tension in Olivia's voice on the phone last week.

Once inside, and with the flowers and champagne presented, Olivia took over. 'It's so lovely to meet you properly at last, Jake. Please sit down and make yourself comfy. Dinner will be in half an hour.'

Mandy whispered in Jake's ear. 'You OK, babe?'

'Of course I am! It's hardly the Alamo. Everything will be fine, just relax.'

Soon the whole family were seated on sofas and comfy chairs, drinking champagne, nibbling at crudités and chatting. Mandy couldn't believe how well things were going. There were no awkward pauses or uncomfortable silences, and eventually Robyn and Milly both came out from behind the sofa and sat next to their granny.

'Well, girls, now that I can finally see how beautiful you both are, I was hoping you would let me give you a present?'

The two girls smiled broadly. 'We love presents, Jake!' they squeaked excitedly.

At this point all the adults looked at each other and burst out laughing.

Milly ripped open her package, quickly dressed, and

looked so pretty as she twirled around in her fairy outfit. Robyn sat close to Mandy, inspecting her case, asking her what all the make-up was and how you used it.

It wasn't long before the children were moving closer to Jake and asking him questions about anything and everything. Jake laughed at their random questions and answered them as best he could.

Dinner was superb. Olivia had set the table beautifully, the food and wine were excellent and everyone was full to the brim by the time they had finished.

'Good grief, Olivia, that was amazing,' said Mandy as she placed her arm around her sister's shoulders. They were moving over to the main sitting-room area. 'Marco Pierre White, eat your heart out!'

'I have to say I've been looking forward to this day all week. You know me, I love to be the hostess with the mostest!' replied Olivia. 'And the best is yet to come; Mum's got the photo albums out.'

Mandy looked heavenwards. 'Oh no!' she groaned.

Olivia and the children had taken to Jake like ducks to water. When Mandy told them it was bathtime, their faces dropped in disappointment.

'When you're all clean and in your nightclothes you can come back down for five minutes,' said Mandy firmly.

Mandy loved to bathe the children and get them ready for bed. It was something she hoped would happen for her one day, but that seemed unlikely. However, she was content at the moment to share her nieces with her mum and sister.

Downstairs, Valerie had relaxed, and in spite of her reservations about Jake she couldn't help but warm to him when he showed so much delight in the photos of her two girls and their childhood. One particular photo attracted his attention, and he made a mental note to speak to Olivia about it.

Mandy came down the stairs with Robyn and Milly. They wanted desperately to say goodnight to their new friend Jake. Spontaneously they jumped on his lap, kissed him hard on the cheek and thanked him for their wonderful presents.

Olivia looked tired, and Mandy knew it was time to leave.

'You will visit us again, won't you, Jake?' pressed Olivia, almost purring. 'We'd love to spend some more time with you.'

'I'd love that too,' replied Jake honestly.

Valerie accepted his goodbye kiss on the cheek, and as Jake gathered their coats and made his way to the car she took the opportunity to hold Mandy back for a few moments. She looked uncomfortable.

'He's a lovely chap, Mandy, and he obviously loves you very much, but sometimes these things don't work out.'

'Mum, for God's sake, why do you have to spoil the evening by making that remark?'

Valerie paused slightly and pulled Mandy closer to her,

lowering her voice. 'Because I know. I've not always been old and sensible, and sometime long ago in the past I was wild and threw caution to the wind. I had an affair, Mandy, and when I finally came to my senses and all the lust and laughter had gone out of the fling, I begged your dad to take me back, and thank God he did. Sometimes you only want what you can't have, simply because you can't have it.' Valerie played with her necklace nervously.

Mandy was stunned, even though she knew her own hypocrisy and that she didn't really have a leg to stand on.

Valerie continued. 'I don't want to harp on about it now. I just want you to know that sooner or later the spark dies out. I was lucky: even though I'd been foolish, I loved your father. It was when he took me back that I realized how much I was loved by him. When your dad died, I wished I'd spent more time with him in reality than with someone else in my head. I wish I'd never cheated on him, and I thank God that something made me see sense, because he was the love of my life. He was also sure, dependable, my best friend. But as you grow older you finally know the true meaning of love.' Valerie crossed her arms. 'Just always remember he belongs to someone else, Mandy.'

Mandy was truly surprised: she had never known any of this. But the sound of the horn from Jake's car meant they had to leave, though she wanted to know so much more.

'Bye, Mum. Look after Olivia, she seems a little hyper-active – is she coping OK?'

'She seems to be. And don't worry, I'll keep my eye on her. But think about what I've told you, hey?'

Mandy kissed her mum and made for the car. Despite the honesty from her mother, she put the revelations out of her head. She was with her man; he was never going to leave; and she would never give him up. Of that she was sure!

The next week flew past. Mandy had a big job on that took up all her time and thought. She had put her conversation with her mum completely out of her mind. Right now, work was vital and she needed to get this new party event organized. With her new concepts and enthusiasm over catering and wine, Michael was over the moon.

Finally the party came round, and it was a resounding success. Mandy moved up even higher in Michael's esti-mation. Relieved it had all gone so well, she looked forward to a weekend with Jake. Her calls to him had suffered a little due to her heavy work schedule, but the texts kept her sane in the time she had to spend without him.

When he arrived on the Saturday evening, he looked gorgeous and smelled warm, familiar and sexy. She had missed him so much. He was eager to take her in his arms and love her.

Eventually breaking away from her slightly, he pulled

out a large package from his briefcase. 'This is for you, my darling.'

Mandy looked at the package, perplexed. It was covered in bubble wrap and tied with a huge red bow.

'Well, open it!' urged Jake.

Mandy pulled the bow apart and ripped the bubble wrap off. She looked at her gift and tears welled up in her eyes.

'How did you do this? Where did you find it? Oh, darling, it's the best present I've ever had.'

'Well, between Olivia and me, we managed it.'

'Olivia!' muttered Mandy. 'She knew about this?'

'Couldn't have done it without her!'

The silver Tiffany frame was gorgeous, and as she gazed at the photograph within it she couldn't believe it. There was her dad, a young Dad with a full head of hair, in faded blue denim flares and a stripy shirt. Perched on his shoulders was a dark-haired child, a beauty even then. With her hands placed on his shoulders and a face full of laughter, there sat Mandy, a young girl of six or seven. The picture was faded but it had been enlarged, and all the marks and scratches that were still there made it extra special.

Mandy burst into tears of happiness.

'I love you, Jake Chaplin.'

FOURTEEN

The Apartment

MAND, IT'S ME, I HAVE SOMETHING I WANT TO SHOW
YOU. ARE YOU FREE FOR LUNCH AT SCOTT'S, AROUND
2.30, LET ME KNOW, LOVE YOU BYE

Mandy loved a bit of a mystery. She texted him straight
back.

LUCKY YOU, I'M FREE! SEE YOU AT 2.30, I LOVE YOU X.

She closed her phone and put it in her bag. She was
wearing a pretty white, loose A-line vest dress with silver
studs all over it, and silver ballet pumps. Her hair was
extra-wavy due to the humid heat and her oversized
brown Christian Dior sunglasses gave her a Jean Shrimpton
edge.

She jumped in a black taxi: 'Mayfair, please.' She
rummaged through her soft snakeskin bag, which she
adored. Assia had brought it back for her from a trip to
Morocco. She had found the bags for a bargain price, but

would always call to check that the other girls wouldn't be using the same bag on their nights out together.

It had taken time, but the gang were together again, with no more atmospheres and secrets. They had sat in the Bluebird café the night before for a good girlie chat.

Assia had become more open and warm, a nicer person. 'I've decided to leave Marius. The divorce is about to be signed, and I'm only taking half of everything.'

'What do you mean,' gasped Deena, 'only half? On what grounds did you divorce him?'

'Sexual neglect,' said Assia pouting, as sadly as she could.

'I don't think that's the right legal term,' smiled Mandy.

Deena looked outraged. Some things never changed and Mandy loved it.

'The poor man hardly *ever* got to sleep with you, and when you finally did, you know . . .' Deena was flustered.

'Let him 'ave it,' said Assia, looking bored.

'Well, yes,' said Deena as diplomatically as she could. 'You had to think of Federer's whites just to see you through.'

'Nadal,' said Assia flatly.

'What?'

'Nadal, he's my new favourite. But actually I'd like them both.'

Deena was speechless. She finally mustered, 'You greedy cow!'

Mandy chuckled. 'Deena, you should know by now what Assia is like. What you see is what you get! She's tough and wants a nice life; she wants money and an amazing property CV. She wants it all,' Mandy emphasized.

'But it's not rightfully hers. She's no better than a thief really, is she?'

Assia raised an arched brow.

'Let's be honest.' Deena looked at Assia sincerely. 'You don't even have children with the poor man.'

'The *rich* man,' retorted Assia in the blink of an eye. 'The man is very, very rich, very powerful and so depressed – *bor*ing. You see, he wants to be twenty and isn't. And he is no saint, you know. He keeps trying it on with these nineteen-year-old girls, and I see him do it, right in front of me! Chatting them up with his old-man hands clutching on to his funky cocktail, and he wonders why they don't want him! I feel like saying, "Move on, old man, there are twenty guys behind you, you know. They too are rich and miserable, but thirty years younger!"'

'If you don't mind me asking, if he's so sad and so miserable, why didn't you go for a younger millionaire, Assia?' Deena smiled sweetly.

Assia held her breath. 'OK, I know you girls want me to be more honest, yes?'

'Yes.'

'Well, I didn't want to have to work too hard. Marius made my dreams of a luxurious life so easy for me. And as *I* wasn't nineteen any more, it made me feel good.' Assia looked at both girls seriously. 'I don't have a talent for anything, dharrlings. Sure, I would like to be the queen of my own castle through work and talent alone, but I have no talent. Seriously, I don't!' Assia started to laugh at herself. She knew she was definitely a tad eccentric, if nothing else.

'Actually, I lie,' she said, holding her hand up, trying to make herself look stern. 'I have a talent at charming old men. And Marius is bloody hard work in the bedroom. So I guess I *do* work hard and deserve it all!'

Mandy covered her mouth, trying not to laugh. Even Deena cracked a smile. Eccentric or not, Assia's laugh was contagious. She could be rude, spoiled, immoral, but she was wickedly funny. She had the guts to be frank. The great thing about Assia was that she lived life with her own rules.

As the taxi made its way along Park Lane, Mandy wondered just how much Jake would lose if he left Helen. Divorce. That was something that she hadn't let into her head for a second, until now. It felt scary, and her chest tightened. Grabbing her BlackBerry out of her bag, she rechecked the address for Scott's. 'Mount Street, please.'

Within a few minutes she jumped out of the cab close to Scott's, wrapped her grey silk pashmina over her shoulders and made her way into the restaurant bar to meet her beautiful man. There he was. Every time she spotted him it was as if for the first time: her heart turned over. She never ever tired of seeing the way he would lean or stand. He had such fabulous legs, she wanted to feel his tight arse, and she could tell from the way he was standing that he was in a flirty mood. She was feeling exceptionally turned on. She loved it when he would act as if they had just met. He would ask questions he already knew the answers to, and occasionally, when he least expected it, she would shock him with something completely new, raw and naughty. She knew he loved it; it was part of their foreplay. If only men got that about women! Foreplay starts in the mind, from step one: the calls, the emails, the things a man says, right up to doing the deed. Sincere romance and the unashamed show of true desire is always a turn-on for a woman.

'You look gorgeous,' Jake murmured.

'Thank you. So do you,' she responded, pouting.

'That dress is so sexy, so naughty.'

'I know.'

Jake tried not to smile too much. 'I love it when you're arrogant.'

'I know.' Mandy leaned in to Jake's ear. 'And I love it when you push me against a wall and fuck me.'

The barman came over. 'And what would you guys like to drink?'

Jake tried to stay serious.

'A glass of dry white for me.' He glanced at Mandy. 'And what do you want, trouble?'

Mandy smiled cheekily. 'A slow comfortable screw for me.'

The barman tried to stifle a laugh. 'Ah yes, I know it well.' He left promptly to get their drinks.

Jake and Mandy burst into a fit of giggles.

'I wish I could take you somewhere and rip that dress off.'

'But what about lunch?'

'Fuck lunch.'

Mandy's heart leaped; she loved Jake when he was forceful about wanting her. She smiled sweetly. 'So what's this special thing you wanted to talk to me about?'

'Be patient, and you'll see.' Jake smiled. His green eyes sparkled with adoration. 'How lucky am I?' he said.

'How lucky am *I*?' she repeated.

It was enough to make any bystander feel queasy, but the two of them didn't give a hoot.

At that moment a young man with long floppy hair came in. His navy suit, pink shirt and patterned tie looked like they were three sizes too big for him.

'Sorry for the delay, Mr Chaplin.' The poor boy was clearly out of breath. 'Here are the keys. Any questions or problems, please don't hesitate to call me.'

He was extremely posh. 'Dad sends his love.'

Jake looked at him as if to try and shut him up.

'OK, right, better be off! Take care!'

And with that the floppy-haired youngster vanished.

Jake looked frustrated. 'I told him to bloody leave them at reception.'

'What are the keys for?' Mandy was curious.

Jake smiled, put the keys to one side and grabbed her hands.

'I wasn't sure what you'd make of it, but – well, I've bought you an apartment.'

Mandy was speechless. A million emotions filled her head.

'Now, before you start some rant about being independent, I'm not trying to buy you, or take over, or anything like that. But I noticed you getting a bit frustrated with my stuff mounting up at your place, and the owners were desperate to sell, so I got it at a great price. I thought, Sod it, why not? It's big enough for the both of us, and if or when you decide to sell, it's in your name and it's yours. From me.' Jake looked at Mandy nervously.

She felt overwhelmed, excited, yet cautious. She wasn't used to this kind of gift. Who was?

'You didn't have to do this,' she muttered.

'I know.'

'We were fine as we were.'

'I know,' Jake nodded. 'But Queensgate will always be yours, no matter what. This flat is in Mayfair, somewhere we can meet in the middle; and it can give us an idea of what *us* is like.'

'Why don't *you* want to own it?'

'I don't need it.'

Mandy's pride kicked in. 'Neither do I then, thanks.'

'I know. I just thought it would be lovely for us, that's all.'

'You feel guilty, don't you?' Mandy said firmly. 'Is that what all this is about?'

Jake looked wounded. 'I always feel fucking guilty, and not just about you, Mandy, but about Helen and my boys too. It's become a bloody way of life.'

Mandy looked at his striking, tanned face. He looked back at her, his green eyes sizzling.

'Is this really about the flat, or is it about something else altogether?'

Mandy faltered. She was confused, and didn't know why she felt like this.

'There's so much I can't give you, Mandy, and I'm having more and more times when I'm feeling bad about that, especially when I think of the future. I can't see a way out.'

That remark struck Mandy hard, sending a shiver down her spine. Jake rubbed his brow; this wasn't panning out the way he had planned. Mandy started to feel a tad angry.

'I see. So this way, if you buy me a fancy flat, it will make you feel better about the fact that you can't see us having a future together, and that ultimately one day I will be paid off and dumped, guilt-free. Is that it?'

'No!' Jake lowered his voice. 'For God's sake, if you want to think like that, I could have felt guilt-free about the diamonds, the holidays, the dresses. For Christ's sake, Mandy,

I didn't *have* to buy you a flat in Mayfair, I just wanted to go to the next level. You deserve it, we deserve it, and I want to be with you in a place where there is room for us both.' He sighed, exasperated.

Mandy felt terrible. He was being completely honest, but she still felt used.

He shook his head, confused. 'All I'm saying is that I could have got what I wanted for a lot less, couldn't I?'

He was pissed off. Jake knew as his words hit the air that they were so wrong.

Mandy felt cheap. For the first time ever, he made her feel like she had been paid to provide a service.

'Fuck you!'

She grabbed her pashmina and bag, and marched out of the restaurant.

Jake chucked some cash on the bar, leaving the two drinks untouched, and ran after her.

'Mandy, stop!'

She ignored him.

'Mandy, come on. You know I didn't mean it like that.'

'Piss off!' she shouted back at him, hurrying forwards.

The doorman of Scott's was watching now, entertained by all the drama. He saw the good-looking man run after the beautiful girl in the flimsy dress, and watched as he kissed her passionately. They looked in love right enough. 'Those were the days,' he mumbled. 'Those were the days.'

Jake took a still pissed-off Mandy to the new flat. As he

guided her through the lobby and into the old-fashioned lift, he pressed the button for the first floor. He opened the front door of the flat closest to the elevator and led Mandy into it. It was beautiful, simple, clean and elegant. There were lots of ornate wood panelling, high ceilings, French windows. In the bedroom a great big sleigh bed stood in one corner, looking so inviting with its fresh white cotton pillows and cushions. There was a white marble bathroom, plenty of storage and heated flooring throughout. Naturally it needed a woman's touch, but the pieces Jake had placed in the flat were, without question, exquisite.

'Do you like it?' Jake looked about ten years old, waiting for Mandy's approval.

Mandy nodded silently.

'Really? I'm sorry, you know I would never hurt you on purpose.'

Mandy smiled sadly. 'I love it, Jake, and I love you too. I'm grateful, I really am.'

'So what's wrong?'

'It's true what you said earlier, about thinking too far ahead. It's difficult and upsetting. Someone is going to be hurt. I mean, can all of this really go on for ever? How can I enjoy this moment without the hope that we could have a real future in this place? Not the odd night, or a weekend, but a proper grown-up relationship. Be honest with me, Jake: did part of you pick here because it's nowhere near your family, but still close enough for your balancing act?'

'Yes.'

'Did you choose *not* to introduce me to that young guy with the keys because he knows your wife or family?'

'Look, that was tricky because—'

Mandy cut him short. 'Tricky or not, right or wrong, you have to be honest with me. I love you, I love this flat, but I can't let myself love you any more than I do now until there's more of a future for us. We've moved on in our relationship to a place where we *need* to know our future. I can't change that, and neither can you.'

Jake looked at Mandy and sighed heavily. His heart was breaking. 'I know what you mean, and none of this is easy. I guess I just wanted to enhance what we *do* have and shut the rest out.'

He looked at her sad face. God, she was beautiful. Her vulnerability made her even more so now. He walked over and slipped her bag off her shoulder, bending to kiss her bare flesh tenderly. He gently unwrapped her pashmina and placed it on her bag. Then he took her hand and silently led her across the room. They entered the bedroom and he walked her over to sit on the bed. He turned Mandy to face him.

Silently, as he gazed at her, he removed his jacket and undid three buttons of his shirt. Then he knelt down on the soft cream carpet, at eye level with Mandy perched on the bed.

Mandy's whole body tingled with expectation.

Raising her little dress to above her waist, he gently tugged down her white lacy knickers and pulled her tanned, toned body towards his face.

He kissed, licked, stroked and sucked her. God, he was good with her, and he knew it. Mandy grabbed his head and rubbed herself up against his warm lips and expert tongue until her whole body shuddered with immense pleasure. She came over and over again.

She felt weak, happy and helpless, her anger ebbing away.

Falling back on the bed, she sighed, raising her arms above her head. This was heaven; a great orgasm was so underrated. Either that or so easily forgotten. If everyone in the world could feel the release and happiness Mandy felt at that moment, anti-depressant sales would plummet.

Jake climbed up on to the bed; he put his hand on her stomach. 'Was that nice?' he smiled.

'Nice? Nice is too modest a word,' she grinned. 'It was out of this world.'

Jake smiled, pleased.

'One of the best actually.' She was still tingling all over.

Jake kissed her and she could smell herself on his lips. No one had ever made her feel the way he made her feel. The whole time she was with him, she always wanted more, and she knew Jake felt the same.

'Sometimes, when I'm lying next to you and holding you, I still want more,' he whispered, and then kissed her again.

'Funny,' Mandy smiled, 'I was just thinking that same thing.'

Jake cupped Mandy's little heart-shaped face with his hand. 'Sometimes I wish I could just jump right inside you and be with you for every single breath, do you know what I mean?'

Mandy smiled and her heart flipped. 'That's one of the loveliest things you've ever said to me,' she said as she snuggled up to him.

'We can do this. We can get through it, I know it.' Jake kissed her head. 'I love you.'

On that hot afternoon, they fell asleep entwined with each other.

Bleep bleep bleep!

The sound of a phone buzzing woke them and Jake popped open an eye. 'What the hell is that noise?'

Mandy jumped off the bed and went to run to her bag to get the phone, but with her knickers still around her ankles ended up waddling like a penguin and falling head-first through the bedroom doorway.

She jumped bolt upright. God, that hurt! Pulling her panties up, she got to the phone just in time. Breathlessly she answered, 'Hello?'

At first Mandy thought there was something wrong with the phone. All she could hear was a screeching noise. Finally she could make out her mum's voice.

'Mum, calm down! What is it?'

'I need you to come to the hospital, and fast,' she shouted hysterically. 'It's Olivia . . .' Valerie sounded like she had something stuck in her throat. 'Olivia has taken pills!'

'Where is she?' Mandy responded, shocked.

'Chelsea and Westminster.'

'I'm on my way.'

It was four-thirty in the afternoon. Both she and Jake had been asleep for an hour or so, but now Mandy was alert, panic-stricken. She grabbed her dress, shaking, her heart racing.

'What's wrong?' asked a sleepy Jake, rubbing his eyes.

'Olivia, she took pills . . . She's in hospital.' Mandy was trembling and couldn't breathe.

'Steady, Mandy, let me get you some water,' Jake said, jumping to action.

'No, I don't have time.'

'Do you want me to drop you somewhere?'

'Yes please, the Chelsea and Westminster Hospital.' Slowly she could feel that her body was present but her head was still somewhere else.

Jake grabbed his jacket and keys and wrapped his arms around her.

'Come on, let's get you to her ASAP.'

They jumped into a taxi that took them to the Fulham Road, and Jake watched her go.

'I'll call you later,' said Mandy over her shoulder, rushing away.

'I'm out tonight, babe, at a big work do at a theatre, and then on to dinner.' God, suddenly that sounded so shallow, so unnecessary and superficial, Jake thought.

Mandy nodded and headed through the large double doors of the hospital.

'I love you,' Jake shouted, but she had disappeared.

Mandy's mum was there to meet her. She looked pale with shock. There had been far too much heartache recently.

Mandy found a sudden strength. 'Come on, Mum, take me to her.'

Mandy walked into the hospital room and saw Olivia in the bed, tubes leading out of her arms. She looked so tiny on the big bed. She was sleeping but still wore full make-up, now smudged, and fake lashes.

'She's exhausted,' Valerie said, looking crumpled. 'The doctors have pumped her stomach and are feeding her with saline and glucose. She woke up crying, but not for long. She's very dopey and could only say a few words.'

Mandy sat on a plastic chair next to Olivia's bed. She held her sister's limp, almost lifeless hand in hers. She wanted to cry, but didn't. It was important that she held it together.

'What the hell happened, Mum? She seemed to be doing so well.'

Valerie paused.

'Robbie wanted to introduce the girls to his new girl-friend. He rang yesterday.'

'The redhead? From the car?' replied Mandy.

'Yes. Robbie and Olivia arranged to meet at Blake's Hotel to talk things through. To be honest, Mandy, it sounds as if he's been mucking her about a bit, hinting he wants to come back one minute and disappearing the next. Olivia has met no one, she's just struggling to sort herself out and, of course, Robbie's only been with the redhead for seven or eight months. As far as we know, that is. Anyway, he never arrived at the hotel, and it's the third time he's done that, stood her up.'

'So that's why she's wearing all that make-up,' Mandy sighed sadly, understanding suddenly. She wanted to look beautiful for him.

Valerie looked puzzled. Mandy left it, it wasn't impor-tant.

'Thank God one of the hotel maids found her. I didn't want to tell you, Mand, but the local GP put her on anti-depressants about a year ago. He changed them recently for stronger ones when he saw how bad she was. She took them all, the whole bottle. The receptionist from Blake's rang me: I'm in Olivia's diary as an emergency contact. That's why she's here.' Valerie looked bitter. 'Anyway, Robbie had phoned her at the hotel and told her it was serious. He and this woman wanted to be engaged!'

'What? What the hell is he thinking of?' Mandy was

stunned. 'Robbie must be having some kind of mid-life crisis, that's for sure. Does this redhead have a name?'

'Sarah.' Valerie shook her head. 'It's very easy to blame the other woman, Mandy, but she isn't the one who owes Olivia and the children loyalty and commitment. Robbie does. He took an oath, didn't he? He legally agreed to love her until death parted them. This woman, well, she owes us nothing!'

'How did Olivia seem to you before? Did she give you any sign of what she was feeling? Was she angry, especially depressed – anything?'

'No, of course not. She made out that she was pleased to be finding herself. You've seen her – she's started yoga, running, even talked about studying interior design.'

Mandy smiled. 'She certainly goes for it, doesn't she?' she said, squeezing Olivia's hand.

Olivia stirred and then her eyes fluttered open.

'Mandy?'

Her voice was frail and trembling, but she smiled weakly at her sister.

'Hello, my darling.' Mandy saw such pain in Olivia's eyes. 'How are you feeling, my gorgeous?'

'I don't really know. I feel so stupid being here.' Olivia's eyes welled up and she began to cry.

Mandy gently stroked the tears from her face. 'Come on now, enough tears, you've had enough sadness,' she said, caressing her sister's soft skin. She was desperately trying to think of something to make her happy. 'We'll have you home soon and feeling fine, I promise!'

'I find it all too hard, Mand.' Olivia started to sob.

Mandy felt so upset for her sister but she held her composure – she was certain it wouldn't do Olivia any good to see her weak.

'We all find life hard, darling. It can be tricky, no doubt about it, but we can't just give in to it. I know you're stronger than that.'

'I just don't *feel* like I have the energy to fight any more.'

'You don't have to, Olive.'

'What do you mean?'

'You don't have to fight any more. Just let it be: you need to let everything go. Me and Mum are here, so you're not alone.'

'I want to be with my daddy!'

Mandy swallowed hard. That last statement threatened to trigger a river of tears from all of them, but Mandy tried with all her might to hold hers back.

'Dad doesn't want us with him yet. You know why? He wants us to do him proud down here, so we can be with him once we've achieved even more great things.'

'I feel useless, so useless – and ugly and weak.'

Mandy stood and leaned over to her big sister, determined to comfort her. She squeezed on to the bed and cuddled her, trying to avoid the various drips and tubes.

Olivia whimpered, calmed by the contact, and slowly her tears subsided as she slipped back into sleep.

Mandy felt too scared to leave her. She didn't know this Olivia, and as a result had no idea as to what she would try to do next. She too was searching for strength.

Valerie went to get a coffee for Mandy. 'Listen, get this down you and then get yourself home. I'll stay with her now.'

'Are you sure, Mum? You look exhausted.'

'Yes, darling, thanks. Knowing I can keep an eye on her will help me feel more relaxed. You know what I mean?'

'OK, Mum. Do you want me to check on the girls?'

'No, all done. Robbie's mum has them. They're fine, and clueless – unaware of all this, so happy as Larry. I mean it, don't worry.'

'OK.' Mandy looked at her sister. God, she felt helpless. 'Tell her I said goodnight, will you?'

Valerie smiled. 'Go and get yourself home. I'll call you.'

After Mandy left the hospital, she decided to call George. 'I need to see you.'

'Are you OK?' asked George, alert to the strain in Mandy's voice.

'No, I've been at the hospital. Olivia took some pills. She tried to overdose!'

'Oh my God! Where are you now?'

'Wandering aimlessly, and I've ended up in Covent Garden for some reason.'

'I'm in Covent Garden too, honey. Meet me in that little Moroccan bar you like. See you in ten.'

'What's the time now?'

'Six-thirty.'

'Perfect, see you shortly.'

'Bye, darling.'

'And, George? Thank you.'

'Don't be such a silly cow and get yourself here!'

Mandy wandered past the Drury Lane Theatre. It was a beautiful evening, warm, still light, with a fresh breeze. It was a real tonic after seeing Olivia.

A throng of people stood outside in the street, spilling from the bars and restaurants. Mandy loved people-watching, and her thoughts ran away with her. Where had all these people come from? She passed the queue at the Royal Opera House. Something special seemed to be going on: men were dressed in tuxedos and the women looked absolutely gorgeous in a variety of ballgowns and classy cocktail numbers.

In particular Mandy noticed a fair-haired woman wearing a beautiful flowy black chiffon cocktail dress. It was completely backless, and her back was taut and defined, her neck long and elegant, her skin pale. Her blonde hair was pinned up elegantly in a cluster of diamanté slides. She looked so elegant, so beautiful, so effortless.

The woman turned around and her diamond chandelier

earrings sparkled in the light. She smiled and walked up to a man, who had obviously rushed to make it in time. His hand touched her back, and she placed her arms around him, kissing him lightly on each cheek. Mandy thought they looked such a beautiful couple as she made her way closer to them. They parted from their public display of affection and held hands, walking to the nearby entrance. There was a large group of people and they all greeted each other, laughing and chatting amiably. Mandy crossed over the road to get a better look, somehow mesmerized. There were paparazzi bulbs flashing now, and Mandy stopped to take it all in. The man and his lovely lady turned around, and suddenly Mandy froze to the spot. She felt sick.

'Oh my God,' she gasped.

The man pulled away. His smile was unmistakable. He put his hand on the elegant woman's back to introduce her to someone. They looked like a dream couple, smiling, happy, beautiful. No doubt about it, it was Jake and Helen! It had to be her. Mandy felt overwhelmed; she couldn't catch her breath, her stomach was churning and she didn't trust her feet to keep her standing, but she couldn't stop watching. The two spoke, calmly smiling. There was no sign of Jake being unhappy with this beautiful woman.

'Oh God,' Mandy repeated, sighing. 'Oh God, oh God, oh God.' Suddenly she couldn't help it, tears poured down her cheeks. Walk away, a voice in her head whispered. Quick, run. Find somewhere, find somewhere to hide.

Mandy ran up the street sobbing. Her stomach churned still, she couldn't see through the tears, and suddenly she vomited violently, retching into the gutter. It was just bile: she had not eaten all day, she felt so weak and tired. The day had proved too much. She kept thinking about the love-making, her smell on his lips and the scent of sex on their bodies. And then Olivia, distraught and pale on her hospital bed.

She collapsed and sat on the kerb, regardless of how she looked.

People walked by, ignoring her.

Being so sick was actually a relief. She fumbled in her bag for some tissues and wiped her face. Then she heaved herself up and threw the damp tissue in a bin.

She walked in a trance to the Moroccan bar to meet George.

'Darling.' George threw his arms around her. 'What's wrong? You look like you've seen a ghost.'

Mandy was speechless.

'Darling, what is it? Are you OK?'

The room spun. All the sparkling tealights and Moroccan lamps and carpets swirled around and around her until it all became too much, and Mandy fainted.

When she came to, she felt that someone had placed a cold, wet serviette on her forehead. George and a kindly-looking waitress were watching her with concern. They had placed her gently on a low bench.

Mandy blurted out, 'I'm sorry. As well as Olivia trying to kill herself, I've just seen Jake with his wife down the road, and I'm so depressed. She is so beautiful!'

'Christ,' said George, 'no wonder you passed out!'

'And Jake met me today. Suddenly decided to give me a treat – he's bought me an apartment in Mayfair.'

'Jesus!' exclaimed George.

Sitting up slowly and perching herself on the edge of the bench, Mandy continued.

'We went there, we had some lovely sex, dozed off in each other's arms and then I got a call about Olivia. From Mum, screaming from the hospital.'

'Fuck me, Mandy! You don't do things by half, do you?' George spluttered. 'Where did you see Jake and his wife?'

'The Royal Opera House,' Mandy explained. 'She was wearing such a beautiful dress, and that's why I noticed her. Then he came up.'

George didn't know what to say. He put a hand on her knee. 'Tell me, what the hell has happened to Olivia?'

'Robbie's decided he wants to marry someone else.' Mandy shook her head, still so confused. 'She seemed to be moving on so well, getting to know herself again, and deep down I truly believed Robbie would be back.'

'So she's still in hospital?'

George looked at Mandy, really worried about her. She didn't deserve this, none of it. It was all such crap. Mandy was the most unlikely mistress, she didn't fit the stereotype of a ruthless, selfish woman out for what she could get. She was sweet and kind, good all through. George looked at Mandy's face and knew she was somewhere else. Today had been way too much. He gathered up their things and, with the help of the waitress, called a cab to take her home.

Tucking her in bed later, he worried for her. An element of him was scared for her, of what had happened that day. He knew Mandy would want to put things right, but on her terms completely. Deep down, George knew, she was never a girl who was going to settle for second best.

The doorbell rang at around twelve-thirty.

It was Jake, in a tux but with no tie.

A bleary-eyed George opened the door, rubbing his eyes. He was staying the night, watching over Mandy.

'I've tried to ring Mandy, but no luck. Look, I know about Olivia, but wanted to check and see how bad things were.'

George just stared at him, speechless.

'Is Mandy in?'

'Not really.' George sighed and leaned heavily on the door. 'She spotted you, you know, you and your wife, at the Royal Opera House. Not a good day for her. But I suppose you'd better come in. I can't stop you.'

Jake followed George into the flat.

'Tea?' George asked as he made his way into Mandy's kitchen.

'Please.'

Jake sat with his own thoughts for a couple of minutes.

'Here you go.' George handed him his tea in a white mug; he'd made it strong.

'So,' he sighed, sitting down, not wanting to beat about the bush. 'I don't want you hurting her, Jake. I mean that.'

'I don't want to. Hear me out, George, please.'

George leaned forward. 'I don't doubt that you love her a lot, Jake, and I know she loves you to death. But in the end someone is going to get hurt. And I don't want it to be her.'

Jake looked worried. 'Was she upset about seeing Helen?'

'Of course, who wouldn't be?' George said. 'She said she was beautiful.'

Jake's heart melted. 'Oh God,' he sighed, then pulled himself together. 'How is Olivia?'

'Terrible. No one's sure what she'll do next. She gave an Oscar-winning performance of someone getting their life back on track, and yet nearly managed to commit suicide.'

George paused. 'It's all so much to deal with. Jake, Mandy has way too much on her plate.'

Jake looked at George, staring him straight in the eyes. 'I love her, George. She knows all about my wife and kids. I told her right from the beginning. But if I was to leave them, it would devastate me, and them. I can't do it.'

George shook his head. 'But what you don't realize is that the time will come when those decisions *have* to be made. You can't keep putting things off, you can't pretend they're not there. Trying to put off the situation won't make it go away. And on another note, it's one thing *hearing* all about your wife, but actually seeing her – well, it puts it into perspective. Now it's completely different, much more real.'

Jake nodded. George was right. Deep down inside, Jake knew it all, all too well.

'Mandy was so upset, she was physically sick,' George added. 'She was on her way to meet me when she saw you both on the red carpet, near the entrance of the opera house.'

Jake put his head in his hands.

'What am I going to do, George?' His voice was tired and throaty.

'I don't know, mate, that's for you to decide. But just remember that Mandy loves you, and because she loves you, she might pretend to be tougher than she is. Do you not think she, too, has the right to be a mother, to have another life?'

Jake was dumbstruck.

George felt, rightly or wrongly, that he had to say it. He studied Jake.

'She would be such a great mum. Haven't you ever thought about that?'

Jake had to be honest. 'That's something I haven't even thought about yet. She's young and ambitious.'

George cut him short. 'True, but doesn't she deserve the choice?'

'Yes, she does.'

'Can you give her that option?'

'At the moment, no, but that doesn't mean I've ruled it out,' said Jake, completely torn. 'It's hard enough for me to think about these things in a normal situation, but even saying that has made me feel guilty for Helen and the boys.'

There was silence for a few moments.

'I love her, George, and I have to go on this journey and hope the right thing will unfold, for everyone's sake.'

Mandy appeared in the doorway of the bedroom. She looked pale and sleepy.

'Hello,' she said.

'Hello back.'

George looked at Jake. His love for Mandy was undeniable.

'Right, I'm off.' He smiled sweetly. 'I shall leave you two to it.'

In silence, Jake and Mandy walked to the bedroom, both too tired to speak. She was hurt and exhausted, and he knew it. They had so much to discuss, but somehow now wasn't the time. Instead, Jake enfolded Mandy in his arms, comforting her in the best way he could. He held her to him tightly, trying to find a way to say that he was sorry for everything.

As Mandy pressed herself against Jake's chest, his mobile

phone rang again and again. It was Helen, Mandy just knew it, and so did Jake. He didn't answer, but his body felt tense.

An awkward silence filled the air and neither of them could think of anything new to say to distract themselves from such an uncomfortable but familiar moment. Mandy closed her eyes tight and prayed for some kind of change.

Helen hung up, putting her head in her hands. She sighed heavily. She had to admit it, the problem wasn't going away. Simply ignoring it and focusing her attention on Jake wasn't working. For the first time she felt fearful and out of control. She couldn't deny her feelings any longer; they swirled around her like a thick, heavy blanket. Suddenly, Helen threw her phone across the room. Hitting the wall hard, it smashed and fell in pieces on the floor.

Helen took another deep breath and tried to think straight. It wasn't over yet, far from it . . .

FIFTEEN

Back at the Office

The hot September passed and the autumn leaves were beginning to fall. The days shortened and the light became more muted with the season.

Michael and Mandy walked back to the office after successfully clinching a deal in the City. Mandy had booked a Christmas party for a client, a large magazine company. They were both very pleased and excited.

'Mandy, I wanted to ask you something,' Michael said, puffing as they walked briskly to the office.

'Yes?' enquired Mandy brightly.

'How would you feel if I asked you to be a director of the firm?'

Mandy's feet stopped suddenly, her walk faltering.

'Are you joking?'

'No. You've been fantastic this year. I love working with you, but I want to do less work and take a back seat, spend more time with my darling India. You're clearly capable of doing more, and I feel I can trust you. So why not?'

241

Mandy flung her arms around Michael. 'Thank you, thank you, thank you!'

Michael tried with great effort to push her off him. He'd never seen her so excited.

'Get off me, you madwoman!'

After squeezing even harder, Mandy let go.

'Come on,' barked Michael, 'let's go back to the office and celebrate with a bottle of bubbly. But don't get me to talk about money when I'm pissed, I'll end up bankrupt.'

Mandy giggled, ecstatic with happiness. This was so unexpected, such an unforeseen development. She wasn't entirely sure of herself, but somehow she knew she deserved this break.

'Gather round, gather round,' yelled Michael now that they were back in the office building.

Michael's team gathered.

'Earlier today, after clinching yet another great deal in this rocky financial climate, I realized that Mandy Sanderson seemed to be my lucky charm. But it's not just luck. It's been her commitment to this company and a dedication to be the best at her job always. We all know our work is unusual, our schedules all over the place, we all work late, pretending we are doing it for the love of it, but this girl here paces herself and delivers account after account when it matters most. She never moans and is always ready to step up to the plate, and she loves what she does, which is why . . .'

the Mistress

Andrew and Maggie looked at each other. 'What the hell is going on?' whispered Andrew.

'Which is *why* I have asked her to be a director of the firm,' said Michael, a huge grin on his face.

Everyone cheered, including Andrew, who was whooping and clapping ecstatically.

'I don't know why you're whooping like an idiot,' said Maggie, looking outraged. 'You won't have your crush sitting next to you day after day any more. She'll be in her ivory tower,' she added spitefully.

Andrew suddenly stopped clapping, and crossed his arms.

'Get used to it, loser,' Maggie hissed, and with that made her way to the ladies' toilets to let out her own sobs of pure jealousy.

'Three cheers for Mandy!'

'Hip hip, hooray! Hip hip, hooray! Hip hip, hooray!'

Then champagne corks were popped and everyone was hugging Mandy, offering her their best wishes.

Michael took her into his office and discussed her new role within the firm and her new wage. Mandy was full to the brim with excitement.

India, graceful and charming as ever, hugged Mandy. 'I'm so thrilled for you, darling. I just know you're going to be amazing.'

*

Mandy ran to the main front door on Mount Street and let herself into the reception. Cripes, it was cold! She had left a message for Jake on his mobile: 'I know it's random and it's not been planned and is very last-minute, but I have had the most amazing day at work and I just want to celebrate. I'm at our flat and will meet you there unless I hear otherwise. Call me if you can't come. I want to celebrate with you, and only you. I love you, byeeee!'

Mandy dashed into the lift and made her way up to the flat. She let herself in and ran a hot bath. The flat was now like a home from home, full of her things and photos of her and Jake, and some special pictures of when they had had some fun-filled nights out. Her favourite picture was of her and Jake on their first anniversary at the Wolseley, at the bar where they'd met; it was such a beautiful evening.

The only sad thing was that Jake had been unable to see her on her actual birthday that year. James had been in a play, and Jake had promised to go and see it.

Mandy had completely understood, but felt sad and a bit angry as Jake had only remembered the day before. But she had taken it all in her stride, biting her lip. She had become very good at that!

All her friends had made plans to see her the night before and she had felt embarrassed to admit to them that Jake had made a mistake and had got his dates mixed up and double-booked to see both her and his son's play.

So on her actual birthday Mandy had made arrangements to go and see her sister. They went to a lovely little place called Cedar House. It was candlelit and cosy, the perfect place for Mandy to catch-up with Olivia. It had been another excuse also to keep tabs on her. They had become remarkably close.

It had been three months since Olivia had tried to take her own life by overdose, and she had been seeing a therapist. Deena had recommended an amazing healer and it all seemed to be working. Bit by bit, Olivia's spark was coming back. Mandy and Valerie stayed over often. Valerie had almost moved in, and slowly Olivia started to explain more about why she had felt the way she did three months ago. During her recovery she had realized that life was for her to live to the full. She was a wonderful woman and a wonderful mother. It was as if in the last few months she had found her core, her own being, and she felt free from the trappings of her previous persona. She had discovered a real belief in herself.

Recently, Olivia had been to Dubai for five days, and while there had been asked out by a man called Adam. He was gorgeous, but married. She had loved being chatted up and having an outrageous flirt, and it made her feel like she was truly alive again, rather than just existing; the difference it had made was miraculous, but she had principles; she wasn't going to get involved yet. She had her own boundaries.

When they met for dinner at the Cedar House, Olivia looked stunning, and Mandy felt so much pride at the sister she thought she had lost. She was back to her yoga classes and looked fantastic in her dark blue flares, crisp white shirt, gold hooped earrings and numerous bangles, which showed off her tan perfectly.

'Can't believe that Christmas is just around the corner,' she said, eating her bread with gusto.

'I know, this year has really flown by!'

'Hardly surprising,' smiled Olivia. 'It's been like an over-the-top soap opera for our family!'

It was good to see her like this, confident, cracking jokes and on top form. She was magical when she just relaxed, even slightly.

'So, where's Jake tonight?'

'Watching his son's play.'

'Sweet . . . you OK with it?'

'I have to be, don't I?'

'Are you happy, Mand?'

'I'm in love with a married man; how happy can I be? I feel like I'm treading water, only to drown in act two!'

'Listen, if that's the case, you had a life before him, so . . . you can have a life after him. Take it from me, I know.'

'I know you do. Thanks.'

Olivia grabbed Mandy's hands. 'Nothing is worth giving up on *you*. You know what I think.'

Mandy looked at her expectantly.

'Get on with your life. Keep going with Jake, but if ever someone else comes along who can offer you the full relationship you deserve, then go for it.'

Mandy nodded. 'Thanks, darling. You're right, I suppose.'

Mandy thought quietly for a few seconds. She didn't want anyone else to give her the full relationship; she wanted Jake to give her that.

Now Mandy checked her phone. No texts, no messages, no missed calls. She perched on the bed in her fluffy white bathrobe; her cheeks were pink after her heavy soak in the hot bath. Surely Jake would have texted or left a message if he wasn't coming.

She padded around the flat, lit some candles and put on her favourite Fleetwood Mac album. Then she popped some champagne in the fridge to chill and waited.

In the end, she sent a text.

ARE YOU COMING TO MEET ME? THOUGHT YOU WERE
GOING TO LET ME KNOW IF YOU COULDN'T? M X

It reached midnight, and Mandy was fast asleep on the sofa with a box of chocolates scattered over her. Something woke her, so she opened her eyes and checked her phone. Still nothing!

This had been starting to happen more and more, recently. Jake was always good at keeping in touch with her by phone, or a brief text if he couldn't call, but this no longer seemed to be the case.

Mandy hated this feeling of being a slave to someone else's wife, to someone else's children and family life. She loved Jake, but, after yet another disappointment, she wondered was this really any way to live?

Jake looked at his beautiful boys from the doorway to their room. They were now sleeping, but Alex had been crying most of the night.

'Don't go, Daddy, you're always leaving me.'

Jake felt racked with guilt. He hadn't seen them as much as he should, and they were starting to notice.

Helen came in and rested her head on his shoulder. 'What's wrong, darling?'

'I've not been here for the boys enough, or for you as much as I should. Alex crying like he did tonight has left me in pieces.'

Helen gently brushed a piece of fluff from Jake's shirt.

'Well, make some more time then!' She smiled gently, looking in his eyes.

Jake nodded slowly. 'So simple, but so true,' he smiled. 'You always make good sense.' He kissed her on the cheek and walked away.

Helen smiled to herself. It would all work out. She knew it.

SIXTEEN

Family Comes First

Jake felt increasingly guilty, and as a result was less and less consistent with Mandy. He tried to be kind: his love and his addiction to Mandy were slowly withdrawn bit by bit over a few months. His loyalty started to sway to the 'other side', as George had called it.

But Mandy knew Jake far too well. She sensed he had been intimate with Helen, and it felt like a slow painful death. What could she do, what could she say? She had known the deal all along, avoided asking certain details. She had accepted a difficult situation, she hadn't set her standards from the beginning. Now she realized she'd been duped.

What a fool!

Sometimes she had a picture of Helen and Jake in her head. Flashes of them furiously making love would hit her like a thunderbolt. What was going on? Mandy was clever, attractive, a director in a successful firm. How did she ever end up in this mess?

She did all she could to distract herself from her natural

reaction to all this worry; she was also irritated with herself for feeling so weak and helpless. Pathetic!

It was a bright, but chilly Saturday in January. Christmas and New Year had been spent without Jake, yet again. Jake now took his boys to football most Saturdays, so Mandy sat cross-legged in Jake's baby-blue boxers, black socks and grey sweatshirt. She opened her Mac laptop, ripped her pencil from her oriental-style hair bun and checked out holiday destinations. She deserved a treat, and Olivia was like a *Wish You Were Here . . . ?* presenter these days, up for a trip anywhere and at any time.

'Wow, what a fab deal!' Mandy muttered to herself. There was a bargain to stay seven nights at the best resort in Mexico. 'Go for it, Mand.' She felt excited.

The phone rang.

'Mandy, it's Michael; can you get out to LA?'

'When?'

'Tenth to the twentieth of February. There's an event there that Margaret wants us to work on.'

'Course, count me in,' Mandy said enthusiastically. 'But would you mind if I squeezed a week's holiday in before I get there? I'd like a break in Mexico, and its pretty close by, isn't it?'

'Mandy, you worked like a bloody steam train all over Christmas and New Year, and I already told you to take a break ages ago.'

'Is that a yes?'

'Yes, darling. Enjoy, but keep fresh for the Americans. It's taken ages, but I feel we can make our mark there.'

'No worries,' replied Mandy.

'Bye, darling. India and I are off to the country for the weekend.'

'Enjoy.' Mandy hung up and started to dial Olivia.

Call waiting. Jake!

Mandy left it. He didn't leave a message; he hardly ever did any more.

'Shit, what did I do that for?' she yelled at herself.

Bleep bleep! The sound of a voicemail came through. Perhaps she had jumped the gun a little there.

'Hi, Mand, I'm freezing my bollocks off watching the boys play football, badly. Gladys Knight came on the radio in the car earlier, and I thought of you. Are you free next week? And the weekend of the seventh of February? Bell me when you can. Bye.'

Mandy found herself dialling before she could speak.

'Yes, let's meet Monday night. Ffiona's at eight.'

That was it!

Jake and Mandy sat in Ffiona's, comfy, cosy and warm. They had just finished eating the famous chicken Kiev and were now knocking back the red wine, but the conversation wasn't flowing like it normally did. They were both nervous.

Mandy's heart was aching. Something had switched off

in Jake, and rather than stepping back and just letting things unfold, she felt desperate and needy. Her mind was full of uncertainties, what-ifs and maybes. Had her reaction to the flat been to blame? Or did she trigger something off when Olivia had overdosed? Maybe all this had frightened him off. Was sex with Helen better than it was with her? Now she'd seen her, Mandy's confidence was undermined. She pulled herself apart bit by bit as Jake gulped down his wine.

God, why wasn't she allowed to be imperfect? Her life was no different from anyone else's; shit happens. Was this rollercoaster all too much? Had he brought her here to end it all?

'So,' Jake said, 'are you free the weekend of the seventh?'

Oh God, yes of course. He had mentioned it when he phoned.

'Yes,' she blurted.

In actual fact that was the week she had booked to go to Mexico and LA. She was juggling dates in her mind. Then she pulled herself together: no, enough was enough, she had her life away from him too, didn't she?

'Oh God, actually no. I have a work thing on in America, and a trip to Mexico. Olivia booked it,' she lied.

'Oh, how long for?' Jake looked completely thrown.

'Not sure yet.' Mandy took another swig of her red wine.

Jake glanced down at his glass, the same look on his face that he'd had when they'd first met at the Wolseley. Mandy had hoped she would never have to see that look again, but there it was. Was she the cause of the unhappiness in his eyes now, not Helen?

'We're not right, are we, Jake?'

Jake looked up at her, and she felt scared.

'No, we aren't right, but we can't be right all the time. It's not possible to be perfect all the time, is it?'

Mandy smiled as convincingly as she could, but she felt her throat close up. The voice in her head wouldn't stop, pleading, Please don't leave me, please don't leave me.

She twiddled with her bracelet and laughed. 'No one could ever say it's dull with us though, could they?' she continued. She needed to get things off her chest. 'Don't you sometimes think it's too hard? We find our good times a relief because the bad times are there in the background?'

'That's not true, or fair,' Jake replied.

'Why not?'

'Well, you're being so negative.'

'No, Jake, I'm being honest,' Mandy said firmly.

'Well, if that's the case, then I'm truly worried.'

Mandy looked down at her lap. This is it, it's going to be over, she thought. I just don't suit him any more. But I need to hear it from him direct, from his own lips, then at least I'll know where I stand.

Mandy looked at him hard. 'So, what do you want to do?'

'I think we should go to Paris.'

'What?' She was taken aback now.

'Well, we clearly need some quality time together, and I think Paris will be just beautiful this time of year. It'll be the weekend before Valentine's, and we'd be in Paris together, having an early celebration.'

Mandy wasn't sure what to feel, confused by a barrage of emotion.

Jake really didn't want to let her go, he wanted to take her to Paris with him; but it was blindingly clear to Mandy why it was the week *before* Valentine's. He was obviously having his Valentine's Day with Helen.

'OK,' she whispered sadly, suddenly feeling exhausted by everything.

They went to the Mayfair flat and, for the first time ever, Jake didn't make love to her.

He slept on his side, on the edge of the bed, and Mandy lay awake, feeling angry about the whole affair. She wanted to roll over to him, to hug and cuddle him, but she felt he didn't want her to. Had he slept with Helen recently? Had he liked it? It was hard for Mandy to know what to think.

'Helen wants another baby,' Jake had suddenly blurted out over dinner.

Mandy couldn't think straight. Was she dreaming? Helen truly was a good adversary, that much she knew. She was so shocked she couldn't deal with it. She held her breath, squeezed her eyes tight and pretended to sleep.

*

Jake's alarm pierced her thoughts and he jumped out of bed, making his way to the bathroom as quietly as he could, closing the bedroom door so as not to wake Mandy.

Suddenly, the landline rang and the answering machine kicked in on loudspeaker. A little boy's voice left a breathless message.

'Daddy,' his breathing got heavier, 'Daddy, my chest is tight and I can't find my inhaler. I'm shouting down to Mummy, but she can't hear me.'

The little boy was wheezing terribly down the phone, and Mandy made her way quickly to the bathroom door and tried to open it.

'Jake,' she shouted, 'Jake!' But he couldn't hear her.

Panic set in and Mandy could hear the little boy start to cry. He sounded terrible. Instinctively she picked up the phone.

'Hello, I work with your daddy. He's going to call you straight back, is that OK?'

The little boy's rasping voice managed an 'OK.'

Oh God, this was all so awful. Mandy felt worry flooding through her body.

Jake opened the bathroom door in his towel.

'Hold on,' said Mandy down the phone.

She went to pass the receiver to Jake, but before she did she told the boy his daddy was here and that she was going to pass him over. She sounded like an efficient secretary.

'It's your son; he's having a bad asthma attack and can't

breathe. He can't find his inhaler or his mum, he's very distressed and he must have tried your other phone first. I'll leave you to it.'

The whole conversation was still on loudspeaker and continued to fill the flat. Jake's face paled with horror.

Mandy went into the bathroom and closed the door. She sat on the marble floor and put her hands over her ears. Alex sounded lovely, so young, so scared. She could hear Helen's muffled voice in the background, and then Jake calming them both down and telling Helen that the other inhaler was in the top drawer in the kitchen.

Mandy's head fell into her hands and she started to cry. She realized at that moment the consequences of her actions. She realized how huge this all was. The obstacle of his family in her life was getting bigger and bigger, and would always be there. At that moment, part of her died.

Jake opened the bathroom door. He was throwing his jacket on.

'God, that was close.'

Men could be totally unbelievable. Mandy wanted to hit out at him.

He came over and knelt down. 'I have to go home. Alex is very distressed. His asthma has been really bad lately, and I just didn't realize how bad it was. For that, I blame myself.'

Mandy shrugged her shoulders numbly. 'How did he have the flat number, Jake?'

'I gave it to him in case of an emergency.'

Mandy looked at him in disbelief. 'But this is *our* flat, Jake, my home. What *were* you thinking?' Mandy wanted to scream at his foolishness.

Jake grew suddenly white with anger.

'He's my fucking son, my boy, Mandy. Right now he is really unwell. If I was at Buckingham Palace and he wanted to speak to me, I'd still give him the Queen's fucking number. Do you understand?'

'But what if Helen had heard me?'

'I told you, he's my son, and he comes first, no matter what.'

With that Jake got up, looked at Mandy with disdain, grabbed his keys and left, slamming the front door.

SEVENTEEN

À Paris

I MISS YOU. I THINK WE REALLY NEED TO TALK. MEET
ME AT THE FLAT AT 8 THIS EVENING.

Three days had gone by and neither of them had been
in touch with the other.

George had got her into the *Love Songs* album by Barbra
Streisand, and at six-thirty one evening, over a glass of rosé,
the two of them sang their hearts out, using a hairbrush and
a tin of hairspray as if they were doing their own spotlit video.

'I'd go straight for Babs,' George yelled over the music,
his hands moving just like Barbra's. 'This is your and Jake's
song,' he said as 'Coming In and Out of Your Life' played.
'But if Jake keeps being a bastard, he'd better watch out.
Otherwise you'll be singing "My Heart Belongs to Me".'

He spun round and threw himself against the wall
tragically, making Mandy laugh.

'God, George, you're getting more and more camp in
your old age!'

He leaned over Mandy's shoulder as she checked her phone. 'Is that him?'

'Yep, he wants to meet me tonight at eight.'

'Oh bloody hell, he doesn't give you much time, does he? How do you feel?'

'Angry, but I miss him and I'm feeling horny too. The usual.'

'Go, girl, go, a good lustful fuck never does anyone any harm, and it can work wonders!'

Mandy laughed again. 'Well, you're right; words get in the way sometimes.'

George flung his arms aloft in the manner of a diva. 'Make love, not war, and if nothing else it will ease the tension and make you feel relieved. Nothing like a multiple orgasm, babe!'

Jake arrived dead on eight, and seconds later was tugging at Mandy's chiffon peach blouse, pulling it up from the tiny waistband of her leather pencil skirt. She looked like a fifties pin-up, unashamedly glamorous, and boy, did she smell good. As he tugged harder her blouse popped open and the buttons flew everywhere. Her full breasts were bursting out of her bra, ready to be caressed and kissed.

As his mouth moistened her nipples, she gasped. The raw sexual chemistry hadn't gone away. The tight skirt was pulled up to her waist, her legs opened and he spread them far apart.

She looked down at Jake's obvious pleasure. He just looked into her eyes and then yanked her knickers to one side and pushed into her hard. Mandy gasped, again. It was such pleasurable pain; she was loving every second.

It was urgent, immediate sex; they were saying everything they needed to, but without uttering a word. Both of them wanted to punish and pleasure each other at the same time.

Later that night, the exhausted pair found themselves sitting with their naked bodies pressed against the wall in the corridor of the flat. Jake had taken Mandy again by leaning her against the wall. When they finished the two had just fallen down on to the floor, sweating and breathless. They had argued and made up, argued and made up over and over again, and now they were completely spent.

'I love and hate you.'

'I love and hate you too.'

Jake looked towards her with eyes that couldn't lie. 'Can we still go to Paris?'

Mandy knew that saying no was never going to be an option, despite the work trip coming up, and her plan to holiday with Olivia. She knew she had to fight for Jake. They weren't over yet, and he was making an effort again.

'Yes, let's.'

The dreaded call to Olivia had to be made. Mandy felt awful. It was all her idea and now she was letting her sister down.

'Olive, would you mind if we made the trip to Mexico later in the year?'

'Why? What has Jake done?'

'God, am I that predictable?'

'Um . . . yes.'

'He's taking me to Paris and then I have to shoot over to LA for my work thing.'

'Enjoy, babe,' Olivia said generously. 'I'm glad things are back on track. What about our deposits, though?'

'Don't worry, I'll sort all that out. You OK?'

'Great. Not ready to kill myself just yet, so don't worry.'

'That's not bloody funny, Olive.'

'Oh, get your stockings on and lighten up!'

'Love you. Bye.'

'Byeeee.'

'Phew, better than I thought,' Mandy mumbled.

George, Deena and Assia came over to the Mayfair flat, and chatted and ate pizza while Mandy packed.

Deena went over to Mandy as she was tucking her shoes in her bag. 'I have a little something for you.' She handed her a semi-precious stone. 'It's for fertility. Have his baby, Mand. Your babies would be beautiful.'

'Are you mad?'

'Yes.' Deena placed it on the bedside table and whispered, 'It's there when you need it and when you're ready.'

George read out his list as Mandy checked her case.

'Suspenders?'

'Check.'

'Edible knickers?'

'Check.'

'Super-sexy underwear?'

'Check.'

'Nipple tassels?'

'George, for God's sake! I don't have nipple tassels on the list!'

'Oh boo hoo,' said George. 'Luckily I bought some for you!'

Mandy giggled and chucked them in the case. 'Check.'

'Body oil?'

'Check.'

'Condoms, pills, et cetera?'

'Check.'

'Coco Chanel?'

'Check.'

George went on: 'Boots, shoes, normal toiletries, clothes, jackets et cetera?'

'Blah blah blah,' Mandy laughed. 'Check.'

'Bet you're so excited, dharrling?' Assia purred, looking amazing in her new canary diamond earrings and black Yves Saint Laurent blouse. 'At last, dharrling, you will be where the mistress belongs!' The divorce settlement obviously suited her; she was on great form.

Mandy smiled at all her friends as she buzzed around the flat.

Part of her had missed being the mistress, with all its

lustful encounters, romantic holidays and spontaneous sex and excitement. She hoped to God this weekend would put it all right for good.

Early on Friday morning, Mandy stood on the platform of St Pancras Station, looking left and right for her man. She was holding a red rose for him. The train was leaving in five minutes. Where the hell was he? Looking down at her Louis Vuitton travel case, she felt a dread well up inside her, but tried with all her might to push it away. Jake would turn up, of course he would, she knew it.

Quietly she whispered, 'Don't do this to me, please. Please, Jake, don't do this to me.'

She was trying to keep warm, hopping from one foot to the other.

She had honestly believed that, dressed in her chocolate fur coat, with nothing on underneath but a black lace bra and knickers, suspenders holding up her black stockings, and way-too-high sexy shoes, that Jake would see her and love the shock of her naughtiness. Suddenly, this was no longer fun or exhilarating; it felt embarrassing and humiliating.

As people rushed and scurried along the concourse, Mandy's vision blurred. Everyone that walked past her seemed to be staring at her. In fact, they all seemed to have X-ray vision and to be smirking at the fact that this silly woman had the audacity to turn up in a fur coat and little else. The men boarding the train seemed to know just what was beneath her coat. Worse still, so did the women. She felt so cheap, so vulnerable standing in her 'sexy' outfit. Going away with a man, it signalled one thing; standing on her own it gave out another message completely.

Mandy squeezed her eyes shut as hard as she could and opened them again. She felt as if everyone was laughing, except those who felt sorry for her, this pathetic lady with her overly made-up face and over-the-top diamond earrings. She felt like a real-life clown.

She swallowed hard. She was just panicking, she wasn't seeing straight. She must be panicking!

'Please fucking turn up,' she prayed. 'No apologies, no cancellations, no texts, not now, not again. Just please, please turn up.'

The lump in her throat had become so large that she could no longer swallow. She nervously looked at her watch, and checked and checked again. Two minutes now until the train left.

Bleep bleep, bleep bleep.

Mandy's blood was boiling before she even read the text. She pulled the phone out of her coat pocket and read the message.

SO SORRY, I'VE TRIED BUT I JUST WON'T MAKE IT ON TIME. TRULY SORRY. GO BACK TO MAYFAIR AND I WILL TRY AND GET TO YOU TONIGHT, EXPLAIN ALL THEN. J X

'Try and get to me tonight? Try and get to me *tonight*? Oh no, this would never have happened before,' Mandy muttered to herself.

She felt her heart fall hard. All eyes from within the train compartment were on her, looking at her curiously. The platform was now empty. Mandy stood alone, stuck to the spot.

'Fuck you,' she murmured. 'Fuck you!'

Impulsively Mandy threw the rose to the floor, grabbed her case and ran on to the first-class compartment of the train. The guards were shouting to her, but she ignored them.

She felt anger, shock and numbness all at the same time. Stumbling to her seat, she heard the whistle blow as the train slowly pulled away and tears began to tumble down her face. She tried to wipe them away, smudging mascara down her cheeks, but more fell, and many more. An elderly man looked at her, full of concern, smiling kindly. But she didn't notice him.

At that moment everything seemed to die inside her.

On arrival in Paris, Mandy aimlessly followed the herd of people that had disembarked from her train. She wandered around until she finally saw the exit of the Gare du Nord. She had managed to clean her face on the journey, and looked a bit more respectable now. A tall bald man, looking very smart in a light grey suit and blue tie, was holding up a sign saying MR CHAPLIN HOTEL COSTES. She had no idea where Jake had booked, it was a surprise, but she was thrilled to hear it was the Hotel Costes. Mandy walked up to him and he smiled kindly.

'*Bonjour, madame.*'

'*Bonjour.*' Mandy's French was not good at all, so she said falteringly, '*Pardon, je suis anglaise.*'

'Ah, no problem, no problem. I am waiting for Monsieur Chaplin, no?'

'No, I'm afraid he could not come, he had a big emergency, huge,' Mandy explained, spreading her arms wide.

'Oh no, I am sorry for Monsieur.'

Mandy stood awkwardly.

'OK, we go now?'

'Yes please.'

'Your, er, name, *madame*?'

'Mandy. Mandy Sanderson.'

'*Bonjour*, Mandy, I am Jean-Claude. Welcome to Paris.'

'*Bonjour, Jean-Claude*, and *merci*.'

Jean-Claude took Mandy's bags and led her to a waiting Mercedes.

'Hotel Costes, yes?'

'*Oui,*' replied Mandy.

Mandy walked in through the doorway of the Hotel Costes and gasped in delight at the lobby. The first thing that hit her was the richness of the décor: dark shades of red were used for the satin and velvet drapes, dark red roses and candles filled every space. The hotel signature scent seemed strong and hedonistic. She noticed that cool CDs which the hotel's resident DJ had mixed especially for the Costes were on sale, as were their perfumes, candles and shower gels. The whole place was just so chic, and so modern too, and extremely romantic. Such a waste, thought Mandy.

The staff looked sharp in their black tailored uniforms, and every guest looked as though they had just walked off the pages of French *Vogue*. No one batted an eye at Mandy's fur-coat-and-fishnet combo; in fact she felt like she wanted to back-comb her hair and add some dark smoky eyeliner, just to fit in.

This place was fabulous – even though she was alone, she felt more cheered. Reception spoke to her in French, and were not thrilled when she apologized in English for not understanding, but within five minutes she had explained that the room was now to be booked under Mandy Sanderson, and that the bill was to be charged to her card, not Mr Chaplin's.

They took her Amex, swiped it and *voilà*, she was shown to her room.

She put the Hotel Costes CD on the player, had a glass of pink champagne delivered to the room and then danced in her fabulous underwear and high heels across the floor of the suite. Who needs men? she thought. At that moment she felt happy, strong and fabulously chic.

Five tracks later, Mandy sat on her antique bed with its beautiful linen and pretty pillows, munching on complimentary crisps. She hadn't eaten a thing and the champagne had gone to her head. She was feeling melancholy. She decided to change into her rain mac, skinny blue jeans and white Converse pumps. She placed a navy woolly hat on her head, picked up her tan Hermès Birkin bag, and was ready to shop.

As she walked along the Champs-Elysées she gazed at all the well-known stores: Chanel, Dior, Louis Vuitton and finally Cartier. She stopped for a tea break at the Plaza Athénée. It was exquisite. Gorgeous women with cute little dogs were everywhere. Mandy couldn't help noticing how elegant, how understated they were. They seemed effortlessly *soignée*.

Mandy felt sad for five minutes, wishing Jake had swept her back to Cartier to buy her an engagement ring, but then cheered up when the sales assistant brought out a glass of champagne and a stunning selection of diamond earrings.

Later she found a wonderful little store, with second-hand designer pieces and accessories. She had died and gone to heaven. Racks of Hervé Léger, Chanel, Lowe, Azzaro, Valentino and Givenchy were hers for the taking. Mandy squealed with delight: classics like these would never go out of style. Mandy fell in love with a black Hervé Léger dress. It sucked her in and contoured her hourglass figure to perfection. She also found some amazing vintage diamanté and ruby earrings. They were big, but teamed with bright red lips and the dress, the look would be a killer.

The shop owner was pin thin, with amazing shiny blonde hair in a centre parting. She was stunning, cool, calm and collected: Gwyneth Paltrow with a French accent.

'So, where are you going tonight in your fabulous dress?' she pouted.

Mandy suddenly realized she had no idea, no plans.

'Um . . . I'm meeting friends at the Hotel Costes.'

'It's great there – cool, you know?'

'Yes,' said Mandy, nodding and pulling her stomach in. 'Yes, it's extremely cool.'

The owner of the shop introduced herself as Madeleine; she was very good at her job. Mandy left with three vintage dresses, two pairs of earrings and four handbags. She didn't feel one bit of guilt, not one bit – she felt she'd earned this treat.

It was dark now, and Mandy made her way back to the hotel, blissfully happy with her purchases.

A doorman smiled at her. He was handsome. *'Bonsoir, madame.'* Mandy actually took him in. For the first time since meeting Jake she had actually noticed another man. It felt good. Mandy nodded at him and made her way to her room.

She checked her phone. Two messages. The first was from George:

ENJOY YOUR NIPPLE TASSELS! THINKING OF YOU!
GEORGE X PS I KNOW HE'S NOT THERE — I SAW THE
BASTARD WITH A WOMAN I ASSUME MUST BE THE WIFE,
IN A TAXI. PULL A FRENCHIE AND FUCK ANYWAY. IT
WOULD BE A SHAME NOT TO USE THOSE TASSELS XX

message two:

HOPE YOUR WEEKEND IS AS BEAUTIFUL AS YOU! ENJOY,
OLIVE X

'Oh God,' sighed Mandy. So George knew, and bless him.

She started to run the bath, adding shower gel to create bubbles. 'Sod you, Jake Chaplin, and your bony wife. Actually, fuck you!' She played her CD again and turned up the volume.

'Enough is enough, we're over!'

She looked in the mirror and put in some Velcro rollers. 'I don't need this shit any more.'

Mandy knew that the embarrassment, hurt and shame she had felt on that train would never, ever leave her. It had been her own fault: she had let it all go on. She took full responsibility for that, but that time was done, finished, over. She would give up Jake once and for all. In her heart she felt that she had lost him anyway, long ago.

Sitting in the bar at the hotel, Mandy felt like Julia Roberts in *Pretty Woman*. Was that a good thing?

Half of her felt pretty, half felt hooker, but what the hell. She had a devil-may-care attitude tonight, and a sense of relief now it was over with Jake for ever. This way, she had the hope of a complete relationship with someone new.

Her dress looked sexy, her hair was half pulled back, and the lush red lipstick matched the ruby red in her costume-jewellery earrings. Mandy decided to eat soup and salad: the dress was tiny and completely unforgiving.

It was nine at night and the restaurant and bar were busy. The atmosphere was amazing. The people-watching alone was enchanting.

Mandy felt special, but slightly vulnerable. Body language is something that is understood whatever your nationality, and men were certainly looking. The women either smiled appreciatively or turned their noses up and ignored her as if they hadn't seen her.

A man was laughing with a group of friends; he had dark skin, longish wavy hair and piercing blue eyes. He was wearing a low-necked baggy white T-shirt, skinny black jeans and a grey linen blazer. He looked extremely cool and he could have easily been in a band, or an artist or something edgy. He was around six foot one, and Mandy noticed he had cute dimples. He kept looking over at Mandy, and eventually when the group made their way over to the bar he said simply, 'Hello.'

Mandy smiled nervously. 'Hello.'

He introduced himself as Tommy; he was thirty-four, Italian, a photographer.

They chatted happily for half an hour and Mandy explained that she was supposed to be with someone in Paris, but at the last minute they had cancelled on her but she had decided to come along anyway.

'Ah, bravo, Mandy.'

The group of people with Tommy were introduced and were warm and friendly, clapping their hands and saying, '*Ciao, Mandy, ciao*.' They all kissed her dozens of times, and were fun, larger than life and stylish too. Mandy enjoyed the attention. Before she knew it she was invited to dinner. Tommy was smiling. There was something lovely about him, an easy charm and a warm and inviting personality. Mandy felt completely safe with these people, so she agreed to join them, and was grateful for the company.

The food was superb and the champagne flowed. Tommy's English and French were perfect. His friends were all arty, creative types, and the girls were young and so assured. Tommy and Mandy talked the hours away, and long after his friends had said their goodbyes the two of them were still there, completely wrapped up in each other. Everything was interesting and funny, and strangely romantic too. Mandy hardly knew this man, yet she found herself shyly asking him up to her room. He was just so beautiful, and so completely different from Jake. He was light, straightforward, witty, genuine – and single.

EIGHTEEN

The Romance of Paris

As they entered, the fragrances were amazing. Only candles lit the room, and the bed had already been turned down. Mandy had thought she would be nervous, but she felt bold and beautiful. Tommy had made her feel this way all evening.

In the time that had passed between them, Mandy had never once thought of Jake; it was only after a couple of bottles of champagne that Tommy had become inquisitive.

'Mandy, can I be straightforward with you?'

'Yes, of course.'

'Your trip, was it with a man originally? I can't believe that someone as beautiful as you was coming to Paris and this hotel with merely a friend.'

Mandy paused, and thought long and hard. 'You're right of course, but it's a very long story.'

'We have all night, you can tell me.'

'I don't feel I want to go into too much detail, so I'll keep it brief.' Mandy smiled softly. 'I am deeply in love with a man, a married man. Things were great at first, but as time went on his own family began to take back what they had lost, and I was more like a puppet. This trip was meant to be special, meant to help us rebuild, but he never turned up, and, more importantly, he never believed I would come alone. Let's not talk about him. The night is ours.'

Mandy placed her drink on the table and moved seductively towards Tommy. She couldn't believe it: she wanted this man, she *needed* this man, and for the first time in a long time she felt the weight lifted from her. She was with a man with no secrets, no hiding places. It was just her and him.

She took his hand in hers and led him to the bed. She lay on the sheets and held her arms up to him, and he fell to her easily and embraced and kissed her tenderly. She felt a groan coming from her throat and she knew that she truly wanted him.

Their undressing of one another was tender and arousing. Tommy stared at her naked body.

'My God, you are so perfect, such a woman, and so very beautiful.'

Mandy looked at his slim waist, powerful shoulders and hairy chest. His legs were long and lean, and she felt herself aching for this man.

Before long Tommy was cupping her breasts, kissing and caressing them. He moved slowly down and eased her legs open, where he placed his head and licked, sucked and teased her for an eternity. He raised his head to see her pleasure and gently began to turn her body on to his and soon Mandy was pleasuring him in the same way. Mandy was good, too good; Tommy could hardly stop himself and before long Mandy urged him inside her, to love her, to fuck her. He was a safety boy. Mandy was relieved: she wasn't sure she would trust herself otherwise.

As he moved inside her, he caused ripples of pleasure throughout her body. He was slow and caring, but then he thrust a little harder. Soon he was penetrating her quite forcefully, and Mandy responded with her body arching, wanting more. He came inside her, but never stopped, still wanting more. Their bodies entwined, and they moved and changed places and Mandy found herself perched on top of him, writhing, pushing him deeper and deeper. Finally, the two collapsed next to each other. Tommy pulled her close and, together in their last embrace, they drifted off to sleep.

The following morning, Mandy awoke to Tommy singing in the shower. She stretched out her long, slightly aching body. She had slept like a baby.

Tommy entered with a bathrobe on, totally at ease and smiling. 'Come on, *bella*, the sun is shining in Paris and we have lots to see. I'm taking you on a small tour.' He was so sweet, wanting to get out and show off Paris to this beautiful woman who had suddenly entered his life like a charm. He pulled her up gently.

'Come, *bella*, get showered and dressed and let us not miss another minute of this glorious day.'

Mandy was thrilled, she loved his confidence. She jumped off the bed and, wiggling provocatively to the bathroom, looked over her shoulder and blew a kiss to the man who had made her feel a complete woman again.

Tommy laughed.

Mandy looked cute but also elegant as she appeared from the dressing room. She was wearing tight black jeans, and black Ugg boots with the fur trim showing. She wore a cream blouse with a beautiful black cashmere roll-neck jumper over the top. It was freezing and she couldn't afford to be cold on their day out. In her ears she wore plain silver hoops, and six assorted silver bangles dangled on her wrist. With her hair in a simple ponytail, and light creamy make-up with a tinge of beige lip gloss, she looked natural but fantastic.

'You are so cute, so lovely, *bella*. Now come and eat the croissant and coffee I've ordered and we'll leave as soon as you're ready.'

Mandy giggled. 'God, I slept with a gorgeous Italian, and I feel fucking wonderful.'

'Yes, *bella*, you did, and it was wonderful for me too.'

They both laughed out loud.

As they left the hotel, the Paris sunshine almost blinded them. Mandy quickly retrieved her Givenchy sunglasses from her bag, and from the inside pocket of his jacket Tommy took out his too.

Mandy stared at him. Flashbacks came to her from last night. Jesus, he was all man, a sexy man, and so much her cup of tea. For a split second she wished she'd experienced last night with Jake, but it was his choice not to be there, his loss. Now, putting all things from the past out of her mind, she grabbed Tommy's arm as they started to walk. Today would be a wonderful day, she just knew it.

The two looked like a couple happy in love as they held hands and wandered the streets of Paris. It was fantastic to visit small curiosity shops down tiny cobbled streets, and just as exciting to enter Dolce & Gabbana, Givenchy and Yves Saint Laurent. The perfumeries were wonderful and Tommy took her to a quaint specialist boutique where they designed her own unique fragrance. Of course, a trip around Paris would not be complete without a visit to the Eiffel Tower and the Arc de Triomphe.

By this time they were both starving, so Tommy hailed a cab and took Mandy to the Ritz.

With its famous décor and wonderful history, Mandy found the Ritz captivating.

'Coco Chanel used to live here. I've been privileged in my career to actually do a few shoots for fashion magazines in her gorgeous suite. It was a fantastic experience.'

'Wow, that's incredible,' she replied.

'You know what, Mandy? I am not a rich man. I am OK, but I love what I do, so in a way I'm the wealthiest man in the world.' Mandy understood his sincerity; his passion for his work showed in his face.

'One thing I don't understand. How come you're alone, Tommy?'

'Well, it's not a long story. I fell in love with a beautiful American girl, and I still love her now. The saddest part of it all is that I know she still loves me too.' He swept his dark wavy hair off his forehead. 'We tried to make it work, but sometimes things just get in the way. The distance caused the relationship to fail, and despite our love for each other we had to go our own way. It's been six months now, and I still think of her, but now I am very single.'

He looked slightly sad for a moment, but soon his smile was wide and light filled his cornflower-blue eyes. 'Come, *bella*, the day is still young and there is much more to see.'

Mandy noticed that as she walked around the large department stores, including Colette, she felt no eyes on her, no stress. Neither she nor Tommy was having to look over their shoulder in case someone might spot them and realize she was with a married lover. Right now she was free from hiding, free from gossip and free from fear. She felt so liberated, and so comfortable. It was as if they had known each other for ever.

When the day ended, Mandy was sad. It was time for her to leave, but part of her wanted to stay and get to know this beautiful man even more. Paris had been amazing, a great experience, and Tommy would stay close in her heart, tucked away but never forgotten. He'd given her strength, a secret to be cherished. That would stay with her for ever.

Tommy gave her his number and said, 'If you do decide to date single men, I'd love to be the first one you call.' He smiled cheekily. 'Failing that, I would genuinely love to be your friend. I feel a real connection, and I'd love us to stay in touch.'

Tommy took Mandy to the Gare du Nord for her Eurostar train. They kissed passionately and Mandy felt a wobble in her legs as he cupped her face.

'I hope I see you again, my beautiful girl.'

Mandy boarded the train. It was hard to say goodbye, and as she took her seat and the train pulled out for the UK, her first thought was of Jake, and she felt a sudden guilt.

Mandy had left her phone on silent. This had protected her from real life and kept her safe in her own beautiful bubble. Now she finally switched it on.

Jake had left a message. Please don't let him be really nice to me, she pleaded to herself. She listened apprehensively.

'Ah,' said a familiar voice. 'I hear a different ringtone,

which tells me you must have gone to Paris. Listen, I know I let you down, but we do need to talk. I know I didn't make it to the flat either, and I'm sorry. It's just that whenever we need to or try to make this work, something – work, my kids, your family – seems to get in the way. Maybe we need some space, I don't know, but you need to call me. I can't go on like this, we need to talk. I don't know if either of us is truly happy, and you deserve to be happy – so do I, and everyone else involved for that matter. OK, I need you to call me. Bye.'

Mandy's guilt diminished with irritation. She thought back to her night of passion with Tommy. It had been unique, simple yet beautiful. Everything was so complicated with Jake.

Mandy slowly convinced herself that Helen had won, just as Mandy had sensed she always would. Helen was clearly a woman who had a knack of getting what she wanted. She also sensed that Helen knew Jake was having an affair. And in her own quiet little way, Helen had declared war. She had the advantage of knowing Jake inside-out and back to front. She knew exactly how to play him.

Mandy didn't want to call him back tonight, she was shattered. As she reached her flat in Mayfair and opened the door, things were precisely as she had left them. Jake definitely hadn't been there at all.

She changed into her white linen pyjamas and brushed her teeth. She fell into bed, too exhausted to think of anything, but hoping she would dream of Paris.

NINETEEN

LA Confession

For a few weeks Mandy ignored Jake's calls. She wasn't exactly sure how to deal with him or what to say, and every message that she did receive from him seemed to be negative and distant.

If you want to fuck off out of my life, Jake, she thought, then just do it. Don't keep ringing to tell me about it.

Thankfully the LA trip was back on: it had been postponed twice and America had seemed out of Mandy and Michael's grasp until they had finally got the go-ahead from their colleague a few days ago.

It was March, and Mandy had packed a wonderful selection of springtime essentials. The car was downstairs, waiting to take her to the airport. Jake hadn't bothered to turn up to the flat once, even though he had tried ringing her again. It was strange, he seemed to just know that she had switched off emotionally.

Mandy skipped down the stairs, excited to be going to LA. Her phone showed that Jake was ringing again. It was one of those mysteries in life: when you truly have just had enough, it's as if an invisible connecting wire of light between you and the person you love changes colour. When you want them too much it's like a red traffic light, a no-go, a complete stop. When you *pretend* you've had enough, the connecting light tries to go to amber. And when you truly let go and switch off, the connecting light between you goes green.

Typical, Mandy thought. When you don't want it any more, they get the green light and are ready for the journey. These invisible connecting lines of light seemed to change from hour to hour, day to day. It was all very confusing.

Mandy was grateful for the LA job: it was just the challenge she needed and would help her switch off from anything emotional.

Margaret, her host, was wonderful, and met Mandy at the Bel Air Hotel.

'At last we meet!' she said. She wore a beige blazer with pearls, and had ash-blonde, curly, shoulder-length hair. She was vibrant, energetic and a joy to be around. 'I'm a New Yorker,' she smiled, 'so don't worry, I'm not in Cuckoo Land like the rest of this town!'

The next day she and Mandy set out the party strategy, picked the music and organized various press to cover the event perfectly. Mandy loved the way Margaret worked: she had a full life away from her job and she had a rich soul, something Mandy had wrongly assumed people in LA might be lacking.

They worked their arses off and pulled the whole thing together in a week, and it paid off. Everything always had to be just perfect in Mandy's mind. She was like a swan, gliding effortlessly on the surface but paddling like crazy underneath to keep afloat.

The party was phenomenal. A seventy-piece orchestra played many classics, including 'Let There Be Love' and 'Unforgettable'. Mandy smiled, as she felt shivers when they played. It was a nod to her dad without anyone knowing; Mandy also thought of her neighbour Diva.

Tonight was a big deal for Mandy. She had a lot to prove and she was nervous. The party was being thrown for a top movie star's wife, who was turning forty and had also started her own clothing line. Margaret and Mandy had suggested she blend the two celebrations together for one big party. The theme she had wanted was anything classic, because her range of clothes consisted of all the classics: the white shirt, the little black dress, etc.

The theme of black and white, with the music, and classic cars on show and little black Smythson books as a gift, went down well with both men and women. Classic red roses were the punch of colour, and old classic movies played on huge screens.

Mandy looked amazing in a sparkling white off-the-shoulder top with a long white floaty skirt.

'You look stunning,' a familiar voice whispered behind her.

Mandy twirled round and nearly passed out there and then.

'What are *you* doing here?'

'I wanted to talk to you.' He looked at her lips longingly.

'Well, *I* don't want to talk to *you*.'

Jake laughed nervously. 'I gathered that when you didn't pick up or return one of my twenty calls.'

Silence.

Mandy felt angry. 'Listen, you can't just come here and make it all about you. This is my job, and it matters to me.'

'It's not about me.'

'*It's always about you!*' Mandy's eyes filled with tears. 'It's all you truly ever care about, *you*! Your life, your kids, your wife! And occasionally, when it takes your fancy, the thorn in your side, me!'

Jake looked confused, shaking his head. 'That's just not true.'

'Stop lying, Jake!' she hissed, trying not to draw attention to herself. 'For the last six months, you've felt awful about me being around. Just admit it.'

Jake didn't know what to say.

Mandy tried to keep her cool. 'I'm trying to give *you* what you wanted: your old life back – so let me have mine!'

Mandy walked away. Jake grabbed her arm.

'It's not what I want! I have so much to tell you, Mand, so much has happened.'

'Yes, for me too.' Mandy paused. 'I met someone in Paris!' Mandy felt panicked the moment the words flew out.

'What?' Jake looked dumbfounded.

'Yes, you heard me! Someone else wants me, Jake! And he had me, and do you know what? I don't regret it, not one bit, because for once I had a man who wanted to be there one hundred per cent. He didn't keep checking his phone, he didn't rush me, he was completely available for me, just silly old little me. I found myself so grateful that his full attention was on me, without worrying that someone would see us. He made me feel I was something to be proud of, not ashamed of and hidden. You make me feel like one big pain in the arse, do you know that?'

Jake shook his head. 'I had no idea. I'm sorry. What do you want from me?'

'More,' shrugged Mandy. 'More, or nothing at all . . .'

She disappeared into the crowd and all Jake could do was watch her go.

Later Mandy walked back to her room at the Bel Air Hotel. It was so pretty there, full of pastel colours and flowers. Slipping out of her outfit and snuggling into the hotel robe and slippers, she checked her BlackBerry.

CONGRATULATIONS, WE ARE A SUCCESS! MARGARET
LOVES YOU! MICHAEL X

FABULOUS NIGHT, FABULOUS ACHIEVEMENT, FABULOUS
WORKING WITH YOU. LET'S DO IT AGAIN SOON. CALL
YOU TOMORROW BEFORE YOU LEAVE. MARGARET

Mandy felt so happy, but her body ached, for deep down she felt that, wherever she went, her heart quietly cried for Jake.

There was a knock at the door. Mandy rushed to open it: it must be room service with her herbal tea.

There stood Jake. He had been crying; his eyes were red and swollen.

'May I come in?'

Mandy walked back in and Jake followed.

A waiter knocked on the open door and came in with a tray of tea and biscuits. Even he could feel the atmosphere. Mandy signed the bill and he scarpered.

Jake sat, leaning his elbows on his black dress trousers. He looked so handsome in a tux, with his tie undone and his large white-gold watch glimmering. His style was top-class and he was a wonderful clothes-horse. Finally he spoke.

'I love you. I don't care that you've been with someone else – well I do, actually, but I haven't really got a leg to stand on, have I? I've been through a phase of wanting to make everything better with Helen and my boys. I wanted to know I had given it a proper go. I was so wrong to do that and still keep you hanging.' His throaty voice got caught. 'I'm so, so sorry.' He looked at Mandy long and hard. 'I just want us to be honest now, good, bad or ugly.'

Mandy didn't know whether to feel better or worse. This obviously meant that he had been intimate with Helen while he was with her.

'Helen got pregnant and lost the baby. I didn't even know she was pregnant. She lost it on the morning I was supposed to meet you at the train station. I felt so, so terrible, so guilty, I've been such a bastard. She's not stupid, Mand, she knows me and she knows my heart is with someone else. It's been such an awful time. All I wanted to do was tell my best friend – that's you, by the way – but I just couldn't, it was all so fucked up.'

Mandy went and stood by the open window, and tried to get enough breath. Poor Helen, poor Jake, poor everyone. Mandy knew that by being in Jake's life she had already made everything worse.

That evening Mandy and Jake talked and talked, kissed and in the early hours made love. Nothing was truly solved, of course. It was easy to feel things were better so far away from home, but their love-making had deepened, they felt more like friends as well as lovers; it was a different kind of magic.

Jake's phone glowed, despite being on silent. He went to reach for it and check the message.

'Sorry,' he mumbled.

Some things would never change.

Helen hung up. She knew Jake was with Mandy. He had even admitted there was someone else when a letter to Mandy and Jake was sent to his home address in Notting Hill rather than the Mayfair flat. It was a welcome-back discount voucher for the art weekend. They had obviously used his credit-card contact address, despite Jake writing the Mayfair address down for future correspondence.

He had become sloppy and lazy when it came to hiding Mandy. It was almost as if he loved her so much that he wanted to be found out. Love can make you feel infallible, like the rules are there for everyone else except you to follow.

Helen knew deep down that she would never give Jake that kind of love, or vice versa. She had never had it, and therefore she didn't miss it, and anybody she knew who had experienced it seemed extremely weak and foolish. That was not her: she was cool, calm, collected. A part of her would always have Jake. She would wait to see what would happen next.

TWENTY

Changes

The next few months were too hectic – no wonder Mandy was paid so much more for being a director in the firm. She had not stopped; she was in Italy one minute, New York the next. The company was expanding and, whilst Mandy was grateful for the extra work, she felt concerned that they simply didn't have the staff or resources to cover it all, plus this tummy bug she'd had for weeks just wouldn't shift. It was wearing her down.

Jake had been brilliant, but felt the pinch of coming second to Mandy's work. Oh, how the tables had turned!

They saw each other whenever Mandy could make it. She was in the driving seat this time. She hadn't planned for it to be that way, it was just the way it was.

Jake was so unsettled he couldn't concentrate, and his work was suffering. He felt he was living a lie; he couldn't take it any more.

He thought about Helen's pregnancy. Their love-making had not been good, the spark was missing. He felt clumsy, and at times just could not get aroused. Helen had said she felt relieved: trying had begun to wear her down too. Sex had never really been her thing since she was a teenager, and it was last on her list of priorities. Her turn-ons were power, money, accomplishments. The passion for sex was something she just didn't share with Jake any longer; the early days in bed with Jake had been a novelty, but she had only put herself through the ordeal of sex recently to try and get Jake back. She really didn't want that part of him, but she didn't want anyone else to have it either. Losing the baby had been so sad – she enjoyed being a mother – but part of her felt relieved.

The baby she'd lost had been conceived through wanting to control Jake, not through true love. They already had their greatest desires – work and their two boys. Jake sleeping with Mandy didn't bother Helen half as much as the thought of Jake taking her to a company soirée, or to meet her boys. Now *that* she wouldn't have. That was her territory.

Helen was in love with the life they had built together and the material wealth that was guaranteed from it. Many of her wealthy friends would admire her for being with a sexy man who went against the grain. He was originally from the wrong side of the tracks, yet he was now a millionaire, and to them, Helen had it all. And that was just the way that she liked it. Helen's big house in Notting Hill, her holiday homes and luxury cars were vital to her image. She would often tell her friends that Jake had showered her with diamonds, when in fact he had done no such thing. What drove Helen most of all was her need to prove herself to her father, to her extremely wealthy friends, to Jake. She lived the perfect life, or so it seemed, because most of it was made up. She'd spun the yarn that she and Jake just couldn't get enough of each other sexually. Losing Jake did strike fear in Helen, but for all the wrong reasons. It wasn't because of how *she* felt, or that she was in love with him; she was afraid of what others would think. That she would seem to have failed.

A big chunk of her life was a lie, but she refused to let it go. She did love Jake, but in her own way. She hated seeing him so unhappy, but being without him was something she would never countenance.

Mandy checked yet another stick.

Six of them couldn't be wrong.

She rang Deena.

'You fucking witch, I'm pregnant.'

Jake walked into his stuccoed house in west London; the Filipina nanny was leaving for the evening.

'Good-night, Mr Chaplin. The boys are in bed.'

Jake didn't respond, but took a deep breath and kept on walking into the kitchen.

Helen was wearing white jeans and a cream polo-neck jumper. She turned, smiling. 'Hi.'

'I don't want this any more,' Jake said.

The smile faded from Helen's lips. She stared at him coldly.

'Then leave.'

'Can you honestly say *you* still want this, Helen?'

'I don't want *you* in this house any longer.'

'I just want to kiss the boys goodnight.'

Helen's mouth became tight with anger. 'I. Said. Leave.'

Jake turned on his heel and kept walking, not looking back. He couldn't bear to.

Tears ran down his face as he got into his car and headed straight to Mandy.

Mandy opened the door. Jake came through and sat himself on the sofa, looking edgy. What the hell was he doing here? They hadn't planned to see each other tonight. Mandy felt like the world was spinning off kilter, that somehow she was an outsider looking in.

'Did Deena ring you?'

'No.'

'George?'

'No, why?'

'No reason.' Mandy didn't want to be rude, but what did Jake want?

Both were completely unaware that the other had something huge to tell, life-changing news. No wonder that both felt so odd.

Mandy had already decided that Jake had to believe that she alone was enough to start a life with. She didn't want the sympathy vote, or for him to 'do the right thing'. She wanted what she had wanted for a long time, longer than even she had realized – for him to want to have a full-time relationship with her 24/7. If they did not try, they would never know if it would work. The pain of them fighting their feelings was what was causing the problems, not being honest and accepting them. She knew it wasn't a decision he could make lightly, but the way they were living was all wrong. Especially with a baby on the way.

Jake rubbed his head in his hands. 'I have something to tell you.'

'I have something to tell you too.' She swallowed. What the hell was his news? She sighed. 'You go first.'

'I've left Helen.'

Mandy's eyes widened.

'I hate living like this. I hate lying to myself and everyone else, from work colleagues to friends and family.' Jake went on, 'I want to show you off without worrying, and I don't want to feel bad about something that feels so right. It's ripping me apart. Being without my boys rips me apart too, but I am going to find a way to make all this work, I know it.' He exhaled a long breath. 'Do you still want me, Mand?'

Mandy smiled gently. 'Yes. Yes, I do.'

Jake nodded relieved. 'OK. Now you. What's your news?'

'Erm . . .' She faltered.

'Oh for God's sake, Mandy, spit it out! Whatever it is, it can't be as drastic as what I've told you!' He looked lighter, happier, relieved to be able to live his truth. He had no idea what was coming.

'I'm pregnant,' she said quietly.

Jake's eyes nearly popped out of his head.

'Well, say something!' she cried.

'Oh wow,' Jake puffed. 'Oh wow!' Tears filled his eyes. 'Well come here! Let me hug you!'

Mandy walked over to Jake and fell into his arms. They both kept crying and laughing and crying again.

'I can't fucking believe it!' he smiled. 'Are you shocked?'

'Er, yes!'

'Have you told anyone?'

'Being honest, I have. I've told George and Deena as I wasn't sure how to handle it or how to break it to you.'

'OK. More importantly, are you happy, Mandy?'

'Yes. I feel like it's right, the right time in my life. I can manage this and work.'

She gazed at him. It was the most happy she had ever seen him. 'How about you? How do you feel?'

'I feel ecstatic! Scared for my life once Helen and her father find out, but ecstatic too.'

'Well, let's leave it a while before we tell them, eh? I don't want them thinking you left her for me just because I had a bun in the oven.'

'No, you're right.' He held her face; it was his favourite thing to do in the whole world.

'I love you, Mand.'

'I love you.'

Jake had to laugh out loud with happiness, then he shouted, 'WE'RE HAVING A BABY!'

In early November Mandy and Jake were shopping in Harrods. It was approximately one month until their beautiful baby would be born. They were looking at gorgeous little blankets now, Chloe, Dior: they all had the most amazing baby ranges.

'Yoo-hoo!' Olivia and Valerie arrived, with the girls and bags of Christmas shopping.

'Bloody hell, you're huge, Mandy! I can't believe how much bigger you are than two weeks ago!'

Mandy felt like a great big happy elephant. Pregnancy suited her: her hair was glossy, her skin glowed and remarks like that went right over her head.

Jake and Mandy were so happy. She had turned Queensgate into extra office space, and the spare room at their flat in Mayfair was now a beautiful bedroom, ready for their eagerly anticipated baby. Mandy and Jake had had no desire to find out the sex of the baby; the surprise made it all the more exciting. The two of them had decorated the nursery together; it was their little joint venture.

One day, Jake had sung into Mandy's tummy while she

had a scarf around her head and a paint roller in her hand:

'Be my, be my baby.'

The baby had kicked furiously, and Mandy jolted.

'Bloody hell, the baby loves it, Jake.'

Jake was also looking for a house for them. 'I want the baby to have a garden to wander in, and a playroom.' He was wonderful. This baby was already such a source of delight for him.

He had explained the situation as best he could to his beloved boys, but they missed their dad, and he missed them even more. However, they liked the idea of having a little brother or sister to play with.

Understandably, Helen hadn't taken the news well. He had broken it to her just before picking up the boys one Saturday.

He was greeted with a stony silence. Then:

'I don't want my boys staying with you and Mandy,' she had said firmly. 'They've met her now, and that's fine, but I don't want them staying over with you yet.'

Jake was livid, but Mandy remembered how upset Olivia had been, and tried to get him to understand.

'Think how she feels, Jake. In love or not in love, you're the father to her children, and to her I'm a home wrecker. Let's face it, she's got a point. I've already taken you, something she thought would never happen. Let her hold on to her boys. Try and walk a mile in her shoes.'

'I just miss them desperately; the flat is so quiet compared to the house.'

'But you knew that you wouldn't be able to have it all.'

Mandy knew how much he had given up for her; she hoped that one day, for the children's sake if nothing else, she and Helen could be civil. She remembered Diva, and the chat she'd had with her long-term lover's wife. It was amazing how brilliant women could be when they had to.

'Shall we have lunch?' Olivia said now, bringing her back to the present.

Olivia had been wonderful: she'd been guarding Mandy's bump like the rarest treasure for the last few months. She looked great too, beaming as she sat on the roof terrace of Harrods. Eating a scone, she suddenly announced:

'I've met someone!'

'Oh my God! Who?'

'He's called Nicholas, he's from Barbados, and he's the most handsome man I have ever laid eyes on. He's a top hairdresser,' she said, flicking her hair like she was in a L'Oréal advert.

'Your hair looks fabulous, by the way,' said Mandy, trying not to laugh.

'Thanks. He did it for me this morning . . . before I left. He is so cool, Mandy, and so much fun, and he has a huge—'

'Enough!' jumped in Valerie, covering Robyn's ears. 'I

love you but this is too much. Come on, girls,' she said, taking them by the hand, 'let's go to the ladies' and freshen up.'

'But we only just got here, Granny,' said Robyn, exasperated.

But Valerie was leading them off before they had a chance to argue. There was no messing with Granny.

Jake chuckled. 'Well, I have heard it's true that black guys put us to shame in the portion department.'

Mandy and Olivia laughed.

'Put it this way,' said Olivia, 'my eyes watered when I saw it!'

Mandy was falling about laughing now, holding on to her big belly.

Olivia beamed like she'd won the Nobel Peace Prize. 'And guess what?'

'What?'

'Robbie wants me back!'

'No!'

'Oh yes! He's been driving me nuts.'

'What are you going to do?'

'Nothing. I really like Nicky.'

'Really, you feel completely OK about it? You don't want him back?'

'Mand, the man had his chance. I'm not his fair-weather wife. Yes, I went a bit bonkers, but he should have tried to help me, as my friend if nothing else, but he couldn't handle it and ran away. I would never have deserted him like that, *ever*. He didn't act like a man, or the kind of husband that I want. He was a coward, Mandy.'

'So what happened to the redhead?'

'He caught her in bed with another woman.'

Jake nearly spat out his scone. 'Crikey, it's never dull with you lot!'

But Mandy wanted to check that her sister truly was OK. 'Don't you love him any more?'

'Of course! But I want to be able to rely on him. Even when I had my really bad spell, I knew it was best he didn't know. He couldn't handle it – it's like having another baby!'

'So Robbie doesn't know about all that?'

'No, not all of it; he doesn't need to. His mum just believes I had some women's problems and was rushed into hospital. He lost out on knowing my secrets the day he dipped his wick elsewhere.'

Mandy sighed. Jake nodded and said, 'Fair comment.'

Olivia looked embarrassed. 'Sorry, Jake, I know this could all be a little too close to home.'

'No, you're right. If Helen wanted to move on with her life and be happy with someone else, I'd only be able to wish her the best.'

Mandy kissed him on the cheek. She was pleased that Jake was trying to be fair.

*

Nearly a month later, on 8 December, Jake and Mandy heard: 'Congratulations, it's a baby girl.' The nurse handed over the little bundle and placed her in Mandy's arms. She was overwhelmed with emotion. Jake leaned over and kissed her; his eyes filled with tears, and he couldn't have wiped the smile from his face if he'd tried. His baby girl was absolutely beautiful. He was mesmerized by her. Her skin was olive, just like his. She was wrinkle-free, her big black mop of hair stuck up on her little head, and her face was just like a china doll's.

'She's a bonny little thing,' remarked the midwife.

Jake stroked her little nose. 'She is beautiful, isn't she?'

'Yes,' Mandy sighed. 'She's the most beautiful thing I've ever seen.'

It was the best moment of Mandy's life.

'What shall we call her?' Jake asked. He wanted to leave the final decision to Mandy.

'Bonnie,' Mandy smiled. 'Because she is. My beautiful, bonny baby girl.'

The first Christmas with Bonnie was amazing, but exhausting.

Olivia, Valerie and the girls came over for dinner and Jake's mum and nan even popped in for drinks later on in the evening. Just when Mandy thought she knew Jake, there was something more to discover. He had never said anything about it but his mum explained how, without fail, he would pop by to see them once a week. He had paid for their house outright, and took his nan to bingo whenever he could.

Jake didn't have much in common with his family any more, but he undoubtedly loved them very much.

'It's lovely to meet you at last,' his mum had said. 'And Bonnie is beautiful.'

Mandy was not sure what his mum thought of her deep down, but she was very polite and sweet.

Underneath the tree was a box wrapped in silver paper. Jake gave it to Mandy.

The card read:

To the love of my life, thank you for giving me such a beautiful baby, thank you for taking me on, and thank you for being you. Merry Christmas, Jake x

Mandy opened the box, and took out the Cartier diamond bracelet.

Everyone in the room gasped.

It was beautiful, he was beautiful and, with their perfect little baby, the future was looking bright.

TWENTY-ONE

Baby Blues

Bonnie was crying, screaming the house down actually. This was the norm in the Mount Street household. Even the neighbours Mandy passed in the lift looked exhausted and pissed off. Bonnie had lungs as loud as a megaphone. Jake slept like a log.

'How can you *not* hear that?' Mandy mumbled.

She dragged herself up out of bed and shuffled to Bonnie's room. She was exhausted; the last six months had been tough, and being a mother didn't always come as naturally as she had expected. She had been breastfeeding and her figure was almost back, but she was shattered all the time and highly emotional.

She missed work like crazy. She felt guilty for feeling like that, but it was true. Mandy's work was a huge passion, a massive chunk of who she was, and giving it up for the last six months had knocked her confidence and lowered her self-esteem.

Mandy felt far more cautious about everything. Bonnie

was so precious to her, and protecting her from everyday problems made Mandy a nervous wreck. There was so much to remember, so many things to do and pack before she even left the house. Thankfully she was organized. However, lists that used to be half a page long were now two pages or more.

Bottle – check.
Nappies – check.
Wet wipes – check . . .

How things had changed.

Mandy had gone back to Queensgate to check up on emails in peace from time to time. This time, Michael desperately needed her help with finding an old contact, and Mandy was thrilled to lend a hand.

She tried folding her pram with one arm and leg while holding her little princess.

Diva twitched her net curtains. 'Mandy!' she mouthed through the window. She vanished, only to reappear on the steps of her front door.

'Let me see the little beauty!'

She made her way down the stairs and pulled Bonnie's little sun bonnet back from her chubby face.

'Oh, she just melts my heart,' she sighed.

Mandy was hot and bothered: it was June and London was experiencing a scorching few days.

'Are you OK, darling? You look tired.'

'I am. This one is only sleeping for a couple of hours and my body clock is completely out of whack. Just as I adjust, or think I've got her sussed, she changes her routine! She's a little minx.'

'I remember it, vaguely!' Diva laughed. 'Do you fancy some cold orange squash and biscuits?'

'Would be rude not to. Just need to email my partner some contact info, and then I'll be up.'

Diva's face lit up. She loved a good natter. 'OK!' she said. 'See you shortly!' She skipped up the stairs like a thirty-year-old, then skipped back down. 'Shall I take the bubby for you?'

Before Mandy could answer Diva had grabbed the buggy with one arm, took the baby with the other and marched up the stairs. She looked back at Mandy.

'My leg's much better. I feel like a new woman.'

That woman was unbelievable!

Mandy contacted Michael, caught up with emails and instantly felt more human. She walked up to Diva's and was buzzed in.

'Come in, sweetheart!'

Mandy sat sipping her cold orange squash and nibbling a Bourbon biscuit.

'What's wrong, Mandy? When I last saw you you seemed so content and happy. Now you seem so edgy and nervous.'

'I'm fine,' Mandy sighed.

'Really? I *am* a woman; you don't have to keep it together for me, you know.' She was a wise old soul.

'The thing is that admitting it to you means admitting it to myself, and I'm not sure I'm prepared for that.'

Diva smiled kindly. 'Whatever makes you happy.'

'It's just that I miss the old Jake. I miss the old me.'

'That's completely natural, darling. You're only six months into your first baby.'

'I love Bonnie – more than life itself. I wouldn't change her, ever, but I miss being creative, I miss being with adults during the day, and I miss Jake loving me. Since the baby's been born he's hardly ever romantic with me. I feel like he doesn't love me any more.'

'But Mandy,' Diva leaned forward earnestly, 'what did you expect? Love and romance are two different things. It's a huge change for you both. It's normal – you're both exhausted!'

Mandy shook her head sadly. 'But we've never been normal, that's just not me and Jake. We are both intense, passionate, volatile, everything *but* normal. And because I'm feeling a bit unattractive, and heavy, I want him to want me more than ever!'

Diva sighed. 'Mandy, you're a mum now. You're still a woman, a beautiful one! You're still an amazing clever girl, with a great full-time career, when you're ready for it.' She smiled. 'Goodness, you remind me of myself. You want life to be a fairy tale, you want it all!'

'Is that bad?'

'No, darling!' Diva laughed. 'I just don't know if what you want is possible.'

Mandy loved talking to Diva. She was like a friendly, glamorous priest! Mandy could confess anything to her now, and she felt safe. Right, wrong, naïve or reckless, Diva never judged.

That evening Jake came home and really made an effort with Mandy. He knew she was struggling. He ordered a Chinese take-away and rubbed Mandy's feet. He spoke to James and Alex, and briefly to Helen, then he ran Mandy a bubble bath.

Later that evening, both he and Mandy, wrapped in their dressing gowns, looked into Bonnie's cradle. They felt like the happiest parents in the world. Bonnie started to stir.

'Jake, would you mind seeing to her while I tidy round?'

'Tidy tomorrow.'

'I can't. If I don't do it now, I won't get the chance. You know what she's like, she's non-stop. I'm thinking of taking her to see Dr Dawkin. Olivia said Robyn was exactly the same when she was a baby, and that she was hyperactive and fidgety because of something in her food. I want to get it checked out. This isn't normal, Jake.'

'Really?'

Mandy felt rattled. 'Yes. I'm not making it up.'

'OK, calm down. I'll get her to sleep, then we can kiss, cuddle up and make love.'

Mandy's face lit up and her tension eased.

'That would be lovely. I've missed you.'

'I've missed you too, but I've been scared. Helen didn't want to be touched at all for a long time after each birth. Whenever I go to touch you I feel I'm being selfish. I just don't want to upset you.'

Jake kissed her on the forehead, and then on the lips, before taking Bonnie out of her crib and trying to comfort her.

Mandy sorted bottles and dishes and got organized for the next twenty-four hours.

She checked herself in the mirror and pinched her cheeks. Walking gracefully, sexily into the bedroom and dimming the light, she dropped her robe to the floor and turned towards Jake.

There he was on the bed, fast asleep with Bonnie snuggled up to him.

Mandy's heart jumped. It was so beautiful, but she was sad.

'You ungrateful cow,' she mumbled under her breath. 'He loves you; you have a beautiful child; he left his wife and family for this.' Mandy bit her lip and stopped the tears forming. But this wasn't what she had thought it would be. What the hell was wrong with her? Why did she feel upset, why did she miss Jake when he was in the relationship with her? Why wasn't she a better mum? She was so confused.

Maybe she'd had the relationship she hoped for with Jake all along? As his mistress.

She tried to get in the bed, but neither of her beauties stirred.

'Jake,' she whispered. 'Jake.'

He didn't wake up; he was out for the count.

Mandy grabbed the blanket on the sofa and snuggled up in it, trying to make the most of the peace.

'Nobody tells you about this bit,' she said quietly. She closed her eyes and dreamed of when she and Jake would be their own version of normal and happy. So far, it always seemed just out of reach.

TWENTY-TWO

Choices

Mandy was not down for long, once she had spoken to George. Who better?

'Right, get yourself back to work, get yourself a tread-mill, get yourself a nanny, get a grip.'

Bonnie was now such a happy baby. It turned out she was allergic to cow's milk, and since it had been taken out of her diet she was a completely different baby – happy, bright and completely in love with George.

George had been Mandy's rock. He had helped inter-view various nanny applicants and went jogging with Mandy every Wednesday and Friday morning. With Bonnie better and Mandy feeling like her old self, the baby blues had become a thing of the past. 'You were definitely depressed, darling. I think the word "humour" had dis-appeared out of your vocabulary completely!'

So at last everything was perfect.

Well, perhaps not *quite*.

Mandy would have evenings out once or twice a week,

with work and the girls if nothing else. Jake was working very hard, and never seemed to want to take Mandy out any more. On many occasions she had hinted about a new restaurant opening, or shown him a pretty dress in the hope that he might want a night with her to himself, but it never happened. He became very comfortable, extremely so, almost to the point where he didn't seem to want to make the effort any more. He was starting to take Mandy for granted. It was almost like he had settled into a way of life that was familiar to him; the life he'd had with Helen was being recreated.

Mandy was in love with Jake, but the last few arguments they had had, she had tackled him.

'What is this all about, Jake? Why are you ignoring me? I've worked so hard to make everything perfect, I'm confident because I'm back at work, I have a fabulous routine with Bonnie, and I run every morning to keep my figure just how you love it. Yes, I do it for me, but I do it for you too. But you only ever want to stay in. You don't seem to notice I'm there any more. I'm only visible when you need something or want to tell me about something that's happened at *your* work.'

Jake yawned. Mandy was having one of her rants.

'Look at you – you're like an old man! This isn't what we're about. I'm not Helen, I'm not happy falling into that trap – that's the life you had with her. If that's what you want, go back to it, but *we* are about being in love, the romance, the passion. Where's it all gone, Jake?'

The two of them had got stuck in a rut. Rows would flare up but nothing would budge. Nothing would change unless Mandy forced it.

It was 8 a.m. and Bonnie was happily beating her drum. Mandy was making her some breakfast. George had his fingers in his ears; he was looking after Bonnie as it was the nanny's week off.

Jake had Bonnie's sick on his work shirt and was trying to change as well as talk to Helen's father on the phone.

'OK, that's not a problem. No, I can handle it. Look, this is my deal and I should see it through really. I'm sorry, I can't hear you.' Jake looked frustrated. 'Sorry, I can't hear.' He covered the mouthpiece with his hand. 'Mandy, for God's sake! Can't you calm her down? I can't hear myself think with all that bloody racket.'

Mandy stuck various bottles, bowls and utensils under her chin and tried to juggle them as she walked through the lounge. A toy on the floor tripped her up, and Bonnie's breakfast landed on the carpet.

George tried to take the drumstick out of Bonnie's hand, but she snatched it back. She started beating her drum as loudly as she could; she was loving it.

George started giggling. 'You're a minx, just like your mother.'

Jake was still trying to have a conversation. 'Alastair? Alastair?'

Alastair had hung up.

'Well, that's just fucking great, isn't it? Brilliant! Let's just show my bastard of a father-in-law that I can't handle my girlfriend and a loud nightmare baby, never mind a MULTI-MILLION-POUND DEAL!'

George pulled a face as he helped Mandy pick up the various bits and bobs scattered on the floor. Crikey!

Jake was furious and shouting at the top of his voice. Mandy shot him a look.

Typically, Bonnie was now bored with the drum and was examining a plastic spoon.

'Well, welcome to my world, Jake!' Mandy yelled. 'I've been late to work every day this week because I've been dealing with Bonnie, without you most mornings because you've had more breakfast meetings than I care to mention. Helen's so-called amazing nanny has never showed to fill in, so thank God for George.'

'Look! I've got vomit all over me!'

'So do I! And poo, so think yourself lucky.'

'I've had enough of this, this is bollocks.'

'And I've had enough of you, treating me like I'm the ex-wife!'

'Well, don't act like her then!' Jake stood there fuming. 'I've had enough of this,' he repeated. 'This isn't fun any more. I don't know what it is.'

Jake walked out, slamming the door; he always did when he was truly angry. Men were good at that.

Mandy started to cry. Bonnie joined in, and George felt hopeless.

'Oh, my darling girls! Oh, my darling girls.' He spun round, looking for something he could do to help. 'Let's just sit down, calm down and listen to Babs.'

'Yes! That would help!'

Mandy sat on the sofa in her work outfit, bouncing Bonnie on her knee while George ran to the stereo and slipped Barbra into the CD compartment. He often played it to Bonnie and danced around the room with her. She would laugh, gurgle and smile.

The music started to tinkle, then Barbra's pure, poignant voice hovered in the living room.

'It's not going to work, George, not like this. I have to face it: it's just not working.'

'I know, my darling. Too many tears, too many tears.'

A huge change was on its way, George could feel it. He held Mandy's hand and did what he was good at: loving her no matter what.

The car pulled up at the elegant house in Notting Hill, and Jake stepped out tentatively. His boys ran out and hugged him.

'Daddy!'

Helen stood in the doorway, for once not sure how to react. This was the unknown.

Jake opened the boot of the car and pulled out his suitcases. The housekeeper came to help.

'Welcome home, Mr Chaplin.'

And with that Jake walked back into the life he had left.

Ten days before, an honest, brave and truthful conversation had taken place between two people who loved each other very much. Their rules were their own, and trying to live by everyone else's just didn't work for them. It was time to do things their way.

Lying on the bed facing Jake, Mandy had held his hand.

'So what did Helen say?'

'She was her usual calm, collected self, and thought it all made sense, you know. It's silly me being away from both the boys and Bonnie. The house is huge, so I don't think we'll get under each other's feet.'

Mandy nodded. 'Has she met anyone else since you?'

'Not that I know of, and the boys have never said anything, have they?'

'I think she'll be glad to have you back in the house.'

'Well, if she will be, she didn't give much away. You know what she's like, she's a dark horse.'

She knows you'll never stop loving me, Mandy thought.

'No doubt all her friends and her dad will think that we'll be back together properly, but what they don't realize is that "properly" hasn't existed for years. She's told the boys and they're excited. She knows I just want time to get you sorted properly. When were you happiest, Mand?'

'Well, the beginning was lovely, and Verona, and when you were outside my little flat at Queensgate after that awful night at the casino. I was so happy to see you. The art weekend was hilarious. God, there are so many! How about you?'

They both loved to play this game, but this time it was different.

'The night I laid eyes on you. You were this beaming light that made everyone else there look faded in comparison.'

Mandy smiled and rested her head on his shoulder. This was the Jake she loved.

'The night at the Whitechapel Art Gallery. God, you were stunning.'

Mandy giggled. 'I loved the night we first did the deed, and I will never forget your face the first time you laid your eyes on Bonnie.'

Jake felt a tear swell; he squeezed his eyes shut and blinked it away.

Mandy felt emotional too. 'What do you think people will think, Jake?'

'Do you really care?'

'No, not really.' She meant it. 'We've never been normal, why start now?' She laughed lightly. Then her face became more serious. 'But I will miss parts of this phase of us.'

Jake sighed. 'I don't know any other woman who would be OK with this change, you know.'

Mandy smiled thoughtfully. 'Yes you do. They exist, and not just the women, the men too. They're just not as honest as we are.'

'That's what I've always loved about you, Mand. You just don't give a fuck, do you?' Jake kissed her head; he had always thought that.

'I do, but I have to be true to us now. It is an odd concept, but you and I are meant to be.'

Jake stroked her arm. 'Yes. It's in our own unique way, but at least we know where we stand with each other. Everyone, including Helen, knows the score. I know marriages that have been going twenty years, and they've turned a blind eye just as many times, or are completely unaware, just because they don't *want* to acknowledge it. Does that make their relationship better or more serious than ours?'

Jake held her face.

'Definitely not.'

He kissed her. 'I thought you wanted the fairy tale?'

'I do, and I've got it. I've realized that what I've wanted – and what suits me, what suits us – I had all along. In my mind, I have the best of both worlds. No one else would think that, but I just don't care.'

Jake would go back and live with his wife and boys. From now on, Mandy would be the mistress. She had experienced the love and the passion that only Jake could give her. Even if she had met Jake after he had divorced Helen, there would always be a history and a life away from her that she would have to deal with, especially with his two boys. Infidelity would always go on; it seemed to be a part of human nature. Mandy and Jake wanted to live their lives openly and truthfully, and if people didn't like it then that was just tough. She was content: it was her choice to be part of Jake's life now, and how it always would be. They couldn't live without each other, but living together 24/7 simply hadn't worked. This way, they would be happier. This way, they would always be together.

Jake and Mandy held each other. At last they had found what worked for them, and now they felt that nothing could touch them.

TWENTY-THREE

The Wedding

Beep beep! Beep beep!

Mandy waited in her new four-wheel-drive outside the house in Notting Hill. Bonnie was strapped into the baby seat, chattering away in baby-talk.

Mandy looked gorgeous. She had treated herself to a full-length Temperley dress. It was cream, with beautiful beading. She had braided her hair the night before, and she looked like a Bohemian princess.

The door opened and Jake walked down the stairs with Alex and James.

'Hi, Mandy!' they yelled as they jumped into the car, kissing their little sister hello. 'Hello, Bonnie,' they cooed.

Helen stood in the doorway and waved goodbye. She gave Mandy the usual stare. She would always dislike her, but to be fair, she put up with her. Helen was dating a handsome tennis coach. It was early days, but she had loosened up. She and Mandy even exchanged a few sentences when needed. Progress was slow, but hey, they were trying.

Mandy and Jake's own crazy little family headed off to the event of the year.

In Henley, the sun shone for the special couple. The vast house was completely adorned with flowers, and lanterns hung from a huge tree next to the river. A gazebo covered in cornflower-blue hydrangeas was a beautiful feature. Everyone took their seats, waiting to watch the happy ceremony that was about to take place beneath it.

Deena came over, full of the joys of spring. She had flowers in her hair, and wore a long dark-green dress.

'Hi, my darling, this is Joseph.'

Joseph looked just like Deena – an expensive hippie. He bowed and kissed Jake and Mandy. They tried not to laugh.

'Hello, my friends,' he said gently.

He kissed everybody three times and walked off bowing. Deena was ecstatic. She whispered loudly:

'It's been two months. He is phenomenal at tantric sex, he's a spiritual angel, and he's a crisps heir!'

Deena dashed off after him.

Jake burst out laughing. 'I hope it's Walkers . . . they're my favourite.'

Mandy elbowed him, but even Alex and James were laughing their heads off.

Assia looked over her shoulder. She was wearing an over-the-top ruffled canary-yellow gown. She winked at Mandy. She had seated herself in the second row with the rest of the family, and had her twenty-two-year-old boyfriend sitting next to her. He looked as fresh as a baby's bum. She smiled naughtily, blowing a kiss.

'Speak to you later, dharrling!'

Olivia came running in with Robyn, Milly and Nicky. She looked fabulous. She was wearing a pink Matthew Williamson dress with a Philip Treacy hat. Her hair was wavy and shiny.

The girls both looked so cute, dressed in white broderie anglaise dresses. They were swinging off Nicky's leg. They had taken their time, but now completely adored him. He was such a handsome man; he was wearing a beautiful linen suit and he looked cool. He had a smile that would warm even the coldest of hearts.

Valerie followed, holding pretty confetti and a camera.

'Wow, new haircut, new mum!'

It was lovely to see her mum looking so assured and happy; she was radiant and smiling. They all waved, then sat in any seat they could find.

The music started. Barbra Streisand blared from the speakers.

Pedro stood up and made his way to the gazebo. Once there, he looked back at the love of his life.

George, dressed in a beautiful light-blue suit, was walking down the aisle to join him.

The chaplain blessed them and they read out their own special love letters to each other as part of their vows.

George's letter said:

To the man I love,

I thank God for the day I met you. I was searching for you for so long. I lived a life like others and pretended I was happy, but when I met you, only the truth would do. I know we will explore our dreams together, and witness the highs and lows, always offering comfort and support. I hope to God we rock the boat of the status quo, and look back when we are old and say, in the words of Sinatra, 'we did it our way'. I love you more than life itself. You are my best friend, my lover, my everything . . . for now, for ever.

Jake reached for Mandy's hand. She looked at him and he smiled a contented, peaceful smile. They couldn't have put it better. Love is such a complex, personal, wonderful thing, and they were blessed to have it – their way.

Acknowledgements

Firstly I would like to thank Jonny Geller and his team at Curtis Brown. Thank you for your belief in me and your wisdom. I respect you so very much. To all at Macmillan, thank you for all your support every single step of the way. Extra special thanks to Imogen – I can't thank you enough for your time, patience and guidance, and, most of all, thank you for believing in me so much as a writer.

Thank you to Kirsty and Andy and all at Insanity Management. You guys rock! Thanks to Stuart Higgins Publicity, Gerard Tyrell and everyone else who helped make this book a reality. Thank you to Dave Clark and all the gang at D.P.C. Media. Your support and advice have been invaluable.

Thanks to my wonderful family, especially Mum. You are a never-ending source of entertainment and insipration – I will never forget us giggling at four in the morning with too much coffee in our systems at a very unfortunate misprint. Thanks for your typing skills Mum, you are a life saver! LJ and Alan – I adore you both.

Thank you to all my friends. My life is so much richer because of you all. The list goes on and on, but you know who you all are, and I'm truly blessed to be so loved by you all. You make my world a great place. And to the great McManus family, many thanks for your support.

extracts reading groups
competitions books new
discounts extracts extracts discounts
competitions extracts
books new events
events reading groups
books books reading groups
new extracts new
titles reading groups
interviews extracts events
events extracts extracts books
discounts interviews new books
new books events events extracts
events new interviews new books
discounts extracts discounts books
www.panmacmillan.com
extracts events reading groups
competitions books extracts new